MAGIC CITY Blues

ADVANCED PRAISE
MAGIC CITY BLUES
BY BOBBY MATHEWS

"Calling back to the best of Robert B. Parker with a wit that reminded me of Gregory MacDonald, Bobby Mathews introduces two great characters in his page-turner *Magic City Blues*. The first is veteran-turned-low-level-street-thug Kincaid, and the second is the city of Birmingham, Alabama, a city that has deserved its time as a worthy crime-fiction locale. It's a city of barbecue and soul food, of racism and gentrification, of power and money and secrets – the perfect setting for what will hopefully be an ongoing series of novels."

> —**Jordan Harper**, Edgar-winning author of *She Rides Shotgun* and *Everybody Knows*

"*Magic City Blues* by Bobby Mathews is a down and dirty exaltation of what I love best about crime fiction. Bad people doing bad things for what they think are the right reasons. Bobby has written a fantastic book."

> —**S.A. Cosby**, New York Times bestselling author of *Razorblade Tears* and *Blacktop Wasteland*

"The action comes early and often in *Magic City Blues* and the energy of this spellbinding novel cannot be denied. Bobby Mathews is a first-rate writer point blank and the crime poet laureate of Birmingham. A master craftsman of new-south noir, who deftly balances crackling dialogue, sly humor, grit and tenderness with smart and wily plotting paired with hardboiled suspense and the kind of complicated (anti) hero in Kincaid we can all get behind. Somewhere at the great poker game in the sky, Donald Westlake, Robert Parker and James Crumley are raising a glass to *Magic City Blues* … as should we all."

> —**Peter Farris**, award-winning author of *Last Call for the Living* and The Devil Himself

"*Magic City Blues* is a straight shot of classic crime fiction reminiscent of Donald Westlake and Robert B. Parker. With one-liners galore, and sharp, punchy writing, Bobby Mathews' latest novel is not to be missed!"

> —**Eli Cranor**, author of *Don't Know Tough* and *Ozark Dogs*

"A twisty, propulsive read led by a witty, compelling narrator. I couldn't put it down!"

> —**Cassandra Rose Clarke**, author of *Star's End* and *The Mad Scientist's Daughter*

More Praise
for MAGIC CITY BLUES

"*Magic City Blues* is a slick, fast-moving crime novel that fans of Robert B. Parker and Donald Westlake will want to get their hands on. Murder, blackmail, romance—this story has it all. With just the perfect mix of brawn and brains, bodyguard-for-hire Kincaid is a narrator you won't soon forget as he navigates the seedy underbelly of Birmingham, dealing out ass-kicking justice and wit in equal manner. Bobby Mathews pulls no punches with this burner."

—Scott Blackburn, author of *It Dies With You*

BOBBY MATHEWS

MAGIC CITY

CITY

Blues

a novel

SHOTGUN
HONEY
2 0 2 2

Published by **Shotgun Honey Books**

215 Loma Road
Charleston, WV 25314
www.ShotgunHoney.com

Cover by Bad Fido.

First Printing 2023.

ISBN-10: 1-956957-10-3
ISBN-13: 978-1-956957-10-5

9 8 7 6 5 4 3 2 1   23 22 21 20 19 18

For my mom, Mavis Mathews.
I wish she was still around to see this.

And for Parker, and Noah, and Spenser.

I love you all.

MAGIC CITY
Blues

ONE

ON THE BIG SCREEN above the bar, two teams were playing for the World Cup, and I'm sure somebody somewhere cared about it.

Not me. I was drinking a cold bottle of Carta Blanca and listening to the pair next to me. Their heads were close together, but they'd had a couple and were talking the way nearly drunk people do—just a little too loud—and they were much more interesting than the TV.

"Man, I still can't believe she threw you out like that," the guy nearest me said. "I hate to hear it."

"Yeah," his friend said. "I mean, I guess I knew it would come sometime. She thought we was in a relationship; I thought we's just fucking."

And now they're neither, I thought. But you keep your nose out of other people's business, right? Things are tough all over. My bottle was empty, so I gestured at the bartender for another. The beer was going down smooth and cold, and the bar was mostly dark except for the overheads that glinted off the glassware hanging from racks mounted to the ceiling. And the TV, of course.

Neither one of them was what you'd call big. The one farther away from me—the one who'd thought that he and his woman were just fucking—was what you'd call wiry. Not six feet tall, but the cords in his forearms stood out every time he moved to lift his glass.

They were drinking gin martinis with not very much Vermouth, and I could smell the alcohol from where I sat three stools down. It was the middle of the afternoon and they were tipsy going on drunk. I looked at my beer. Most of it was gone. If I wasn't careful, I'd get tipsy, too.

But I had things I needed to do, work that couldn't wait much longer. Maybe I'd made a mistake with the beer. There was some pressure south of my belt buckle, and I remembered that old saying: you never really buy beer, just rent it for a little while. I stayed put. Of course I did. Being patient is part of the job, and I pride myself on being professional. When the one nearest me shoved away from the bartop and said, "I gotta break the seal," I slid from my own stool and managed to stumble into him when he tried to pass.

"Oh, hey," he said as he grabbed my arm to keep me from falling. "You all right old-timer?" I didn't say anything. I couldn't. While he was helping me stand, I put my hands on him, too. A quick dip into his pockets, a nudge to the ankle with the side of my foot.

No gun.

That was good. I don't carry on jobs like this one, not since I got arrested and my attorney had to do a little fancy footwork to keep me out of jail on a weapons charge about five years ago. But I still worked all the time around people who carried a gun, and it made me cautious when I wasn't carrying one.

He headed to the men's room and I followed about two steps behind him, giving him just enough space to step through the door before I came through like a freight train. I had my fist tight against my shoulder and I drove the point of my elbow horizontally into the base of his skull.

He stumbled forward, trying to catch himself on the white porcelain sink. But it was slippery with water and his hands skidded along the smooth slick surface. I got a right hook into his kidney and he kind of slumped down, an agonized chuff of wind exploding from his mouth. I caught a glimpse of myself in the mirror and didn't recognize the man looking back at me. There were two bright, hard red spots high on my cheekbones, right underneath my eyes, but other than that my face was as pale and emotionless as death itself.

I got a hand under his collar and turned him around to face me, slapping one rough palm over his mouth before he could scream. His eyes were wide and sweat trickled down his forehead. His hands were locked on my forearm and he made little mewling sounds against my palm.

"I don't know if you're wearing a wire," I whispered, spitting the words like venom from a snake's mouth. "I don't care, either. We have a mutual friend. He'd like you to shut your piehole. If you don't do it yourself, he's gonna send me around again, and we'll have to work out a more permanent solution. Nod if you understand."

He nodded. Snot trickled out of his nose and onto my hand. I let him go and punched him. Just the belly. My orders were clear: Leave no marks on his face. So I pounded his ribs with a couple of shots, and when he turned away, bent over and clutching his abdomen, I aimed a kick right between his legs, getting up under him hard, doing my best to punt him like a football. That was the closest he came to screaming, but there wasn't enough air left in his body to actually make the sound. Instead his mouth was drawn out in a silent rictus of pain.

It wasn't enough.

While he knelt puking on the floor, I stepped on his ankle with my thick-soled shoes and heard a bone crack.

I washed my face at the sink and used the paper towel on the bathroom door handle. If the cops wanted to, they could get my prints from either of the bottles I'd used. But I was betting there wouldn't be any cops. I opened the door and walked out. The afternoon sun glaring into the bar looked a few shades darker. I left a couple of bills on the bar to pay my tab, and then I walked past Mr. I-Thought-We's-Just-Fucking and out the door. It was summer, so the sunlight was still strong, even though it had dropped deep into the western sky.

I walked a couple of blocks to a little pocket park over on 76th Street, where I sat down on a green-painted wrought iron bench and texted the client. Message delivered. Only time would tell if the message was received.

I'm muscle for hire. You need someone protected? I can do it. Somebody owes you and doesn't pay? I can collect. And sometimes I run a messenger service, like today. Better than a certified letter. My messages tend to stay with people, even after they get out of the hospital.

I put the phone back in my pocket. Sat on the bench and watched the world come back into focus. It was deep in summer, and the green world around me was abuzz with bees and butterflies. Somewhere nearby a woodpecker hammered percussion in a band no one else could hear. Nature red in tooth and claw.

The phone buzzed, a notification of payment sent to an app, which would eventually be electronically transferred to my bank. All clean and tidy. It made me think of the early days on the street, scrapping. Poor white boy, no money in his pockets, fight anybody over anything, without the slightest provocation. Of course, I still didn't have any money in my pockets. Money doesn't mean what it used to. It's no longer a wad of cash concealed in a handshake once the job is done. Now it's electronic transfers, all ones and zeroes. I don't understand it. All I know is that I still don't have any cash in my pockets.

The platinum card in my wallet isn't bad, though.

That was the year I was living in the Sky Inn, a not-quite-condemned pile of cinderblocks, shingles, and roach-infested carpet on the 6000 block of First Ave. on the east side of Birmingham. Yeah, I could've lived somewhere nicer if I'd wanted to, but the place had its charms. Each room came with its own drug dealer. And in that neighborhood, no one gave a damn about my comings and goings. Gunshots and knifings and clubbings went unremarked and unreported. My neighbors tended to be like me: gentrified right out of the Crestwood and Avondale neighborhoods, looking for a permanent place to light. I rented by the week, a cash-only deal that would probably get the manager fired if anyone ever found out about it. A hundred bucks due every Sunday before noon.

I was sitting in the glowering darkness of my room early on a Monday afternoon, staring at the gray blank screen of the broken TV when Carlton Doyle called me.

I carry the standard twenty-first century communications device, a small black flat rectangle that makes me feel dumber every time I look at it. I don't spend a lot of time on it, but it's got the usual slew of social media apps, something that told me the weather, and everything I needed for online banking. It tracked every incoming and outgoing call. Somewhere in a data center in Bumblefuck, Nebraska, there would have been a record of Carlton's call.

But he went through the motel switchboard instead. There's a reason he runs most of the organized crime in the greater Birmingham area. He ain't dumb.

When the phone rang, I gave it the surprised and ultimately suspicious look that most of us living in this new century use. We don't talk on the phone anymore. Texts and instant messages—in an emergency, emails—are the way we reach out and touch someone these days. But since I'd grown up before all that, I still remembered how to answer the phone.

"Hello?" I said. My voice sounded rusty, like a gate with hinges long unused.

"Do you know who this is?"

I didn't have to lie. I'd been in Doyle's presence four or five times over the years, fixing problems he needed solved.

"Yes."

"My office. One hour."

The line went dead. Self-assured prick. Maybe I didn't want to go to his office. Maybe I had big plans, sit here in my room and watch the gray TV screen while the window-unit air conditioner droned in the background and hum *Desperadoes Under the Eaves* to myself. Warren Zevon would be proud.

But this wasn't the Hollywood Hawaiian Hotel, and I wasn't going to drink up all the salty margaritas in Los Angeles. I wasn't even sure you could get to LA from Birmingham. Might as well see what Doyle wanted.

I took a quick shower and shaved carefully. In the alcove that passed for a closet, three suits hung. I took the best one down, a charcoal gray number with narrow blue pinstripes, and paired it with a shirt that nearly matched the color of the pinstripes. I put on gray socks and a pair of black tasseled loafers that needed a shine. I threaded a black belt through the loops of the pants and put a spring-clip holster at the small of my back. An Airweight .38-caliber revolver went into it. It's a little hammerless number, easily concealed. I figured it would be perfect for a trip to downtown Birmingham. If I ever decided to go on safari, I had a .357 Magnum locked in the portable safe beneath the hotel room bed. It doubled as an elephant gun when I needed some real stopping power.

I tried not to think about the differences between the message I'd delivered the day before and my appointment with Doyle, but it was impossible to ignore. Even under the best of circumstances, Carlton Doyle was dangerous.

I spent a few minutes debating what kind of tie to wear, but finally decided the hell with it. On an hour's notice, Doyle probably didn't care what I looked like when I got to his place.

That was one of the differences between us. I cared. It ain't just what you do; it's how you look while you're doing it.

I heard that from a Boston P.I. one time, and I've never forgotten it.

The drive downtown was a reminder that I wasn't from Birmingham, I just lived there. People who knew the city, who lived with it and made up its beating heart, knew the surface streets much better than I did. That's why I always took the interstate, much to my chagrin. It wasn't any faster, with orange cones blocking some exits and guiding the off-ramps to others. The Department of Transportation was still hell-bent on fucking up traffic in central Alabama for the foreseeable future, and was doing a fine job of it. I got off before Malfunction Junction and found the John Hand building right where it was supposed to be, at the corner of 20th and Second Ave.

A private elevator took me to the eighteenth floor, where a bubbly blonde receptionist took my card, looked at the name discreetly, and told me that Mr. Doyle would be right with me. I'd seen the secretary a few times before. Maybe one day she'd remember my name.

I took a seat on a white leather settee that looked more expensive than the entire motel I lived in and checked my appearance in the mirror. The suit fit well, even though I'd lost some pounds—or maybe because I had—but my sandy blond hair needed a cut. My teeth were white and mostly even, but the lines in my face were etched deep by sorrow or time or both. I'll never look forty again. My complexion was too pale, the color of skin that doesn't see a lot of daylight.

Doyle's reception area was tony, with a lot of gold leaf and real plants, the kind that needed to be watered regularly. There was an old-fashioned water cooler that advertised Poland Springs water. I could get a cupful and sit back on the sofa with it. Have something to do with my hands.

On the receptionist's desk, a discreet chime sounded. She

looked down once, and then back up to me. Her smile was brilliant and charming and devoid of any independent human warmth.

"Mr. Doyle will see you now."

She dropped her gaze without a second's hesitation. So much for the good suit. Maybe if I'd worn the tie. I went past her desk—I knew the way—and opened a frosted glass door.

TWO

CARLTON DOYLE WASN'T quite what anyone would expect a crime boss to be. Today he wore what I always considered his professorial look, a pair of starched blue jeans, crisp white shirt, and a corduroy blazer with actual suede patches at the elbows. He sat at a table beside a floor-to-ceiling window, a thick leather-bound book in one hand. He'd marked his place by closing the book on his index finger and holding it there. No dog-eared pages for him. He didn't rise. Didn't extend a hand to shake. Our relationship wasn't like that. But he motioned for me to sit in the other chair at the table with him.

This was unusual. Usually Doyle gave his orders from behind the large mahogany desk at the end of the long room. The peon comes in, gets his marching orders, and leaves.

But now Doyle was different. I couldn't figure out what it was at first. His receding hair was still worn long in the back with a little fluff of curls at the nape of his neck, and his rusty-gray beard was clipped close to his face. He pulled a limp white handkerchief from his breast pocket and dabbed at his narrow, wolfish face. That's when it hit me.

Doyle was sweating. Something I'd never seen before.

He didn't waste any time. No small talk. He didn't offer me a drink or ask how I was doing. It would have been out of character. Instead he went directly to the matter at hand.

"You know my business," he said.

"Not all of it," I said. "But I know some. I can guess at the rest."

My answer startled him. He wasn't prepared to be interrupted, but I was never good at rhetorical questions anyway. He paused for a moment, looked out the window. In the clear light filtering in through the glass, his pale green eyes were the color of old dollar bills.

"I've made enemies," he said. "You make your mark in this world, they're gonna find you. They'll hate you just because you built something and they didn't."

Doyle started to say something else and stopped himself. He wasn't used to trying to justify himself to a two-bit thug like me. Just another moment that was out of character for him. He looked out the window again and breathed deeply. We were coming to it now.

"I have a daughter," Doyle said. "She's twenty-four. Still lives at home."

I didn't say anything. There was so little air in the room that I was scared to breathe.

"She's not ... connected with what I do. Never has been. Not once in her life, you understand? And now. Now she's been threatened. Not because she did anything. Because of who her father is."

I waited.

"I want you to protect her."

I opened my mouth to turn him down. Instead, what I said was "All right." Somewhere, Sancho Panza was holding my horse so that I could mount it for another tilt at the windmill.

Doyle rose from his chair without a visible sign of effort and strode to his desk. His steps made no noise on the polished marble floor. He pressed a button on the console of his desk.

"Bring her in."

A few seconds later, a small mountain range opened a hidden door near one of the floor-to-ceiling bookcases behind Doyle's desk and stepped through. I'd met the mountain before. His name was Ralph, and he was nearly seven feet tall and must have weighed better than four hundred pounds. Maybe his mother couldn't pronounce Alps. Who knows. He stepped aside for a slip of a girl with auburn hair and eyes as green as the Irish hillside.

In the movies, a girl like that would be beautiful. Doyle's daughter couldn't be identified so easily. Her features were strong, and her teeth were small and white and perfect in the grin she flashed automatically. She was somewhere past cute and nowhere near lovely. Striking. That was the word for her.

The mountain stayed where he was as she came forward and extended her hand. Breeding. I shook it gently.

"Abby," she said.

She held my hand a moment too long, a slim girl in a yellow sun dress. Her legs were muscular and lean. In a pair of cork-soled wedge sandals, she very nearly reached my shoulders.

Doyle spoke before I could.

"This is Mr. Kincaid. He'll be responsible for your personal safety for the next little while."

She looked me over like a butcher appraising a wormy scrap of meat.

"I'd think Ralph is enough," she said. "If something happens, I can always hide behind him." The corner of her mouth turned up slightly, and her eyes sparkled with self-amusement.

"Yeah, but is he handsome and charming?" I said.

She shook her head.

"No, but at least he doesn't talk much."

"Thank God for small favors."

Behind Abby, Ralph was giving me the dead-eyed stare of the professional tough guy. He looked at Doyle and then back at me.

"You don't want to get too cute," Ralph said. His voice was a low burble like a diesel engine set to idle. He was right, of course. Without a lot of room to maneuver, The big man's size would make him a lot of trouble to handle. I let my hands relax at my sides, very conscious of the gun against the small of my back. In that moment of crystalline stillness, I felt I could see everything, even the pores of Ralph's face and the diamond solitaire on Abby's left hand.

"Stand down," Doyle said from behind his desk. His voice carried the tone of utter command. He was watching us both carefully. I'm sure he saw the tension in my shoulders as I considered what to do if Ralph decided to make a move.

"Ralph, you've done your job. You can go."

The man-mountain turned around and went out the door he and Abby had entered. I was a bastion of restraint. I didn't stick my tongue out at him when he left.

Abby was looking at me thoughtfully.

"What would you have done if Ralph kept coming?"

"Shot him five times in the upper lip with a .38-caliber revolver," I said.

She raised an eyebrow. Her eyes were a deeper green than her father's, full of fire where his were dead calm. Life hadn't beaten her down yet. I kind of hoped that it never would. The devilish grin still lurked around the corners of her mouth.

"Only five times? Doesn't that kind of gun hold six shots?"

"If the first five didn't do the job, I was saving the last one for myself." I inclined my head toward her father. "Let him explain it to the cops."

She laughed, and that changed things. When she laughed, she was no longer just a striking-looking woman. In the moment when humor and intelligence animated her features so perfectly, she was finally beautiful.

I was very aware of Doyle behind us, hands flat against the top of his desk. He was watching us intently. I cleared my throat and turned away from Abby.

"You'll go everywhere with her," Doyle said. "I don't want her out of your sight."

"If you want 24-hour protection, it will cost more."

Doyle knew my rates. He didn't blink.

"Her building is secure. Pick her up every morning. Stay with her until she's safe in the building at night."

He reached under the desk and brought out a brown paper bag, the kind of sack a normal person might bring their lunch to work in.

"You'll want something for a retainer," he said, digging out bundles of hundred-dollar bills. He put them on the desk, and I made them disappear, a neat magic trick I've had to practice once or twice in the past. Once the greenbacks were salted away, I turned from Doyle's desk and took his daughter's arm.

"Come with me," I said. "I'll take you places you've never seen."

She laughed, her head casually bumping against my shoulder.

"I hope we'll stop at the club first. I have a tennis lesson."

Doyle's voice cracked behind us.

"I'm tired of jokes, Kincaid. If anything happens to her, I'll make sure—"

I turned back to him. We stared across open space at one another. The space between us felt charged, as though lightning could strike at any moment, as if the intensity of our stares were flint and steel and the open space between us was dry kindling waiting for the spark.

"If anything happens to her, I'll already be dead," I told him, my words flat and hard. "You know how I work."

We left him leaning against his desk with a look on his face that said he wasn't sure what he'd just bought.

It was a look I was used to.

THREE

"TENNIS LESSON" didn't quite describe what Abby Doyle did at the Magic City Racquet Club. She spent nearly two hours chasing down balls, hammering groundstrokes, chipping little spinning backhands and charging the net, and finished up by practicing a serve that looked ready for Wimbledon. Her coach, a wiry, medium-sized guy with the dark tan of a man exposed always to the sun, was hard-pressed to get to many of her shots, and sometimes they were so far out of reach, he didn't try at all.

I was wearing a pair of wraparound sunglasses and listening to the steady beat of her work on the court. The sun warmed my face, and I knew I'd have to be careful not to burn. My usual jobs kept me out at night, sometimes all night. I was used to sleeping through most of the day, so the sun and I weren't as well acquainted as we could've been.

Around us, other women were busy with private lessons, too. There were sixteen courts at the club—some covered in grass, some in composite, and a few like this one, covered in Alabama red clay. As a protection detail, it was pretty easy. No one could approach the court without being seen. Of course, if they'd hired a sniper ... the thought made the back of my neck itch, but the chances were remote. By the time Abby came off the court, she was sweating hard, her shoulders and biceps glistening in the afternoon sunlight. Her top was damp and see-through in several places. I maintained eye contact until she moved to a courtside bench and sat down.

"You took off your coat," she said, zipping her racquet into a gym bag where two others already rested. "You must be burning up. Let me get changed and we'll go up to the clubhouse and get a cold drink."

I slipped my coat back on despite the heat. I was aware, as I always was when I wore a gun, of the holster at the small of my back. We stepped into the clubhouse and felt the blessed cold of the air-conditioning hit. I waited outside the women's locker room as she changed.

The racquet club's main building housed locker rooms for men and women, a private bar, a swanky restaurant that took up most of the second floor, and a gift shop. Security was pretty good. I was asked twice by uniformed women why I was lurking around outside the locker room. Each time, the security guard stepped into the room to verify that I was a guest of Abby Doyle. Each time they returned, they were courteous.

It took a little more than thirty minutes for Abby to decide she looked presentable. When she rejoined me, it was worth the wait. Her makeup was understated, and she was wearing the same dress that she'd been wearing earlier. This time, though, she was in flats.

"Do you want a drink, or are you hungry?"

"Both," she said, laughing. "Every time Len trains me, I have to work a little harder out there. He's very good."

"You seemed pretty good yourself," I said, and she nodded in assent, and that made me like her even more than I already did. She didn't demur from the compliment, simply accepted it as a fact she already knew. She *was* very good.

It was mid-afternoon, well past the lunch rush, so we didn't have to wait for a table. Abby had a glass of white wine. The club didn't carry Carta Blanca, so I settled for Sam Adams in a tall glass. One makes do.

The round cocktail table where we sat was so small that our knees nearly touched underneath it. I drank a little of my beer and studied the menu briefly. As I did, I kept flicking my eyes around the room. We probably weren't going to come under attack at a fancy-schmancy lunch, but I'd learned a long time ago that you had to prepare for what someone might do, rather than what you think they will do. I had my sunglasses perched on top of my head. Our server brought a bread basket, and Abby attacked it with knife and butter.

After she'd put away a couple of rolls, she calmed down a little and drank some more wine.

"Sorry," she said. "Carbs are my weakness."

"Nothing to apologize for," I said. "People gotta eat." Now that I was certain I wouldn't get my hand chewed off, I felt confident in reaching for a roll of my own.

"Dad always wants me to be ladylike, take small bites. Small sips. Be dainty. I haven't been dainty for a long time."

It made me grin.

"What?"

"You're hungry. You don't have to justify how you eat. If I'd expended the energy you just did, I'd be so hungry I'd probably take a few bites out of the table."

"Well, you know, I have *some* self-control." She made a show of examining the table. "It's probably got a lot of fiber, though."

She polished off another roll and looked longingly at the empty basket.

"Oh well," she said. "It was good while it lasted."

"I'm sure we could get some more."

She sat back and shook her head.

"No, I only excess in moderation."

The rest of lunch proved her out. She had a steak salad, the beef cooked rare, and drank another glass of wine. In between, she drank several glasses of water. Outside of the carb-lusting first ten minutes, she seemed to have iron willpower. When our plates were clean, she sat back with a contented look on her face.

"Do you like tennis?"

"I liked Jimmy Connors."

Abby rolled her eyes.

"Would you like to play sometime? I could get you a guest pass."

I thought about it for a minute, then shook my head.

"I don't think so."

"Why? Scared a girl might beat you?"

I was on my second beer by then. The bubbles rose slowly in the glass and popped when they reached the surface.

"No," I said. "You're very good. You must know that. I wouldn't be a challenge for you, so I wouldn't feel badly about losing. Just like you can't bench press three hundred pounds, and you shouldn't feel bad about that, either."

Abby cocked her head at me.

"So why?"

I shrugged.

"No interest," I said. I watched her take a sip of wine. "Besides, who wants to lose to a girl?"

It got her. Abby laughed in mid-swallow. She coughed—in a less elegant woman, it might have been a snort—and some of the wine ended up back in the glass. Some of it ended up on the table, too. She dabbed at the mess with her napkin as she giggled. Tears of laughter stood in her eyes.

"Good lord," she said. "You're supposed to be protecting me, not trying to kill me."

The server came by to check that everything was okay. Abby thought about another glass of wine, and then changed her mind.

"Bring me a margarita, rocks, lots of salt," she said. The server looked at me.

"I'm good, thanks."

When the server left, Abby looked askance at me.

"Working," I said.

"Oh," she said. "Right. We were having such a nice time that I forgot."

"That's all right. I didn't."

It was pleasant duty to sit there and talk with this lithe, attractive woman as the afternoon sped on to early evening. She took pictures of everything, clicking away with the latest and greatest smartphone. A couple of times I had to shy away as she tried to get me in the pictures, and I had to explain that my work went better if I didn't show up on social media. We were still at the table an hour and two margaritas later when a frat boy from central casting showed up. As he approached the table, I stood and blocked his path, keeping my body between him and Abby.

"Get out of my way," he said, and tried to step around me.

"Not gonna happen."

Abby hadn't moved from her chair. After the wine and the margaritas, she was very relaxed.

"It's just Britt," she said behind me. "My fiancé." The alcohol had brought out her Southern accent, and Britt's name gained another syllable. She put no heat into the word fiancé, but I detected some disdain in her voice. Or maybe that was just me.

I looked at her.

"Can he join us? Or would you prefer to drink alone?"

That spark of amusement glinted in her eyes, just a flash before it vanished.

"What would you do if I said no?"

"Remove him from the premises."

"Not bloody likely," Britt said. He tried to step past me again, but I was too quick. I moved with him, like a dance partner matching his steps.

He was taller than me, nearly as slender as Abby, and the suit he wore looked like it had been tailored to fit. Bespoke, I think they call it these days. His hair was razor-cut, thinning at the temples, and it was easy to see the kind of older man that he'd relax into one day. King of the yacht club, terror of the golf course, and master of the nineteenth hole.

"Come on, Abs, cut it out," he said. "This is childish."

Abby was diligently drinking the last of her margarita. She placed her glass back on the table with a loud click.

"It's kind of fun, though," she said.

I stepped away from Britt then. "Sit down," I said. He looked at me, puzzled.

"I hired on to protect her," I said. "I'm not here for entertainment value."

Abby looked away from the table as Britt dragged up a chair. This time there was no amusement in her emerald eyes. Now the eyes were hard, and I could see the resemblance to her father.

"You don't have to be so damned smug about it," she said. I didn't say anything.

The server came by again, and Britt ordered a gin and tonic. Once the waiter went away, Abby explained who I was. He turned back to me when she was done.

"And you're just letting her get drunk in the middle of the day? Some bodyguard."

"I don't control what she does," I said. "My job is to follow along and mitigate any danger that might appear."

Britt didn't say anything. His drink came, and he took a long pull from it.

"I'm here now," he said. "You can take off."

I shook my head.

"You don't pay the bill," I said. "I stay until she's safe inside her apartment."

Britt made a face, as though he'd tasted something foul in his drink. But it was me he found objectionable.

"I can take care of her. I've got a black belt."

"Goes lovely with your black shoes," I said, and Abby giggled, despite her snit.

"You think I'm not tough?"

"I think you're a lawyer," I said. "Or an accountant. I wouldn't come to your office and tell you how to do your work."

He took another long pull from his drink and set the empty glass down. He frowned for a moment, making up his mind. Then he stood up.

"On your feet," he said. "You think you're some kind of tough guy? I'll show you what I can do."

The truth was that I didn't care if Britt was tougher than me. I didn't care that he had a black belt. If he beat me up, it wouldn't be the first time I'd lost a fight. I had no interest in proving I was tougher or better than him. But if I didn't do something, he was going to keep pushing. He stood there in front of me, his belt buckle about eye level from where I was sitting.

I punched him in the balls, hard, following through with the punch and using a lot of shoulder. He yipped and doubled over, his hands cupping the front of his expensive slacks. I caught him by the shoulders and kept him from falling long enough to help him back into his chair. He clutched himself and sat there with his head down, his breathing ragged. Abby was watching, her eyes bright with mirth and avaricious interest.

"I don't want to take anything away from your black belt," I said to Britt, "but I'm sort of what you'd call a professional thug. I do this kind of thing for a living."

He didn't look up at me.

"I wasn't ready," he said. His voice was low and hard, as if it was an effort to speak.

"That's the difference between a professional and an amateur," I told him. "My job is to be ready."

We sat in uncomfortable silence for a few minutes while Britt tried to collect his little Britts and pieces. I thought about ordering another beer, this one from the bottle. If he lunged at me, I could hit him over the head with it. Can't take me anywhere nice.

When he finally got his breathing under control, he said, "I'll sue you for that."

"For what? I didn't see anything" I looked at Abby. "Did you?"

"No," she said. "Truthfully, Britt would be a lot nicer person if someone would punch him in the balls on a weekly basis."

I nodded.

"My rates are reasonable."

"Oh, you two think you're fucking funny," Britt said. "We'll see, tough guy. One day you won't be ready, and I'll be there."

He was trying to make himself feel better, trying to reclaim some of the manhood he felt I'd taken away from him. I'd just punched him in the balls in front of his fiancée, and instead of seeming miffed, she was entertained. Maybe I'd be angry, too. But it wasn't the time to let Britt live under delusions of revenge.

"Do you know Hamlet?"

Britt looked confused.

"Hamlet," I said. "It's a play, written around 1600 by a guy named Will—"

"I know what fucking Hamlet is." Beside us, Abby convulsed in silent laughter. Tears spilled down her cheeks as her body shook with seismic giggles.

"Good for you," I said without hesitation. "Hamlet said 'Readiness is all.'"

I waited a beat, until Britt looked directly into my eyes. When I was sure I had his full attention, I continued. My voice was as flat and hard as a Republican's heart.

"I will always be ready."

He snorted and stood up from the table. I didn't get up. He brushed the front of his pants sort of gingerly, turned his back on us, and walked away.

"He's a pleasant fellow," I said. "Friend to all who meet him, loved by small woodland creatures everywhere."

Abby got herself under control. Sort of. She dabbed at her eyes with a napkin, and every now and then her shoulders shudder with repressed giggles.

"I'll pay for that later tonight," she said. "But God, it was worth it."

"What do you mean?" I said.

"It's nothing."

She stared at the diamond solitaire on her left ring finger. So did I. It was a very large diamond.

"Sometimes," she said, and paused. She wouldn't meet my gaze. "Sometimes this thing weighs a ton."

I didn't know what she meant. I'd never been engaged.

"Does he hurt you?" The words were out before I realized they were coming. I didn't mean to ask, because I really didn't want to know. It wasn't any of my business.

"Probably not as much as I hurt him," she said. She looked around for the server. "I think I'm going to have another margarita before dinner."

"Up to you," I said. "Wither thou goest, I go."

We sat and she drank while I kept an eye out for a busboy carrying a shank. Or an Uzi. The dining room, which had been nearly empty when we first arrived, began to fill up for dinner service. I asked her if she wanted to stay at the club or go somewhere else for dinner.

"Here is good," she said. She had a little trouble with the sibilant s sound. On the other hand, between the wine and the margaritas, she'd had enough alcohol to anesthetize a horse. I walked her to the restroom twice and stood outside the door each time.

She talked very little about anything but her tennis game and the charitable work she did. Abby was something of a normal Birmingham WASP, just like the rest of the ones that had moved from the city proper out into the suburbs. She didn't have to work, so she didn't. She'd been to college—the University of Alabama, naturally—and had a degree in public relations. Mostly what she did was help raise money for worthy causes, play tennis, and enjoy an active social life.

Toward the end of the meal, she tried to turn the conversation toward me.

"You're not exactly what I thought you'd be," she said. "You're not just quiet when I talk. You're really listening, aren't you?"

"It's a way to learn things," I said.

"So tell me about yourself."

"No," I said.

"No? What do you mean, no?"

"You know what you need to," I said. "I'm competent. I'll stand up for you. I won't try to direct what you do unless you endanger your own safety."

She took a final swallow of her drink. She must've been beyond drunk by now, but I couldn't tell it just from looking at her.

"That's cutting it pretty fine," she said.

I shrugged.

"I could make something up, if you'd like. The truth is that I'm not very interesting. What you see is what you get."

She played with the ice in her glass, stirring it around with a swizzle stick, looking for any last bits of tequila she might have missed.

"What about your hopes and dreams?"

"Don't have any," I said.

"Really? I don't believe you. Everyone has dreams. Everyone wants something."

I saw the server and asked for the check. When it came, Abby was still sober enough to sign for everything, which included Britt's drink. She added a tip while I took a big breath and let it out.

"It doesn't matter much if you believe it," I said. "As long as you understand that I believe it. I don't hope. I don't dream. I see what's there. That's all there is."

Abby stood up from her seat, placing her hands on the table. In that moment she reminded me of the last time we'd seen her father, palms down on the big mahogany desk in his office at the top of the John Hand building. Unlike him, she was simply trying to keep her balance. I stepped around the table and took her arm and we went out of the racquet club. Her apartment was too far away to walk, so I opened the passenger door of my Mustang and bundled her inside. She was asleep and snoring lightly by the time I got into the driver's side.

She lived in the Pizitz Building on 19th Street North, a white brick mixed-use building with the bottom floor taken up by an eclectic mix of food stalls, a favorite of the white hipsters who seemed to be flocking back into Birmingham as the city's urban renewal plans hit their stride.

Most of the WASPs who called Birmingham home didn't actually live in the city. They lived in suburbs like Hoover or Homewood or Vestavia Hills. The filthy rich lived in Mountain Brook. It said something about Abby that she chose to live in Birmingham proper. Maybe there was something more to her than the spoiled little rich girl I'd seen so far during our time together. I hoped so. I liked her.

I parked on the deck next to Abby's building and shook her awake. She looked a little embarrassed to have fallen asleep, but neither one of us said anything. We walked across to the Pizitz, got in the elevator, and went up to her apartment.

I knew something was wrong the moment we got off on her floor. Gunpowder leaves a particular smell, and it was fragrant in the hallway. Abby's apartment door was open. I hustled her back down the hall to a stairwell, checked the door, and pushed her inside it. I pressed my keys into her hand.

"Go sit in the car," I said. "Lock the doors. Don't open up for anyone who isn't me or a cop."

"What's going on?" She asked. Her voice was still thickly clotted with sleep and booze. "I don't understand."

"Me either," I said, "but I can't check it out if you're here with me. I don't have any way to keep you safe."

She moved off down the stairs, her movements slow and languid, swimming under the influence of the distillery she'd ingested. I waited until she was out of earshot before stepping back into the hallway. By now my nose was getting used to the smell of gunpowder. There was something else underneath the smell, as unpleasant and wormy as the underside of a crawling kingsnake, and I knew what I was going to find when I went into Abby's apartment.

I just didn't know who.

Abby's apartment was immaculate. The floors were silvery ceramic tile polished to a near-mirror shine, and the walls were a creamy white. There was no dust in the place, no dirty dishes in the sink. Fresh flowers stood in fluted vases, and the art on the walls wasn't done by anyone I'd ever heard of, but it all looked original. A pair of matching leather sofas sat in the living room, where a glass coffee table had been shattered by the body's fall.

Britt lay face up, halfway on the ceramic tile floor and halfway on a white shag rug that would never come clean again. He wore an expression of surprise forever etched on his face. Blood seeped from behind his ear onto the floor.

I didn't need to touch the body to tell that he was dead. The hole in the middle of his forehead told me that. Sometime after he'd been shot, his colon and bladder had let go. That was the smell underneath the odor of the freshly fired round. There wasn't a ton of blood from the wound, but I could see powder burns on his skin. Someone had held a small-caliber pistol to his forehead and pulled the trigger.

I knelt next to the body and found the source of the blood that trickled from his left ear. A bullet hole behind his left ear. There was no exit wound.

Guns kill. It's what they're made to do. That's just a fact. Larger calibers mean larger holes. But sometime back, some gangster film had shown that hired killers preferred smaller caliber weapons. It was supposedly the mark of a professional. I don't know how true that actually is—it's never been my preference—but some of the people who saw those kinds of movies apparently took the idea to heart.

Britt had been the victim of the ol' double-tap: one behind the ear, and one to the forehead, just to make sure. The killer used a small-caliber weapon, nothing bigger than a .25, so that the first shot—the one that actually killed Britt—bounced around in his skull for a little while, turning his brain into so much tapioca.

The second shot was just a way to show off. Like the flourish on an autograph.

Finally, I put my fingers to the big artery in his neck, just as a formality. No pulse, of course. But his body was still warm. It had happened not too long ago, maybe even while we were in the car. We'd missed the killer by no more than a few minutes.

By the time I hit the hallway, I was running. I sprinted down the stairs two at a time, my sweating palm squeaking against the handrail. I hit the exit door with my shoulder and stumbled out into the humid night. The parking deck loomed ahead of me, and I streaked for it.

Abby was locked in the passenger seat, safe and sound. When she saw me, her eyes grew wide. I motioned for her to open the door.

She got out and I told her about Britt. I don't know what I expected, but she took it calmly. Maybe it was her natural demeanor. Maybe it was the booze. I still don't know. But she came with me when I went back upstairs.

I ushered her into the apartment, keeping myself between her and the body, and we went to her bedroom. I checked her closet, the bathroom, and even under the bed. When I was satisfied she was alone, I shut the door.

I slipped my phone from my pocket and dialed 911. Almost before I hung up, I could hear the sirens in the distance hurtling toward us.

FOUR

IT WAS PAST TWO A.M. and the crime scene people weren't finished yet. The cops had questioned Abby for more than two hours before they called it quits with her. She'd taken some Valium and was now asleep in her bedroom. I leaned against one of the spotless white living room walls and ran through it with the detective again. No, I hadn't seen who did it. Yes, I'd had an altercation with the defendant earlier in the day. Yes, I could account for my whereabouts. The questions were tedious, and I'd answered them several times over the course of the last few hours. My eyes felt like ground glass, and all I wanted was some sleep.

"You're not exactly the kind of company Miss Doyle usually keeps."

The detective was a woman in her late 30s, with an expensive pantsuit tailored to fit. She wore her badge on her belt. Her brown hair was streaked with expensive-looking blonde highlights that fell to her shoulders, and her nails were lacquered with clear polish. She wore cop shoes, thick-soled, good quality leather uppers.

Her appearance told me a couple of things about her: She was feminine, but professional. She was someone to be taken seriously. I heard one of the crime scene techs call her Detective D'Agostino.

But she hadn't asked me a question, so I didn't say anything. Something I learned a long time ago, when I was younger and dumber: If a cop doesn't ask you a question, don't answer them. Never make their job easier.

D'Agostino tried again. "Why don't you tell us what you were really doing with her today?"

"I've answered all of your questions," I said. "Miss Doyle is tired. I'm tired, too."

My answer didn't phase her. If she was irritated, I couldn't tell. Here we were, well past the time of night when any reasonable person would be in bed. The detective looked fresh as a daisy, ready to be pleasant and persistent until she got what she wanted or until the trumpet sound of Revelation, whichever came first.

Just looking at her made me even more tired. Of course, that was part of the affectation she wore. I wondered what it would take to pierce that kind of armor. I kind of admired her.

"I don't like this," she said. "You're a known thug, a legbreaker, been violent all of your life. I like you for this."

I spread my hands.

"Alibi," I said. "You can like me for it all you want. But three things: One, I didn't do it; two, I got a witness who swears she was with me the whole time; and three, I bet you'll find closed circuit cameras that show I was at the racquet club with Miss Doyle until we drove here. Then you'll find security footage of when we arrived. I'm covered."

She crossed her arms over her chest and tapped her front teeth with one lacquered fingernail. It gave me pause. I'd known a woman, a long time ago, who used to do the same thing when she was thinking.

"What, exactly, were you doing with Miss Doyle?"

"Family friend," I said. "Just passing the time."

She tapped her teeth again. "You're a liar. And a bad one."

Maybe so. But I don't spill to the cops. At least not when there's nothing in it for me.

"We know who her father is," she said. "We know what you are. You think we won't find a way to connect the dots? Tell me what's going on here."

One of the techs told D'Agostino that they were done with the crime scene. A couple of paramedics zipped Britt's stiffening body into a black bag and carted him away on a stretcher. They wouldn't use the sirens on the way to the morgue. Britt didn't need them.

"I met him earlier today," I said. "I don't even know his last name."

"It's Parker. How did you meet him?"

I told her, and she tilted her head at me.

"You punched him out? Why tell me?"

"If you're any good at your job, you'd find out about it anyway. And when you found out, you'd want to know why I hadn't told you."

D'Agostino nodded. She knew I was right. I'd been arrested before, and had gone through multiple interrogations. Although I'd never been convicted of anything, I knew how the cops worked. So when I can, I tell the truth. Nothing confuses cops like truth.

When the last of the crime scene people departed, the detective stuck around. When it was just the two of us, she walked around Abby's living space, not searching, just the genuine curiosity of a stranger in a new place.

"Where's your partner?" I asked. "Don't you guys work in pairs anymore?"

The detective snorted.

"Budget cuts," she said. "You don't get two detectives out to work a domestic scene. Are you going to quit the bullshit and tell me what's going on here?"

I decided I liked her. She was like a bulldog after a bone.

"Not today," I said.

"I can guess some of it. You're protection, aren't you?"

I didn't want to lie to her, so I held my silence, which was as good as an admission. Her face brightened.

"So if you're guarding her body, that raises the question: Why does she need to be protected?" Her eyes narrowed. "She doesn't have a sheet. Not so much as a parking ticket. But her father could buy her a lot of innocence, make a lot of things go away. God knows he's got influence all over this town."

Enough.

"You want a drink?" I asked, and got up to rummage through Abby's kitchen cabinets. I found a bottle of Basil & Hayden bourbon in the fourth door I tried. Ah, well. Beggars can't be choosers. A couple more tries led me to some heavy lowball glasses. I put them on the kitchen counter and poured a couple fingers' worth of bourbon into each of them, then went to the fridge and added a couple of ice cubes. D'Agostino watched me the whole time.

"You're confirming my theory," she said.

I shook my head and handed her a glass. She held it carefully in both hands.

"You're not a friend, and you're not in a relationship with Miss Doyle. You didn't know where she kept the liquor or glassware. You keep shifting about like you're in a new place."

I took a sip from my drink, feeling the liquor integrate down into my body, making me feel a little inflated and whole, as it always did. Some of my exhaustion lifted, even though I knew it would only be temporary. D'Agostino used both hands to lift the glass to her lips. She closed her eyes and took a deep breath, inhaling the smoky aroma of the liquor. Her eyelashes were long and thick, but if she was wearing mascara, I couldn't tell it. She set the glass down carefully.

"Are you wearing a gun?" She asked.

I shook my head. "First patrol guy on the scene frisked me as soon as they found out I had a sheet."

She snorted. "So where did you hide your weapon?"

"It wouldn't be fair if I told you, would it?"

She put her glass down on the counter.

"Restroom is down the hall, right?" I nodded, and she headed that way. A couple of minutes went by and she came back out, a look of disappointment on her face.

"You were hoping I'd hidden it in the toilet tank? Detective, everyone's seen *The Godfather.*"

She smiled—the first genuine smile I'd seen from her—and something that felt like a glacier in my heart cracked. The force of genuine warmth and amusement from D'Agostino was so physical that I nearly staggered.

"Can't blame a girl for trying," she said, and picked up her drink. This time she drank a little whiskey. We sipped in silence for a moment. It was past three a.m. I yawned, suddenly aware of how bone-tired I was. Whiskey is good for a temporary lift, but the comedown is steep.

"I'll want you and Miss Doyle to come down to the station later today to sign your statements."

"Sure."

"You were being honest, weren't you? You don't know who did this."

I rubbed my hands over my face, trying to keep the tiredness at bay.

"No reason to lie about it," I said. "Well, not yet, anyway."

"I don't know how to take that."

"That's okay," I said. "I don't know how I meant it." Another yawn stretched my face. My entire body felt like taffy, pulled and stretched nearly beyond its limits. I watched D'Agostino finish her drink. I tossed mine off, too.

"I'll be more charming when I've had some rest."

"I'll take that as my cue to get the hell out," she said. "But I'm serious. I want both of you at the station tomorrow. Today, I mean."

"Gimme four hours of sleep, and I'm all yours."

She shot me a look, but I kept my face blank. A few minutes later, she left. I took a quick tour around the apartment, making sure the windows were locked and the deadbolt on the door was secure.

My gun was where I'd put it, taped securely to the back of one of the original oil paintings that hung on Abby's walls. I stripped the tape off and checked the loads out of habit. No one else had handled the gun, but it had been out of my sight for several hours. It was a habit that might save my life one day. Then I retrieved my holster from Abby's underwear drawer. She was snoring gently in the bed behind me. I tried not to look at the gossamer bits of barely-there ephemera that passed for her underwear, but that was impossible. She was an attractive young woman, and the knowledge of what she was wearing—or what she wasn't—played in my head.

Sleep. I needed to sleep desperately. I put the holster back on my belt and slid the gun home until the spring pressure clicked and it was secure.

Sitting down on one of the brown leather couches was heaven. I remember leaning back, feeling my neck and shoulders relax. The next thing I knew, it was early afternoon and the sun was shining brightly through the floor-to-ceiling windows. It was just after one p.m., and my mouth tasted like an unwashed army battalion had camped in it. In the kitchen, I scared up some coffee and filters. While it dripped, I poured a short shot of the previous night's bourbon and drank it down. The world came into soft focus. When the coffee finished brewing, I poured a shot of whiskey into a ceramic cup on top of the brew. I stirred with one of Abby's spoons—heavy plated silver—and then went to her bedroom.

I knocked twice. When she didn't answer, my heart rate sped up. I didn't know why. I knocked again. Still nothing. I turned the doorknob, and it moved easily in my hand. I stepped into the inky blackness of Abby's bedroom and flipped on the overhead light.

She wasn't there.

The bed was unmade, the covers bunched at the footboard. At

one end of the room, the door to a half-bath stood ajar. I checked there. I checked under the bed and in the walk-in closet.

No Abby anywhere.

I left my high-octane coffee cooling on the counter and went out the door at a dead run. By the time I reached the stairs, I stopped.

I had no idea where to go. I didn't know her well enough to understand where she might have gone nor what might have happened to her. I called her cell phone, but it went straight to voicemail. Son of a bitch.

What to do? I didn't know. I'm not a detective. I don't find people. That's not part of my skill set. I tried to calm down. Called again, voicemail again. So her phone was either off or the battery was dead. Maybe she'd gone out to get breakfast. Or lunch. Maybe she'd figured she was being thoughtful and let me sleep.

I didn't know enough. All I knew was what my gut feeling told me: Something was wrong. I let myself back into Abby's apartment, forced myself to calm down and take a good look around.

I checked the bedroom. I didn't know enough about her to know for sure, but it seemed to me that there were some empty hangers in the closet that should have held summer clothing. There was no makeup on the bathroom counter. No hairbrush. I couldn't find a purse or a phone charger anywhere in the apartment.

So Abby had left, probably on her own accord. A kidnapper wouldn't have given her time to pack. I sat on the edge of her bed and turned my cell phone on. No new messages. Shit.

I didn't see that I had much choice. I called her father.

Doyle answered on the second ring, and I told him what had happened the day before, and what I suspected about Abby's disappearance.

"What do you mean she's gone?"

"I said what I said. Clothing is missing. Her phone and charger are gone. No makeup in the bathrooms. She left of her own accord."

"Where the fuck is she?"

"I don't know yet," I said. "But I will."

"You fucking find her," Doyle said. His voice was deadly. He didn't scream or shout. He didn't threaten. He didn't need to.

"I will," I said to the empty air. Doyle had already hung up. I looked at my phone and dug out Detective D'Agostino's card. I looked at her name. Laura. Huh. Didn't sound like an Italian name. The lettering on the card was embossed, the card stock heavy. I thought about her name. Laura D'Agostino. I remembered her slightly abashed grin when she came out of the apartment bathroom after checking the toilet tank for my weapon. She wasn't ashamed of getting caught at it; she was ashamed she'd thought I'd be that easy.

Stalling. That's what I was doing. D'Agostino was expecting me to come in and make a formal statement, and to bring Abby with me. I couldn't do that right now.

But I could call her. Why didn't I just do it? Punch in the number, talk to her. She wouldn't know the number, would probably let it go to voicemail.

So I called. Haltingly, hesitantly. When she answered, I almost hung up. It reminded me of when I was a kid and nobody had caller ID. You'd call the person you had a crush on, just to hear their voice, and hang up when they answered. She said "Hello?" for a second time, but I couldn't say anything.

"Third time's the charm," she said, and I could hear the rich undertones of exasperation and amusement in her voice. "I'll say it one more time, but then I'm hanging up."

"Don't," I said. The word croaked out of my lips, barely audible. I could taste the fear on the back of my tongue, an electrical taste like copper.

"Who is this?" She asked. I told her. And then I said something that surprised both of us.

"I need your help."

FIVE

D'AGOSTINO DID EVERYTHING she could unofficially. She didn't put out an APB, but she called on some patrol cops she trusted and sent them to the local hotels. We figured someone like Abby wouldn't stay in a pit. Spaces like those were reserved for guys like me.

I was expecting more, to be honest. You watch the cop shows on TV, they're always triangulating someone's location by the signal from their cell phones. But real life isn't like that.

"I mean, I could do it," D'Agostino told me. "Let me get a search warrant for a material witness, and I could track her credit cards and bank accounts, too, but you wanted to keep this on the down-low."

I ran a hand through my hair, racking what little brains I had.

"I know," I said. "But it feels like we're not doing enough."

"Police work is like that. You do what you can. You comb through the evidence, and you wait. And then you wait some more. You either get very patient or very, very bored."

D'Agostino had breezed into Abby's apartment a little over thirty minutes before. She'd done everything I did, gone over every corner of the apartment, and come up with the same thing I had: Abby had left on her own accord. Hearing her come to the same conclusion as me made me feel simultaneously smarter and more hopeless.

She sat at the kitchen table while I made coffee. When it was done, I poured a mug for her and set it down on the table in front of her chair.

"How'd you know I like it black?"

I flashed my teeth.

"I've known a lot of cops," I said. "Never saw one that took it any other way."

I added cream and sugar to mine and stirred it with a silver teaspoon from the cutlery drawer. D'Agostino watched me with a look of envy.

"It's not being a cop," she said. "I look at half-and-half and I gain three pounds. I don't want to wake up at fifty and weigh three hundred pounds."

I grunted. She had a long way to go to weigh three hundred. Like a whole other person. I bet during her time on patrol that her gun belt had weighed almost as much as she did. But it was none of my business.

Of course, if I'd minded my own business more, I wouldn't have gone to work for the Doyle family, and I wouldn't have a missing client.

"What about her social media?" I asked, but D'Agostino was already ahead of me. She opened her laptop and pecked away for a couple of minutes, then shoved the laptop over so I could look at the screen, too.

"Her Facebook profile hasn't been updated in, like, a year," she said. "She updates Twitter every week or so. Our girl is not very active on social media."

"What about Instagram?"

D'Agostino raised an eyebrow.

"I spent a lot of time with her yesterday. She took pictures of the food, the drinks, the view. She posted 'em somewhere."

There are approximately four thousand Abby Doyles in the United States. Fewer in Alabama, and only two in Birmingham. We narrowed it down to @abbadoo24 within a couple of minutes. She'd posted photos from the racquet club, from dinner, and then, that morning, a photo of a bottle of Veuve Clicquot champagne in a silver ice bucket. The background appeared to be a swanky hotel room that rang a distant bell in my memory.

D'Agostino and I stared at each other.

"I know that hotel," I said. "I've been there before. It'll come to me."

The detective showed how she earned her badge. She used a reverse image search and came up with a photograph taken from a similar angle. It might've even been taken in the same hotel room for all I could tell.

"It's the Tutwiler, downtown," she said. "Hell, it's a ten-minute walk from here."

We drove instead. She wanted to take her car, an official BPD cruiser, a slickback Dodge Charger without the light bar on top, but I talked her into the passenger seat of the Mustang. We were at the hotel in no time, pulling into the circular driveway and parking under the big awning in front of the hotel. The valet started toward us, but D'Agostino badged him and he waved us forward.

The Tutwiler is old Birmingham, a throwback to the lie of genteel white benevolence. The marble floors in the lobby give way to thick plush maroon carpeting in the hallways, and the elevators are still maintained by aged black men wearing the traditional operator uniform that matched the carpet. If we'd known Abby's room number, we'd have headed straight for those elevators. Instead, I let D'Agostino take the lead as we approached the front desk. After all, she was the one who had a badge.

And she knew how to use it. She had the badge and her police ID out on the counter.

"How may I assist you, officer?" The young African-American woman at the counter asked.

"Detective, actually," D'Agostino said, and the desk worker nodded.

"I'm sorry. Detective."

"We need the room number of an Abigail Doyle. Checked in sometime in the early hours of the morning."

Already the clerk was shaking her head.

"Company policy doesn't allow us to release information on past, current, or future guests," she said. The muscles at the hinges of D'Agostino's jaw tightened.

"I'm asking nicely," she said. "I can go get a search warrant and make this very messy for you and your employers if I want to."

The clerk held her ground.

"Perhaps you should do that," she said. Her voice was nearly robotic, and her gaze stayed somewhere in the middle distance between the detective and me. "The Tutwiler complies with all legal procedures. I'm sure a duly authorized warrant would be honored."

A small smile played at the corner of D'Agostino's mouth. Before she could say anything else, I put a hand on her arm and gently pulled her back toward me. Her entire body was quivering with anger.

"Let me try," I whispered. My lips were so close that they brushed her ear when I spoke. I took out my wallet, selected a bill, and folded it into my palm.

"I'm sorry about my partner," I told the clerk. "Sometimes she gets a little aggressive when she doesn't need to."

The clerk's eyes flicked toward me and away again. "I can see that."

"Perhaps we don't need a search warrant?" I moved my fingers to show her the bill was a hundred.

The clerk cocked her head to the side and smiled at me.

"I'm sorry, sir. Information about the Tutwiler's guests is not for sale."

So much for the nice guy approach. I thanked her and stuffed the bill back into my pocket. I steered D'Agostino by the arm, and we went out the front door and down a side alley. She was still fuming.

"Goddamn it," she said. "That little bitch."

I laughed, but only a little.

"She called your bluff," I said. "She's dealt with cops before."

D'Agostino crossed her arms over her chest and leaned against the wall of the hotel.

"Yeah. I'd like a chance to run her sheet sometime."

She paused. I could see her fighting her anger. The battle was all over her face. This was a formidable woman, and one who didn't like being thwarted. But she took a deep breath and set it aside.

"We should've tried your approach first. I screwed it up by coming on too strong."

I wasn't going to agree with her—at least not out loud—because I'd seen what she looked like when she was angry. But I thought it would have made a difference. So we waited beside the locked service entrance to the hotel until one of the maids came out. A twenty got us in the building, and then we cautiously made our way to the rickety old elevators, keeping out of sight of the woman at the front desk. We rode up the first elevator, chatting with the operator who had been on shift since midnight. D'Agostino showed him a picture of Abby from one of the social media apps on her phone. He hadn't seen Abby come in, and was most sorry he couldn't help us. I duked him a twenty to forget he'd seen us, and he made the folded bill disappear as if he were starring in a magic act on the Vegas strip. We rode back down and caught the other elevator. This time we struck gold.

Abby had come up with another guest, and they'd gotten off on the sixth floor. I motioned for the operator to kill the elevator, and he stopped the car on the fifth floor, pushing a button to keep the doors closed.

"I don't suppose you saw what room they went in."

The operator grinned at me, a gold tooth glinting far back in his mouth.

"I did not," he said. "You her husband? Here to cause her some trouble?"

Beside me, D'Agostino smirked. I ignored her.

"No," I said. "But it's important that we find her."

"How important?" He didn't actually put his hand out, but the implication was there. I handed him the Benjamin I'd offered the woman at the front desk. He tucked it away inside the ridiculously formal coat he wore.

"I didn't see what room she went in," he said, "but I seen who she was with, and that's just as good. Martin James keeps a suite on the sixth floor, number 604. She come up with him, she's probably still there. I see a lotta girls come up with him. They usually stay the night."

I gave him another twenty to forget he'd seen us, just like the other operator. He made that bill disappear just as neatly as the hundred. D'Agostino and I got off on the fifth floor and went up one flight of stairs.

Number 604 was a corner suite. A few doors past its door, a cleaning cart stood. I looked at D'Agostino. It was time for her to take the lead again.

She badged the maid, a stout Latinx woman wearing a gray uniform and orthopedic hose. I turned away from the fear in her eyes. It occurred to me that D'Agostino's badge was just as much a weapon as her gun. While the detective distracted her, I went to the cart and found what I was looking for: a magnetic card about the size of a credit card. It was a master key that would open any door on the sixth floor. I nabbed it and strode quickly down to Martin James' suite. I slid the card through, watched the red light on the door lock blink once and then switch to green. I turned the handle and the door swung free.

I left it open a crack while I replaced the key card. D'Agostino kept the maid distracted, and I saw her nod a little at me, acknowledging that everything was clear. I slipped back to Room 604.

My breath came shallow and irregular. I inched the door open and waited, hoping that I wouldn't smell gunpowder again. The scent from the day before had dissipated from my nostrils, but the memory of it was fresh. I breathed out slowly and pushed the door open the rest of the way. I couldn't smell anything.

I moved further into the suite.

Abby wasn't there. Or at least she wasn't in the sitting room. There was a big bouquet of fresh flowers on the coffee table, and the drapes were open to let in the light from the outside. A couple of bottles from the minifridge had been cracked open and left on the bureau where the flat-screen TV stood. The door to the bedroom was closed.

On my way there, I stopped to check the bathroom. I'd look like an awful fool if some guy stepped out of the john and shot me in the back. I flipped on the light. No one sat on the toilet. I checked the shower, too, just to be safe. No one there, either. If someone was in the suite, they had to be in the bedroom.

I was only a couple of steps away from the closed door when I heard a long muffled moan from behind it. I don't remember drawing my weapon, but it was in my hand when I went through the door.

I don't know what I expected, but seeing Martin James naked and tied to a four-poster king-sized bed wasn't it.

James was a developer, a guy famous for getting a lot of the Avondale and Crestwood neighborhoods rezoned and gentrified. He wasn't yet thirty years old, but he owned a piece of three downtown restaurants, a microbrewery, and a couple of bars on Second Avenue. He had friends in the mayor's office and on the Jefferson County Commission.

In other words: James was a big fucking deal in Birmingham.

He was long and lean, except for an incongruous little potbelly that mounded his middle like an Appalachian foothill. His nose had been broken once upon a time and set inexpertly, and his cheeks bore the broken capillaries of a man who likes the liquor a little too much. I knew the signs because I had an early version of that same red-veined road map on my own face.

And here he was, laid out and trussed up neat as a Christmas turkey. Silk scarves ran from his ankles to the bedposts at his feet. His wrists were similarly bound at the head of the bed. He wore a red ball gag in his mouth and nothing else.

I moved over to him and took the gag away. He moved his jaw tenderly for a few seconds.

"Where is she?" He rasped.

"Who?"

He looked even more annoyed, if that was possible.

"Abby Goddamn Doyle is her name. She left me like this, god-damn it. Untie me. I've got to go to work. Ah, Jesus, when I get my hands on that little bitch—"

It didn't take a lot of imagination to see what had happened here. Abby let herself get picked up, came up here to the hotel room with James, and then suggested a little something unusual. Once she had him tied up, she left. The trail was cold.

"What time did she leave?"

"I don't know. Now untie me, motherfucker! I've got to take a piss."

I pursed my lips and looked around the room. A pair of gab-ardine slacks puddled on the floor at the foot of the bed. Beside them, a slim black wallet lay open. I picked it up and thumbed through it. No cash, but that didn't necessarily mean anything. James's ID and credit cards all seemed to be present. I closed the wallet and tossed it onto his naked belly.

"How much cash did she take?"

He wouldn't look at me.

"I said—"

"I heard you. I don't know how much. I keep a couple hundred in my wallet for emergencies. I guess she got that. She took the roll, too."

"The roll?"

"I keep a roll in my pocket." He hesitated. "You never know. I might see something I want to buy."

"How much?"

He was silent for a time. We could hear the cleaning woman. She was in the suite now. D'Agostino was talking to her. They were coming closer. I went to the door and locked it.

"Still time for a little guy talk," I said. "How much did she take?"

"A little less than ten grand."

I guess my face showed my surprise.

"What?" He said.

"Why the hell did you have ten grand on you?"

"I always do."

I didn't know what to say to that, so we sat there for a minute. Pretty soon, though, he shook his hands against the silk bindings.

"Are you going to let me out of this?"

"In a minute. Where do you think she went?"

"How the fuck am I supposed to know?"

Behind me, the doorknob turned. I twisted around and said, "Uno momento, por favor," and the rattling ceased.

"You really have no idea?"

"Of course not. I'd tell you if I did. She took my money, took my car keys—"

"What kind of car?"

"Does it matter?"

I rubbed my face with both hands. It felt like a lifetime since I'd slept last, even though it had only been the night before.

"It'll make finding her easier."

He gave me the year, the make, the model, and the license plate number. I was pretty sure D'Agostino could do something with that information, and she could do it quicker than I could. I stood and grinned down at him. I thought about taking his picture. Somebody somewhere would pay a good deal of money for something like that. But I decided against it. I had Doyle on my back already. Who needed more heat? I stood up.

"Thanks for the cooperation," I said.

"Hey, aren't you going to let me out? I gave you everything you asked for."

I shook my head.

"You got into this mess," I said. "You can get yourself out."

That's when the curse words started.

"Son of a bitch," he said. "I'm going to kill you for this. No, fuck that, I'll have you killed. No motherfucker does this shit to me and gets away with it."

I leaned over him and picked up the ball gag.

"Do you know who I am?" I said.

"No," he said, and paused. "Are you supposed to be someone important?"

"You don't know who I am. How do you expect to find me?"

He struggled as I slipped the leather strap over his head, but Abby had tied him tight. He didn't make it easy, but it didn't take a ton of effort to make sure the gag was in place. I got up and went to the door. Opened it, looked out.

The detective was waiting for me, but the cleaning woman had moved on. Behind me, Martin James screamed into his gag.

"I put a 'Do Not Disturb' sign out and shooed the help away," she said. "Who's in the bedroom?"

"Look for yourself."

She did, and burst out laughing. I went back in and took her by the arm.

"Come on," I said. "Let's get out of here." On the way downstairs, I filled her in on everything James told me.

SIX

PALE EDDIE'S POUR HOUSE is on Second Avenue, a little hole-in-the-wall bar where they pour a good drink and then leave you alone. If you get there early enough, it's quiet and you can talk. D'Agostino was drinking amaretto on the rocks. I had a double shot of Black Bush and water back. She'd already called in Martin James's plate with instructions that anybody who found the car should call her first. I was checking my phone every five minutes for social media updates.

Pale Eddie's isn't much. There's a half-assed bandstand to the left as you come in, and the bar runs pretty much the length of the room on that same side. There's a scattering of tables along the right-hand wall. We were at a table, staring at each other and racking our brains for the next step.

D'Agostino's phone rang. She picked it up and turned partially away from me, so that I couldn't see her face. Her voice was low, but I was right there. I could hear everything.

"I told you not to call me anymore." She paused, listening to the person on the other end of the line. "I don't care. We've been over all that. It's done. You need to let this go." She hung up without saying goodbye and drank down the rest of her drink without pause. I gestured to the bartender for another, and he came over with a fresh lowball glass. D'Agostino's knuckles were white where she gripped her drink.

"Ex-boyfriend?"

"Ex-girlfriend," she said, and took another long swallow. "Together for three years. We broke it off six months ago, but she still calls me all the time."

D'Agostino patted the breast pocket of her shirt.

"Shit," she said, and shook her head. "I gave up smoking about the same time Samantha and I broke up. Just hearing her voice makes me want a cigarette."

"Sounds self-destructive."

She laughed.

"You have no idea. I left my husband for her—you can imagine how that went over—and I thought I was in love for the first time in my life. What I was, was desperate. I hated being married."

Her phone rang again, and this time when she turned away, I didn't listen. Not my business. There was an old-fashioned cigarette machine in the corner beside a newfangled Internet jukebox. I broke a ten-spot at the bar and fed dollars into the juke, picking out some Tom Waits and Dave Van Ronk tunes. Those cats aren't everyone's cup of tea, but I thought D'Agostino might appreciate them. I bought a pack of Camels from the machine and nabbed a matchbook and ashtray from the bar.

When D'Agostino got off the phone, I tossed the cigarettes and matches down in front of her. She looked down at them and grinned.

"Oh, you're a sonofabitch." She laughed, then took a cigarette and lit it. She took in a big lungful of smoke, held it, and then blew it out toward the ceiling.

"Shit."

She motioned toward her phone.

"And that was the guy I'm supposed to go on a date with on Friday. I never meant for things to get this complicated."

"I guess that's being an adult," I said. "Things get out of hand when you don't mean for them to."

She snorted.

"Try being bisexual in the deep South," she said. "We're smack dab on the buckle of the Bible belt. The women who are gay don't know it or won't admit it—it amounts to the same thing—and the guys get turned on because they think you'll be up for a threesome."

My drink was gone. I motioned for the bartender to hit me again, and he did. I wanted to ask him to leave the bottle, but I didn't need to get that drunk. Irish whisky goes down easy, and when you're drinking the Black Bush, it's almost as if the liquor evaporates as soon as it hits your tongue.

"I always thought sex was a one-on-one sport." The words escaped my mouth before I could call them back. D'Agostino blinked in surprise, and then laughed. I looked away.

"Are you hitting on me?" Her eyes were full of challenge.

I thought it over for a few moments before I answered.

"I don't think so," I said finally. "You're a cop, and I'm a crook—or at least the next thing to it—and I don't see what good that would do either of us."

We were staring at each other over our drinks now, a lot of words left unspoken. I could feel the machinery in my head clanking around and around, thinking of witty things to say and discarding all of them. And rightly so.

Ralph saved me. He was so big that when he opened the front door, he had to turn sideways to get inside, and then he had to waddle down the narrow walkway between the bar and the booths to where we were sitting. When he got to me, he glowered down and said "Outside" in that diesel engine voice of his.

"You see," I said to D'Agostino, "the mountain does come to Muhammad."

She snorted, but her eyes were wide. Ralph was nearly seven feet tall, and probably just as big around. There was something prehistoric about him. He wore khaki-colored pants and a white button-down broadcloth shirt so large it probably doubled as a sail down at the yacht club. Each of his hands were curled loosely into fists, and I knew he carried rolls of quarters in his palms. I'd seen Ralph work before. When he wanted to work someone over, they ended up looking like raw hamburger meat.

"I'm not going anywhere with you, big guy," I said. I kept my voice calm. Ralph was like a mean dog; showing fear would only excite him. "I know why you're here, and you can tell your boss that I'm working on it."

Ralph shook his head, and I swear I could hear tectonic plates shift and grind against one another. I could smell the smoke of D'Agostino's half-finished cigarette and the stale aroma of spilled beer and liquor that always seemed to pervade the air in Pale Eddie's. The dark walls leaned closer and I was aware that Ralph could yank me out of the booth at any moment. He was big enough and strong enough that there was no way I could stop him.

"Nope," he said. "I'm here to give you a message."

His hands moved in small circles near what would have been a waist on a normal person. I'm not even sure he knew he was doing it. Of course I knew what kind of message Doyle would send. I was usually the one who carried those missives. But taking a beating here and now would only slow me down. It wouldn't get me any closer to finding Abby. I blew out a breath and looked over at the detective across the table from me. She was studying Ralph as if he were some heretofore undiscovered dinosaur fossil, huge and grotesque, an apex predator from a different age.

"I'd better go with him," I said, and D'Agostino shook her head. She took her badge off of her belt and placed it face-up on the table. Ralph paused and looked at her, taking her in as if filing D'Agostino's features away somewhere for future reference. He shook his head again and looked at me sadly.

"Okay, not right now. Don't matter to me none. But the cops ain't always gonna be around, buddy boy. You got a beating coming. The longer I gotta wait, the worse it's gonna be for you." Ralph turned away from us slowly, a glacier with feet, and moved toward the door. I didn't relax until I watched the door close behind him.

"Jesus Christ," D'Agostino said. She expelled a breath I didn't realize she'd been holding. "So that's Ralph Miller."

I'd never heard his last name before.

"Miller, huh?"

"Yes. He's got a rap sheet longer than my arm. Assault and battery, kidnapping, terroristic threats, attempted murder."

"How many convictions?"

"One fall, five years." She lit another cigarette and blew the smoke away from us. "Nothing recent, though. Witnesses decide not to talk. Some don't show up. One was never heard from again."

"Eek," I said.

"You should take this seriously," D'Agostino said. "People who get crossways of Ralph don't usually come out whole."

I nodded.

"I take him seriously, but I can't do what I do if I'm walking around scared," I said. "I'm sure you've been threatened before, right?"

"Sure," D'Agostino said. "It comes with the job." She was spinning the cigarette pack on the table in slow and nearly hypnotic rotations. Her fingers were agile, the nails cut right down to the quick, with some kind of clear polish on them that gleamed in the dim light. Around us the room had quieted as time passed, and it dawned on me that we were the only two customers in the place. The bartender sat on a vinyl-covered stool at the other end of the long room so that he couldn't overhear us.

"You know the question I'm not asking," she said, and flashed a wintry smile. It was there and gone, blink-and-you'll-miss it, and its fleeting nature made her even more attractive. I pushed the thought away and focused on the task at hand.

"Why did Abby leave?" I asked. "I want to know the same thing. She was safe where she was. The apartment was locked. I was on the couch. There was almost no chance Britt's killer would come back."

D'Agostino shook her head as if waking from a dream. We were both conscious of our surroundings, the quiet intimacy of being almost alone, with the rest of the night open to us. My throat felt close and hot, and I resisted the urge to clear it.

"Almost no chance isn't the same as no chance at all," she said, and we both thought about that for a minute.

"The killer had a key," I said, and watched as the detective nodded along as I said it.

"And knew some way to get in the building, maybe a security code. Makes sense. Killer lets himself—or herself—in, unexpectedly finds Britt. But why kill him like that? It looked like a professional hit."

I didn't have an answer. I had no illusions about bringing Britt's killer to justice. I wasn't a detective, and had no desire to be one. All I wanted was to find Abby again. It didn't matter to me that Ralph wanted a piece of my hide; it didn't matter that Doyle himself was ready to carve me up. I wanted to find the girl and do the job I hired on to do. My only interest in the killer was that he—or she, as D'Agostino said—might be gunning for Abby, too.

The detective—Laura, damn it. I could think of her as Laura, couldn't I?—drained the last of her drink and caught the bartender's attention with a wave. When he brought the check, I scooped it up before she could put a hand on it.

"Hey—"

"Nope," I said. "You're in this because of me. The least I can do is buy the drinks."

Laura shook her head. "As bribes go, that's pretty cheap."

I laughed. The bartender took my credit card and went to the cash register. I kept my eye on him because I didn't trust myself to look at D'Agostino. It felt like we were skirting something between us that could not be said, at least not yet. What it was, I wasn't sure. The bartender came back, and I signed the receipt and added a tip.

"What do I get for two drinks?"

"Some advice: Don't turn your back on anyone."

SEVEN

D'AGOSTINO WENT OUT THE FRONT. She could do that sort of thing, because she was a cop. I watched her climb into the Uber she'd summoned. She showed little effect of the drinks we'd consumed other than a slightly exaggerated roll of her hips as she strode out. I'd known a lot of cops at one time or another, and they almost always have a little bit of swagger. It looked better on her than most. I turned to the bartender and asked if I could use the employee exit. My car was parked at the curb on Second Avenue, but I wanted to approach it from an unusual angle to see if anyone was watching.

There was a squeal of rusty hinges as I stepped out into the alley behind the bar. The door swung shut, and I was swamped in semidarkness. Pale Eddie's was set near the easternmost corner of the street, so that the walk toward the street—toward the relative safety of the sodium-arc streetlights—was short. Instead, I turned away and skulked down the dark alley, taking the long way around.

I don't believe in magic. I don't believe in God. I don't believe in much, other than the money in my pocket and a gun in my hand. But there is something out there, even if it's simply a vestigial leftover of man when he came down from the caves and the other predators had sharper teeth and longer claws. The hairs on the back of my neck rose, and goosebumps prickled the flesh along my arms.

I wasn't alone in the alley.

I still can't tell you how I knew. But there was someone there, and they meant to do me harm. I slid my hand back for my gun, sweeping the tail of my suit coat aside in one motion when something hit me. A hand the size of a dinner plate slammed into my jaw and a whole universe of stars exploded into my vision. My gun clattered to the asphalt pavement, and I staggered in the other direction, away from it, trying to make sense of the Big Bang going off in my head.

In the quiet gloom of the alley, Ralph came for me. He didn't say anything. He didn't have to. There was enough glowering light cast from the streetlamps that I could see the murderous look on his face. This wasn't business for Ralph. It wasn't a beating, or a message. He meant to kill me. I shook my head and wished I hadn't, because the buzz of that first shot redoubled, and I nearly fell. The wall on the far side of the pavement saved me, and I leaned there waiting for Ralph to come. Sweat stood out on my face, and there were tears streaming from the corners of my eyes.

He shifted toward me, slow and implacable. The next shot came whistling down low, a hook to my ribs that would have crushed them if it had landed. Instead, I pushed off the wall with all the force I could muster, bringing myself inside the wide loop of his punch, and head-butted him in the face.

There was a satisfying crunch when his nose broke, and now it was his turn to stagger away from me. My own head still rang, but I knew I had to put Ralph down as soon as possible, so I stayed on my feet, sodden with fury and pain. When he came for me again, I waited until he lunged in close, and kicked him in the kneecap.

He screamed and fell, a tree in the urban forest of a back city alley. He gripped his knee and tried to scramble up. When you scuffle for a living, you can't allow yourself to be on the ground while your opponent is on their feet. It's a good way to get stomped to death. Ralph almost made it, shifting his weight to his good leg and trying to rise, his arms making swimming motions in the heavy summer air as he tried for balance.

His breathing sounded loud and hoarse in his throat. I could hear it over the blood pounding in my temples.

I stomped on his other knee, trying to drive the hard heel of my shoe through the side of his leg, and for the second time in less than twenty seconds, Ralph screamed again. His hands opened as he caught himself on the pavement, and I saw a roll of quarters escape his fist. I scrambled for it—I was faster than the big man, if only because I had two good legs—and when my own hand closed around the roll, it was Ralph's turn to be hunted.

I hit him on the nose again, and he yelped. His hands came up, and I slammed a hook to his ribs, just as he'd tried to do to me. When his hands came down to clutch his midsection, I punched him in the throat. His windpipe closed, and I saw the panic in his wide eyes as he fell back to the pavement and scrambled to breathe. I tossed the roll of quarters aside, The wrapper split when the roll hit the ground, and coins bled liquid silver in the moonlight.

I kicked him once, and then again. And I would have gone on kicking him as long as there was strength in my body if the bartender from Pale Eddie's hadn't intervened. He grabbed me around the shoulders and spun me away from Ralph. I would have hit him, too, but he put his hands up, palm out, and hissed, "Enough! That's enough! You're killing him."

I looked down at Ralph. Even unconscious, with blood on his face and one knee bent in the wrong direction, he looked danger-ous. I wanted to go back at him, to finish the job. I didn't want to have Ralph walking around behind me, waiting for a chance to exact revenge. I breathed in some air, trying to calm myself. The bartender stood between us, his palms wide open in a gesture that begged for mercy.

I was suddenly aware that I was shaking. Just as quickly as the adrenaline rush hit, it also left. My heart felt like it might explode in my chest, and the side of my head felt swollen and grotesque where Ralph had hit me. My breath came in gasps now, and I was aware of Ralph's breathing, too. It was erratic and pitched high like the whistle of a tea kettle.

I turned away from them and found my gun where it had fallen. I checked the cylinder, even though I knew the gun was loaded. It wouldn't take much to finish the job. Just like I'd told Abby, I could put five shots through his upper lip and never have to worry about Ralph again. But if I did that, I'd have to shoot the bartender, too.

My knuckles were white on the .38 as I thought about it for a minute. The bartender's eyes were very wide and glassy, and his Adam's apple bounced up and down as he swallowed. I put the gun back in its holster and walked on through to the end of the alley. When I turned the corner, I could see the Mustang parked at the curb. I beeped the driver's side door open, hauled myself behind the wheel, drunk with pain and anger and frustration, and drove back to what passed for home, too scared and too hurt to care if anyone followed me.

EIGHT

THE POUNDING WASN'T just in my head. At some point between sleep and wakefulness, I realized that someone was banging insistently on the motel room door, and that I'd have to get up to answer the knock, because it didn't look like they were going away.

I sat up and kicked the bedclothes off of my legs. The room swam a little, then came back into focus. I felt like I had the world's worst hangover. My shirt and suit coat hung on the back of the room's only chair, and my shoes had been kicked aside and scattered across the room. My pants were puddled on the bathroom floor. The knocking remained insistent, though, so I padded to the door in my sock feet and boxer shorts.

I peered through the peephole and then unlocked the door. When D'Agostino heard the safety latch moving, she backed up a step and moved to her left. Her hand rested on her gun, and her gold detective's shield glinted at her belt.

I blinked in the harsh, strong sunlight. If I had been a vampire, I'd have turned to ash the moment I opened the door. Or maybe I'd have just sparkled a little. D'Agostino took a look at me and drew her breath in.

"Good lord, Kincaid. Put some clothes on."

Usually seeing me in my underwear makes even the strongest women undress, but D'Agostino was made of sterner stuff. I stepped aside and she shouldered her way in. The door slammed behind her, the sound like a nuclear blast inside my aching head.

"I've been reassigned," she said, no preamble. "Somebody, probably your boss, had me pulled off the Britt Parker case. Did you have anything to do with this?"

I shook my head and immediately regretted it. D'Agostino and the rest of the room swam away for just a second, but I managed to remain standing.

"I said something about it, you know, 'My mistake, I thought we did police work around here.' Got told I needed to take some vacation time before I took a ten-day rip for insubordination. Can you believe that shit? So I'm off the case."

And then she flashed her killer grin.

"It's too bad, too. I've got a lead on your missing girl."

"Hnggh," I said. My jaw wasn't working very well, and at least two molars felt loose in their sockets.

"What's the matter with you?" She asked. "You didn't get drunk after I left, did you?"

I sat down on the edge of the bed and put my head in my hands. It hurt to keep my eyes open. Trying to talk and think was almost impossible. I held up my index finger to indicate she should wait a minute. I tried to get to my feet. I really did. But D'Agostino beat me to the light switch and flipped it. I closed my eyes, but the bright overheads bled through my lids and seared pain into my brain.

Once I forced my eyes open, I could see D'Agostino's mouth drop open in an O of surprise as she took in the swollen, misshapen side of my head where Ralph had slugged me.

"What the hell?"

I tried to grin, but my head hurt too much.

"Ralph delivered his message." My jaw felt tight and hot as the words spilled out, and the words were slurred as though I were coming off a bender. I told her everything that happened after she left—except how I'd nearly shot Ralph as he lay helpless in the street—and when I was through, she stared at me like I was something alien and unknowable.

"My God," she said, and reached up to touch my face. She stopped herself before her fingers made contact, and she dropped her hand to her side with an embarrassed little laugh. "How bad does it hurt?"

"Imagine diving into a swimming pool, but there's no water in it when you land."

"Oh," she said.

"Yeah, it's at least twice that bad."

D'Agostino's mouth quirked up at one corner, but that was the only reaction she showed. That was okay. I was used to people thinking I'm not that funny.

"So I guess you don't want to come with me to find your girl," she said. "I thought you might want to ride along when I pick her up."

I stared at her. If my jaw had been working properly, I'd have had to pick it up off the floor. Now the detective was grinning at me, her face satisfied and beatific like a cat that's been in the cream.

"You think I'm gonna let some administrative asshole tell me what cases I can and can't work? I went home and found Abby."

That was D'Agostino. While I was trying to recover from having my head nearly twisted off, she was out there, working and finding out information, putting everything together, and then coming here to gloat.

"Where?" I asked, finally.

"I'll show you, but you gotta get dressed first."

"Fifteen minutes," I said, and lurched for the bathroom. I needed a shower. I was rancid with leftover sweat and fear and grime from the night before. When I was done, the postage stamp-sized bathroom was thick and close with steam, and I used a black plastic comb to put a part in my too-long hair. I wiped steam away from the mirror and brushed my teeth carefully. Blood stained the sink when I spat, and I decided I could skip shaving for the day.

When I came out—in clean boxers, give me that—D'Agostino was bent over the desk, looking at my little collection of novels lined along the back edge.

"Elmore Leonard, Donald Westlake … don't you have anything where the cops are the good guys?"

I found a clean crew-neck navy blue shirt and slipped it on. My suit choices were down to two, and I chose the tan one. Thanks, Obama.

"That would run counter to my experience," I said, and she spun on me with the speed of a snake.

"Hey, asshole, I'm trying to help you here. You're the next thing to a criminal yourself, and I solved your problem anyway. You could show a little appreciation."

Now it was my turn to grin.

"See what I mean?"

D'Agostino crossed her arms over her chest and leaned her butt against the desk. She didn't say anything, and the strain of not coming back with a hot retort was written all over her face.

I put on a pair of burgundy loafers with understated tassels and slid a matching belt through the loops of the slacks. D'Agostino eyed me carefully as I unlocked my weapon from the closet safe and clipped it to my belt.

"I assume you have a permit for that," she said.

"Would you like to see it?"

D'Agostino showed me her teeth. It wasn't exactly a smile, and there was something predatory about it.

"Not at the moment," she said. "Maybe later, when I'm not on vacation."

I checked myself again in the mirror, then slipped my wallet into my jacket. I stored away the motel room key card and my Swiss army knife. At some point, D'Agostino and I both realized I

was stalling. She flicked her angry-eyed glare up and down, bra-
zenly inspecting me like a piece of meat. I didn't mind. I was very
aware of her as a sexual being at that moment. We were two adults,
alone in a motel room, and the bed was right there. My throat felt
thick, and there was a tightness in my chest that I wasn't used to.

Our eyes met, and I could see the spark of challenge in them,
just like the night before at Pale Eddie's. There would come a time
when I'd find out what that challenge meant, but this wasn't it,
even though I dearly wanted it to be. Finally, she dropped her
gaze and said, "Are you ready?"

I nodded. If I'd tried to speak in that moment, my voice would
have broken like a kid just hitting puberty. It was just as well
that my jaw hurt.. We went out to D'Agostino's car, a late-model.
On vacation or not, D'Agostino still had the department-issued
Charger. It was a slick-top, no light bar, but there was thick steel
mesh between the front and back seats, and a riot gun was locked
vertically to the dash. From the outside, it looked almost like a
civilian's car, except there were no hubcaps on it, and it wore the
telltale buggy-whip antenna of a cop car. She beeped the doors
open, and I got in on the passenger side.

"Wow," I said. "Getting to ride up front is nice for a change."

Laura snorted, an unladylike sound that made me like her even
more than I already did, which was turning out to be quite a bit. A
silver thermos sat on the console between the seats, and I looked
at it with something approaching lust. D'Agostino caught my eye
and said, "help yourself." I unscrewed the cap and poured steaming coffee into the outer lid. I got a couple of sips into me before
she put the car in gear, reversed quickly, jammed it into drive,
and tore out of the parking lot. We detoured through downtown,
slipping through side streets and sliding along alleyways, missing
slower vehicles by inches. The detective had no qualms about hitting the blue gumdrop lights hidden in the front of the car's grille
and blipping the siren to signal cars to move aside. If I hadn't been
so manly, I would've covered my face with my hands and cowered

in fear. Instead, I made sure the cap was closed on the thermos and drank the rest of my coffee. Then I closed my eyes and leaned back against the headrest.

"You okay?" D'Agostino asked, and I opened my eyes in time to see her nearly sideswipe a municipal bus. I closed my eyes again. Quickly.

"Fine," I said through gritted teeth.

"Your face is a mess." She blipped the siren again, and this time I didn't open my eyes. Sometimes it's just better not to know. I sagged down in my seat a little, finding a relaxed position in the Charger's well-sprung suspension.

"Don't worry. I heal up good." If this ride didn't kill me first.

The Charger got up to speed, and I risked a look. We were on Highway 280, eastbound, heading toward the suburbs. Not long after the civil rights movement, white flight had taken over Birmingham. The "good" neighborhoods were over the mountain now, enclaves of middle- and upper-class white families who feared the city because it was too "urban," a polite way of saying that the city was too black. Areas like Mountain Brook and Vestavia Hills catered to rich whites and contained some of the most expensive real estate in the state. We dropped off the highway, heading toward Mountain Brook.

"What did you find?" I asked. Now that we weren't dodging city traffic, I could talk without fear of losing breakfast. Not that I had any to lose. D'Agostino braked hard and took a left turn into oncoming traffic. There was a blare of horns as she skidded into the driveway of a gated community and screeched to a halt at a small hut that contained an on-duty security guard.

He heaved himself out of a pleather rolling chair, grabbed a clipboard and ambled over to the driver's side of the car. D'Agostino flashed her badge and told the guard to open the gate. He hesitated.

"I'm s'posed to call ahead for any visitors, ma'am."

D'Agostino looked at me and bared her wolfish grin.

"If you do not open that gate right now, I will bash it in." She dropped the Charger into low gear and revved the engine. The security guard jumped back a step, and then waddled back to his hut. He opened the gate, and D'Agostino roared through. I looked back and saw the guard writing down her license plate.

"You gonna get in trouble for this?"

D'Agostino shrugged.

"It'll give the captain something to do," she said. As soon as we were out of sight of the security guard, she dropped her speed to about fifteen miles an hour. We were in a neighborhood that featured large homes, three to four stories high, each with a little postage stamp-sized yard. McMansions. There was probably a HOA and a community pool. The American dream.

We pulled into the driveway at 1229 Beulah Lane and D'Agostino cut the engine. The house was four stories, made of fieldstone. Along the front, ivy climbed pleasingly toward the slate-shingled roof. The yard—what there was of it—was impeccably neat. The detective got out, and I followed her. We climbed onto a wide veranda that ran the length of the house, and D'Agostino rang the doorbell. Dissatisfied after a second, she banged her fist on the crimson-painted door.

"Okay," I said, "I give up. Where are we?"

D'Agostino looked over her shoulder and smirked at me.

"Ralph must have really rung your bell or you would have figured it out by now," she said. "This is Britt Parker's house."

There was movement inside, and then Abby Doyle opened the front door.

NINE

"OH," **ABBY SAID,** as if she hadn't been missing for more than a day. Her face was so full of innocence that it had to be fake. "Hey. I just put on some coffee. Come on in."

She moved away from the door, and D'Agostino stepped inside. Her right hand stayed on the butt of the pistol at her hip and she glanced around warily. The foyer was at least two stories high, with a staircase at either end that led up to the floors above. The floor was done in flagstones, and what looked like original oil paintings hung on the walls. A baby grand piano was the centerpiece of the foyer, its black lacquered surface gleaming in the natural light supplied by the tall windows at the front of the house. If D'Agostino was impressed by the place, she didn't show it.

"Miss Doyle, are you alone in the house?"

Abby peeked at me, a quizzical look in her eyes.

"Is there any reason I wouldn't be?"

She was wearing fresh clothes: a pair of gray yoga pants and thick white socks. An oversized blue T-shirt that read Jason Isbell and The 400 Unit covered her upper body.

By then, D'Agostino had stepped further into the foyer. At some point—I didn't see when—she had drawn her weapon. She held her hand up behind her, and I moved to one side of the room. I pulled my own weapon and heard Abby gasp behind me. There was sweat on my brow, even though I could feel the soft breeze of air-conditioning on my face. I opened my eyes wide, not staring at any one thing directly, trying to look obliquely at my surroundings for any sign of movement.

"My God—" Abby started to say. I whispered "Quiet" in a harsh voice, and she obeyed.

Ahead of us, D'Agostino had settled into a classic Weaver stance, her feet perpendicular to one another, weight evenly distributed, the butt of her service pistol cupped in her left hand. It was an old-school thing. Most shooters used a more modern stance, but the Weaver was good for short-range shooting like we might have to do here. D'Agostino's index finger was settled along the barrel of the weapon, not on the trigger. I realized that I'd shucked my own gun, my own stance much like hers. Something—we couldn't tell what—had set off alarm bells for both of us.

"Stairs?" I said, my voice low.

D'Agostino heard me. She caught my eye and shook her head, and I got the message immediately. She was a cop, in a strange place, with every nerve ending screaming at her that something was wrong. She knew what she should do: call for backup. If she went up the stairs with me, she'd be relying on a guy she barely knew to be her backup, and her training wouldn't let her do that. Somewhere ahead of us in the house, a door clicked closed. We both heard it, and our guns swiveled in that direction.

"Stay with her," the detective said, and surged forward.

"Where's she going?" Abby asked, and I shushed her again. I kept my eyes on D'Agostino as she moved through the first floor. Every time she cleared a room, she would move back to the foyer to nod at me. I stayed with Abby, even though my every instinct told me that I should be backing D'Agostino up.

A few minutes later, the detective came back.

"Clear," she said. She put her gun away, and I followed suit. "Miss Doyle, who was here with you?"

Abby's eyes were guileless, their deep green color betraying nothing.

"I was alone," she said.

"Bullshit," D'Agostino said. "But if that's the way you want to do it, fine."

The detective holstered her gun, and in the same motion, moved her hand underneath the tail of her coat. She brought out a pair of gleaming metal handcuffs and caught Abby's wrist in one hand. D'Agostino spun the young woman into a hammerlock, bringing Abby's hand up between her shoulder blades. I heard one of the cuffs ratchet closed.

"No!" Abby yelped, and I moved forward, putting a hand on D'Agostino's forearm.

"You don't have to—"

D'Agostino swiveled away from me, putting Abby between us.

"Move back," she said, and her voice had the cop's cold ring of command to it. Underneath it, though, I could hear a small trilling note of fear. D'Agostino was hyper-alert to the fact that she was the only cop here. She had cleared the first floor, but there were three more floors above us, and neither of us knew if there was anyone else in the house. "Move back unless you want me to run you in for interfering in an investigation."

I backed up a few steps and held my hands wide apart at shoulder height.

"All I'm saying is that you don't have to do this," I said as D'Agostino pulled Abby's other arm behind her and clicked the second cuff into place.

"The hell I don't," she said. "She's already run away from you— some bodyguard, right?—and now she's lied to me. She can be held as a material witness in a homicide investigation, and that's just what I'm going to do."

D'Agostino flipped the hem of Abby's T-shirt up and found her phone tucked into the waistband of her yoga pants. She took it out and placed it on top of the piano a few feet away. I watched in stony silence as Abby began to cry, real tears that welled at the corners of her eyes and began to slip slowly down her apple cheeks. Her whole face began to crumble.

"Please," she said. "I don't want to go to jail."

"Is there anyone else in the house?" I said. "Anywhere?"

"N-no," Abby said. "Not anymore."

D'Agostino and I looked at one another. She still held Abby, her hand on the cuffs that bound the young woman. She'd already lied to us. We'd have to check.

"Only one way to find out," I said, and turned for the stairs.

"Wait," D'Agostino called after me. I stopped on the first step and looked back.

"Your weapon," she said. "Leave it on the piano next to Miss Doyle's phone."

I looked back up the stairs. I had no way to know how many rooms there were, and only Abby's untrustworthy word that we were now alone in the big house. Shit. I stepped down from that first stair, drew my gun gently with just my forefinger and thumb, and went to the piano. I put the gun next to Abby's phone as instructed.

"You have trust issues," I said as I passed D'Agostino on the way back to the stairs.

"Yeah," she said, her eyes steady on me the whole time. "Blame my ex."

I went up the stairs like my head didn't hurt, like a man with purpose. Like I wasn't afraid. The second floor held four bedrooms. Each had an attached bathroom, and there was also a bathroom at the end of the hall. The rich are very different, they piss more. I paused before I went into the first room and drew in a deep breath to steady my nerves. There was an itching sensation between my shoulder blades, and I badly wanted a gun in my empty hands. Reaching around the doorway, I fumbled for the light switch and turned on the overheads. Nothing moved inside the room. I inched my way inside and found a guest bedroom. The wallpaper was rich, maroon accented with creamy white stripes. The duvet matched, only with the color scheme inverted. The headboard of the bed was nearly obscured by decorative pillows. In the room's single closet, I found a set of golf clubs in a rich brown leather bag. I drew the nine-iron and carried it with me when I checked the bathroom. Then I used it to sweep under the bed. There was nothing. I moved the pillows at the headboard to make sure they were pillows.

I repeated the process with every room on the second floor and kept finding a whole lot of nothing. When I went out to the half-wall that separated the second floor from the foyer, I yelled down that the area was clear.

"Good," D'Agostino's voice echoed up from below. "Third floor now."

"Yes ma'am," I called back.

The next set of stairs was in the middle of the second floor, and I took them a little less cautiously. The third floor contained an office at one end and a small theater with tiered seating and a huge projection screen at the other. I checked the closets, checked under furniture, checked every nook and cranny where someone could hide. There was no one. I could've walked back down the stairs at that point and yelled again to D'Agostino that the third floor was also clear. Instead, I took the wrought iron staircase that stood in one corner of the office. It led to the fourth floor.

The staircase opened up onto the master bedroom. It ran the length of the house and featured deep pile carpeting. There was a king-sized platform bed at one end of the room and a heavy bag for boxing set in one corner at the opposite end. There were dumbells and other exercise equipment scattered along the floor, and the walls held blown-up photos of Britt Parker and Abby Doyle. There were nightstands on either side of the bed and a long, low dresser. The walk-in closet was bigger than my motel room. Judging from the state of the bedclothes, this was where Abby had slept.

Again, there was no one there.

I crept back down the spiral staircase still carrying the nine-iron I'd appropriated on the second floor. There was no one waiting for me in the office. I checked the theater again. If I'd missed anyone, perhaps I'd drive them down toward D'Agostino, and she could deal with them.

I went down the stairs to the second floor and did a cursory re-check of every room, just to be thorough. When I was satisfied, I came back down the opposite marble staircase into the foyer.

"No one there," I said. "I checked all the way up to the—"

My voice trailed off. D'Agostino wasn't in the foyer. Neither was Abby. I looked over to the piano where I'd laid my gun. The weapon wasn't there. Neither was Abby's phone. Something rose inside me, a panic I didn't know I was capable of. I tore through the first floor of the house, but there was no sign of D'Agostino nor Abby.

They were gone.

TEN

D'AGOSTINO'S CAR STILL CROUCHED aggressively in the drive-way, its nose forward like a predator ready to pounce. Around me, everything was still. Nothing seemed out of place. I turned away from the front door and went back to the top of the house, moving room to room again and peering around corners as if I expected the boogeyman to jump out at me. I don't know what I was looking for. Nothing had changed. I kept ahold of the nine-iron, bringing it up in a high arc every time I went through a doorway, but my enemy was my own imagination, and I could never get ahold of it.

My mind was buzzing along at a hundred miles an hour: I had to call the local cops. No, I had to call the Birmingham cops. They were better equipped to deal with something like this than the Mountain Brook force, and D'Agostino was one of theirs. I had my phone out, ready to hit the emergency dial button, when I stopped. I was thinking like a civilian. I wasn't thinking like a cop, and I damned sure wasn't thinking like a crook.

Smart crooks don't kill cops. They know that murdering an offi-cer brings down heat like no other. Every level of every operation in the Birmingham metro area would be disrupted. Officers who might look the other way in certain situations would still have their hands out. Only now those hands would be holding a baton. Heads would—quite literally—roll.

So if someone had taken D'Agostino and Abby Doyle, they were smart. They got into the house silently, and took the women while I was upstairs. That told me that the kidnapper—maybe more than one—had bided their time until there was an opening.

That meant D'Agostino was still alive.

"Shit," I said aloud in the empty house, and my voice echoed up the walls. This wasn't a problem that could be solved by punching some slob on the bazoo. It required thinking, and thinking was my worst subject. It's not that I couldn't do it; I just preferred problems that could be solved with an application of well-timed violence.

Think, Kincaid. Think.

I went up to the third floor and found Britt's office. He had a laptop computer on his desk that was password-protected. I didn't even bother with it, because breaking into it would be beyond my capabilities. But I could look through his desk and trash can, so that's what I did. On the desk, there was a photo of Britt and Abby caught in mid-laugh, looking at one another. Happier times. I was aware of Britt's face in the photograph as I plundered through his desk, so I turned it face down as I continued my plunder..

Even so-called paperless offices still generate a lot of paper, and Britt seemed to generate more than most. He liked to have things printed out, and that's where I caught a break. He was an attorney—I'd called that one right—and I found file folders full of transcripts and depositions and legal filings for the past year or two, probably dating back to when he passed the bar exam. There were bank records going back to that same time period that showed Britt Parker was a lot more than solvent. He was rich, with a capital R.

Of course, that would make sense. Abby Doyle was rich, too,

or at least her father was. Two rich kids in love or something like it, no cross-class romance here.

It looked like Britt dealt with a lot of property law, and that pinged something in the back of my head. He helped broker deals between major landowners for shopping malls and mixed-use properties around the metro area. Judging from his bank statements, he made a good living at it. He owned this house and a cabin on Lookout Mountain in Mentone, a small vacation town just outside Fort Payne, and a house on the shore in Orange Beach. He also owned parts of six other ventures around Birmingham, ranging from parking decks to part of the Uptown shopping and dining complex.

I don't know when my brain put two and two together, but when I did, it felt like turning a key in a lock. I sat down in Britt's leather executive chair—he wouldn't be needing it anymore—put my elbows on the desk and held my aching head in my hands.

The intersection of everything came down to money. Money and power, although they were often the same thing. Who had the money? Who wanted it? Gears were clicking forward in my head, slowly. When things began to tumble into place, I got up from the desk and started to move.

The first thing I needed was wheels. I couldn't take D'Agostino's car, because I was pretty sure she'd pocketed the keys. I went outside and checked anyway. The Charger was locked up tight. Next, I made my way to the garage. Hanging next to the door that led to it was a plaque that helpfully read "Keys." Two sets of car keys hung from hooks attached to the plaque: one of them was a more traditional key with the Porsche logo. I grabbed it and stepped into the garage.

The Porsche was at least ten years old, maybe more, an old yellow Boxster S with a black cloth bonnet and six gears on the floor. Inconspicuous, that's me. The leather seats felt perfect, and the rumble of the engine when I cranked it was a nearly sexual thing. I tried not to feel disloyal to the Mustang. There was a garage door opener on the visor, and I punched it. I kept to the speed limit all the way through Mountain Brook and back into Birmingham. The Porsche didn't want to do that. I could feel the engine raring to let loose and unspool, and I desperately wanted to let the top down and fly up along the Interstate with the sun on my face and the wind in my hair.

I forced myself to stay within the speed limit and never got the Porsche out of fourth gear. Damn it. Back at the motel, I keyed in my code on the room safe and got out the big .357 that I kept in case I needed to bring down Donald Trump's ego. It felt too bulky on my belt, so I stripped off my coat and put on a webbed leather shoulder holster. It was uncomfortable and I didn't like the way the gun peeked out from under my coat, but it was worlds better than going unarmed.

At the last minute, I tossed my phone onto the bed. If things got bloody, the cops could ping my phone to try to place me at the scene. At that point, I didn't really care. All I wanted to do was find Abby and D'Agostino and bring them back safely. I caught a glimpse of myself in the mirror as I turned to leave. There were bright red spots high up on my cheekbones, like a man burning with fever, and my hands trembled visibly with barely contained rage. My face was swollen and freshly bruised from where Ralph had struck me. I took one last look around before I closed the door behind me.

No one would care if I didn't come back, and that was fine. I could live with that. I'd been a solitary, lonely man for a long time. Now Laura D'Agostino had inexplicably cracked the walls I'd built to protect myself from the world, and I couldn't tell if I was hurt or scared or happy, or some mangled combination of all three.

I left the Porsche in the motel parking lot with the key in it. It wasn't mine, and Britt couldn't use it anymore. Besides, the Mustang was much more my style. I roared away toward a man who might provide me with some answers.

ELEVEN

THE MAN I WANTED to see had an office on the fourth floor of the so-called Tower Building in Homewood. The building, ugly and blighted like an old scar, was elevated around the rest of its suburban surroundings so that it provided an unobstructed view of downtown Birmingham. As far as I could tell, that was its chief allure. It was located on a hill a little ways off Valley Ave., behind Sammy's, a profitable-but-questionable strip club where I knew Carlton Doyle had a financial interest.

Access to the building was easy. No security guards, no receptionist. I headed for the elevator and went up to the MJ Development suite and didn't knock when I went in.

The place didn't spend a whole lot on overhead. The walls were mostly bare, with only a couple of Daniel Moore prints depicting past glories by the University of Alabama football team. In one corner there was a plastic plant that wasn't fooling anybody, and directly in front of me there was an equally plastic secretary behind a desk that held a computer monitor and phone.

"May I help you?" The secretary asked. Okay, so maybe she was a little more lively than the plant, but not nearly as smart.

"No," I said as I breezed past her. There was a single door set into the far wall, and I raised my right foot and placed a heavy kick above the doorknob. The door sprang open so hard that it banged against the wall. My momentum carried me through, and Martin James looked up from his desk in surprise, his eyes widening with fear.

He scrambled to open the middle drawer of his desk, but I went over it like a swimmer diving into the surf, got hold of his lapels and toppled us to the floor in a heap. I rose to my feet first, and grabbed the front of his shirt in my left fist. The fabric tore as he pulled away, and I caught him by the shoulders and hit him twice low in the gut to try to settle him down. They were mean punches, thrown with a lot of body weight behind them. His face paled and he made an *urk!* sound deep in his throat.

Martin bent over his desk, head hanging, his dark and glossy hair hanging in his face. A stream of saliva leaked from his mouth to the desktop.

"I think I'm gonna be sick," he whispered. With my foot, I shoved a wastebasket from one side of his desk toward him. He bent over it and threw up noisily. His secretary had risen from her desk and peeked in at us.

"Mr. James? Do you want me to call the police?"

I crossed my arms over my chest and looked at him without mercy.

"Yeah, Marty. Let's get the cops in here. What do you say?"

He shook his head, then raised his voice so the secretary could hear.

"No cops, Jenna. It's okay. It's just a misunderstanding. Close the door and go back to what you were doing."

"Maybe drive over to Starbucks," I said. "Get yourself a nice, iced coffee."

Jenna looked bewildered but nodded.

"I, uh, I'll take my break early, then?"

Martin James nodded, not quite meeting her questioning gaze.

"Do that," he said.

Jenna backed out of the room. Out of the corner of my eye, I saw her try to close the door, but the jamb had cracked open and it wouldn't close. She settled for pulling it to.

"You're going to pay for that," James said. It would have sounded much more intimidating if he had been able to look me in the eyes. Instead, he stayed bent over, his stomach heaving a little as it tried to deal with unexpected seismic waves of pain. "I'm going to see to it."

"Gosh, Marty. I thought we were such good friends. Hey, it's nice to see you dressed for a change."

He raised his head against the pain, turning his face toward me, and I could see anger flicker in his eyes. His eyes darted downward and then I saw his hand dive for the middle desk drawer. He raked it open and I hip-checked it closed, catching his fingers in the process. He yelped, a high startled cry, and jerked his hand to his mouth. His left arm was easy to turn, and I did it, pulling the wrist behind his back and up toward his neck with my left hand while pushing his shoulder forward. I reached up and got hold of his hair, the old cop move, and banged his forehead onto his desk.

He was already moving forward with the momentum of my left hand pressing his arm up and up and up, and he couldn't bring his other hand forward to stop the motion. When his head hit the wood, it sounded like a David Ortiz home run.

Martin slumped down to the floor in a kind of swoon, and I reached into the desk drawer Martin had been trying for. There was a Desert Eagle .45-caliber semiautomatic in there that Martin probably kept in case a blue whale wandered in. I ejected the clip and ran the slide back, making sure the gun was unloaded. I tossed it away and felt, rather than heard, it bounce.

There was a private bathroom just off the office, and I went to it and found a hand towel. I ran it under cold water for a few minutes and squeezed it out, imagining my hands around Martin's neck

I went back to the office and squatted in front of Martin James.

His forehead was mostly goose egg and his eyes were unfocused. I folded the towel into a square and pressed it into his hands.

"Put this against your forehead," I said, and he did so, moving slowly. "When you can talk, tell me where they are."

Martin looked up at me through dull eyes. There was blood seeping from his nose, and one side of his mouth was puffy.

"Who?"

I breathed out a little and tried to keep the red ball of rage in the pit of my stomach from rising again and taking over my body.

"Abby Doyle and Laura D'Agostino."

He tried to shake his head, but the pain stopped him.

"I don't know, man."

I wanted to grab him, to shake him until he told me what I wanted to know. But if I laid my hands on him again, I wasn't sure that I could stop myself from killing him. Somewhere deep inside, I knew I wouldn't mind killing him. But that didn't get me where I wanted to go; it didn't get me any closer to finding Abby and Laura.

"Tell me about the deal you've got going with Abby's father," I said.

This time Martin did manage to shake his head. It was a slow movement, languid and detached. I was pretty sure he'd be diagnosed with a concussion when he got to the hospital.

If I let him get there.

"I can't," he said. "He'll kill me."

I stood up, my knees popping from the effort. I kicked him lightly in the ribs, drawing a grunt of discomfort. No pain yet. I wanted him to know it was coming.

"Martin," I said, and my voice was very tired. "What makes you think I won't? You think I'm some kind of good guy here. I'm not. I will kill you and sleep like a baby tonight. I've done it before."

"Please," he said. "I can't. I don't know anything."

My breath was ragged in my ears. I wouldn't have to do much to let the genie out of the bottle. All I had to do was let go just a little. But that wouldn't get me what I wanted. Martin James cowered on the floor in front of me. I wasn't sure how much more I could frighten him until he became useless to me. The bigger question, for me, was how much more I could take. I'd beaten people up before. I'd even killed once or twice—good luck finding the bodies—but I wasn't good at torture. If this went on much longer, I'd end up hating myself.

I would still do it, though. I had to know where D'Agostino and Abby had gone. I needed to find them. It wasn't professional pride, although that was part of it. I couldn't let something happen to Abby, or Doyle would put a contract out on me. And I wouldn't blame him. But D'Agostino was something else. She was a tough, wised-up broad, and I liked her. And I was pretty sure she liked me, too. That was kind of hard to find for a guy like me, and the fact that it was there and unspoken made me happy and scared at the same time.

If something happened to her, it would be my fault. I brought her into this, and she continued helping me off the books, even when she didn't have to. Sure, she was using me. I was her best lead to figure out who killed Britt Parker. But she'd been in my corner, figured out where Abby had gone all on her own.

I hadn't lied to Martin James. If I had to kill him to find out where Abby and D'Agostino were, I would do it with a smile on my face, no matter how it felt afterward.

That's when I heard the door open behind me, and I turned. I thought I was ready for anything, but it turns out that I wasn't. Laura D'Agostino entered the office with her gun drawn, her right index finger on the trigger. He left hand cupped the butt of the weapon, and her feet were at a ninety-degree angle. She was balanced on the balls of her feet, and she was staring down the barrel of her service weapon, her left eye squinted slightly, her right eye wide open and seeing everything. Her face was scraped raw along one cheekbone, and her hair had fallen around her shoulders, greasy and rancid with sweat. Her hands were filthy with dirt, her nails ringed black with the stuff.

"Get out of the way," she said to me. "I'm going to shoot the bastard."

TWELVE

MARTIN JAMES' EYES WIDENED, and he scrambled to get away from the wall and put the desk between himself and D'Agostino. I got out of the way, managing to keep myself between Martin and the big semi-automatic I'd taken from his desk. Sure, it was unloaded, but if he could manage to get to that bazooka and pick it up, he could still do some damage with it as a projectile.

"What. The. Fuck. Is. Going. On." D'Agostino said. "You have about two seconds to start talking before you get a third eye, right in the middle of your goddamned forehead."

Martin put his hands up in front of his face, for all the good that would do him. I'd seen guys shot through the hands before, lying on the ground or on a slab in the morgue. Defensive wounds, they called them. As if a hand raised in the act of begging for your life could ever be a defensive tactic.

I'm not a guy who will die of old age in his bed. Eventually there will be a bullet or a knife blade out there with my name on it, and I hope to God that I go out with more guts than guys like Martin James.

"Don't shoot," he said, his voice cracking. "Don't shoot please for the love of God don't shoot me."

D'Agostino kept the pistol leveled at his head. She glanced over at me, then back to Martin. Her trigger finger was fish-belly pale with the effort not to fire a round through Martin's head.

"What do you have going on with Carlton Doyle?" I asked again. His eyes never left the barrel of D'Agostino's weapon.

"I'm just—I put the proposal together to buy Carraway Hospital. That's all. I don't have anything to do with this—" he waved his hands at us, at the room in general "—whatever this is."

Carraway Hospital is in north Birmingham and its skeletal frame looms like a half-destroyed zombie over the Norwood neighborhood. Its 10-story main building and 52 surrounding acres had been left to fester, die, and decompose over the past decade. The place had a long history in the city as the hospital for Blacks in the city, and during segregation it had even turned away white Freedom Riders who were injured in clashes with racist whites.

Since it closed in 2008, the area had been sold and re-sold as the neighborhood around it stayed mostly working class and very Black. Attempts to gentrify the area had been rebuffed for years by the locals.

"Carlton Doyle owns Carraway?" D'Agostino said, and lowered her weapon a little. "Since when?"

Martin was more at ease when the gun wasn't pointing directly at his face. He was talking about something he knew, now, Birmingham real estate, and the words poured out like a faucet that's just been turned on.

"I mean, his name isn't on it, that's all shell corporations and bullshit," he said. "But he owns eighty percent of it. I got ten for putting the deal together, and the other ten went to, you know, grease the wheels with the city. You don't grease the wheels, they don't turn."

"Uh-huh," D'Agostino said. "Who is involved on the city's end?"

Now Martin shook his head.

"Are you kidding? Be easier to tell you who isn't involved. The ones I know about are the obvious ones, like planning and zoning, a couple of commissioners. You could figure that out by yourself. But I got no idea who Doyle's got on his payroll. I just know everybody's got their hand out on this one."

"That's everywhere," D'Agostino said. "How is this any different?"

Martin took in a deep breath and blew it out while he thought about how to explain the situation to us.

"It's mostly a matter of scale," he said. "It's fifty-two acres in north Birmingham. First time it sold, it went for six million. This time? A hundred and ten. Folks move to Birmingham, they want to live in the city, they don't wanna live out in the suburbs. So Carlton figures buy the property, set it up as mixed-use. Restaurants and entertainment, put in some high-end condos, too. Gated, sure, because the white kids who buy will want to keep the Black folks out. But nobody straight will deal with him because he's a fucking crook, for Christ's sake. Me? They know me. I helped put together Patton Creek, the Summit, rehabbing Brookwood Mall, I got a good rep for getting deals done and making money."

"So you helped him?" I said softly.

Martin looked away.

"I got a little cash-flow problem right now. Nothing major, it's gonna clear up in a couple months. But Carlton solved it for me. I owe him."

He took a deep breath in, hitched a little, and gently rubbed at the spot where I'd hit him. It was already purpling, and the lump had begun to look like an alien third eye.

"You got a punch like a goddamn mule kick," he said. I tried to look modest, which is not always an easy thing for me.

D'Agostino made a rolling motion with her finger. She had Martin talking now, and she didn't want the flow of information to dry up.

"So you helped Carlton Doyle out," she said, "by being the public face of his deal to buy Carraway."

"Sure," he said. "Nothing to it. And you know the thing about developing, right? It's a good place to put your money if you got, say, some extra sitting around."

"Uh-huh," D'Agostino said. "Dirty money goes in, clean money comes out."

"Changes places and handy-dandy," I said. "Which is the justice, which is the thief?"

D'Agostino stared at me, puzzlement on her face.

"You are strange," she said, and then to Martin. "So why kidnap Doyle's daughter?"

"I never did that."

"Bullshit. Was he squeezing you too hard?"

But Martin James was adamant. He was already shaking his head before D'Agostino had finished asking her question. And the strange thing is this: I believed him.

"Wasn't me, I swear. I been here all day. You could ask Jenna, if your gorilla hadn't scared her away. He wasn't squeezing me anyway. I got out of my cash-flow problem, he got the hospital deal. I got nothing to do with whatever you two are talking about."

I put a hand on D'Agostino's arm. She was safe, so I could see it now. Before, when all I could think of was finding her and Abby, the red haze of rage had clouded my vision. But I understood some things now. Martin was a middleman, a guy looking to profit off of whatever scheme he was involved in. He'd make money with Doyle, but he'd also skim some from whatever contractors they hired to complete the renovation and resuscitate the Carraway property. He wasn't violent. I'd proven that before D'Agostino had arrived, and the real fear he'd shown when she stuck her weapon in his face was enough to make him fold like a cheap suit when she questioned him.

"He's right," I said. "There's lots of money here. There's a lot for everybody, right? Mostly for Carlton Doyle, but think about it. Who else would want a piece of the pie?"

It didn't take her long.

"Shit," she said, and turned to Martin.

"Has anyone been giving you a hard time? Anybody really pissed about somebody buying Carraway?"

"I mean, sure. Lots of people in Norwood don't wanna see it get developed. They want their neighborhood hospital back, but that shit's been gone. It's gone for good."

D'Agostino nodded along.

"Yes, but has anyone specific been complaining? Anybody come by to see you?"

James looked at her, his eyes wary. But he'd come too far to back out now. He opened his mouth, and the words came out in a rush.

"Becks Towson sent a couple guys around, tried to muscle in. You know the guy thinks he owns everything from East Lake to Ensley. When I told 'em Carlton Doyle was involved, they cleared out pretty quick."

"Becks Towson," D'Agostino said. Her voice was soft and thoughtful.

"Goddamn," I said. My breath quickened, and the hairs on the back of my neck stood on end. Becks Towson was bad news. If I had known he was involved, I wouldn't have agreed to watch Abby. Hell, I probably would have saved myself time and just shot myself in the head.

D'Agostino went to Martin's desk and picked up the receiver to his phone. She kept her body turned toward both myself and Martin as she reached for the keypad.

"Nine to dial out?" She asked, and Martin nodded.

"Hold on," I said. "What are you doing?"

"Calling the precinct," she said. "We've got a material witness in a money-laundering and bribery scheme. We'll need forensic accountants to go through Martin's files, find enough to bring Doyle in. Money-laundering, maybe even a RICO violation."

I shook my head.

"Don't do that," I said. Then, lower, my lips near her ear so that Martin wouldn't hear. "You're off the case, remember? They've got the skids greased, and that means that some cops are probably involved, too. There's no way you can know who to trust."

"You're talking about people I work with," she said, and even though her voice was nothing more than a whisper, her tone was sharp. I probably should have walked away, or at least softened my tone of voice. From the floor, Martin watched us carefully as we talked. He had an inkling that he might get out of this situation alive, so he was being smart and staying out of the way, making himself as small as possible.

"You know how easy it is to get a cop to look away? We're not talking big money here. Just enough. You know there are crooked cops in your department. There are bent cops everywhere."

"So I'm supposed to trust you instead? You're a goddamned crook yourself."

I nodded. She was right about that. I went through life and did what I did, without a whole lot of thought about right or wrong, lawful or unlawful. I had few rules in my life, and I liked it that way. But now her disapproval stung like an angry wasp.

"You're right," I said. "But you can trust me. I do what I say I'll do. I hired on to protect Abby Doyle. And now I'm in this thing, trying to help you figure out who killed Britt Parker, and it keeps spiraling out of control. This is way more than I ever signed up for. But I'm still here."

"Welcome to police work," D'Agostino said, and I snorted.

"Look, Abby's still out there somewhere. You're probably the only one who can find her. You haven't even told me what happened when you left Britt's place."

"Don't worry," D'Agostino said. "Abby's fine. She's in the car."

She paused for a second, and a grin played at the corner of her mouth as she watched my jaw drop to my chest.

"What?"

"Downstairs, in the parking lot. I parked in the shade. She's fine. Although she *was* kind of mad when I handcuffed her to the oh-shit handle."

I was already on my way out the door when I heard her voice float over my shoulder.

"It's a gray Lincoln Town Car," D'Agostino said. I turned around, and she lofted a set of handcuff keys toward me. I caught them in both hands. "The keys are in it. But be careful. She's angry, but probably not as mad as the two guys in the trunk."

THIRTEEN

THE LINCOLN wasn't hard to find. Neither was the buzzsaw named Abby Doyle. She had reversed herself and shimmied out of the open car window so that she was bent over the door frame. I could hear other, more muted thumps coming from the trunk of the car.

"Hey," I said, and Abby whirled part way around. Her hand was still inside the window, wrist locked to the door.

"You son of a bitch," she said. "You just let some assholes waltz in and *take* us?"

"Not on purpose."

"You're supposed to be protecting me, not acting like some fucking sidekick cop wannabe."

The thumps coming from the trunk were louder now. I walked closer, stepping around to the driver's side door so that I could get access to her wrist.

"What exactly happened?" I asked, opening the door and sliding into the driver's seat. "When I came back downstairs, you were both just ... gone."

Abby shrugged her shoulders and the handcuffs jingled lightly like an off-key wind chime in a soft breeze. I reached over and unlocked the cuff from her wrist first, then from around the—as D'Agostino had called it—the "oh shit" handle on the front roof support. She held her wrist tightly against her chest and rubbed at the red mark where the cuff had chafed against her skin.

"These two guys came in with their guns drawn," Abby said. "They got the drop on your friend and grabbed me. One of them held a gun to my head and told her to put hers down or they were gonna shoot me."

"Got the drop on her?" I said. "You deal with just one pair of kidnappers and suddenly you're Mickey Spillane."

"Who's that?"

"Don't worry about it," I said. "But if you tell me they took D'Agastino's gat, you're going in the trunk with them."

Abby looked at me blankly. She had no idea what I was talking about. Why should she be any different?

"How did they end up in the trunk?"

Abby shrugged.

"I really don't know. One was driving, and the other was in the back with us. Laura—that's her name, right?—told me to duck down in the floorboard and make myself as small as possible."

"What happened then?"

"There was a lot of swerving and cussing. I could feel them shoving around above me, but I couldn't really tell what was going on. It sounded like someone had set a wildcat loose."

"You didn't look?"

"I was scared shitless, Kincaid," she said. "I didn't want to see her die."

Now there were tears running down Abby's cheeks. Red spots the size of fifty-cent pieces had appeared high on her cheeks, and she still held her formerly cuffed wrist between her breasts. She was shaking with fear and fury, and I recognized the signs of both. I held up my hands, palms out, trying to make peace with her.

"The next thing I know, the car's on the side of the road and the two guys are face-down on the pavement. She put these plastic things on their wrists—"

"Zip ties?"

"Is that what they're called? I guess so. She made them get in the trunk and lie down. And then we came here."

"And she cuffed you to the car door to keep you from running off?"

"Says she's going to take me in as a material witness."

It might be the best thing. Abby would be safe, and I would have room to maneuver and find out what the hell was really going on. It had been so easy to convince D'Agostino not to call the cops. Sure, she was on "vacation" but she hadn't called for backup after putting a couple of bad dudes in the trunk of a car. Instead she'd shown up at Martin James' office less than five minutes behind me. If you looked at it in a certain light, she hadn't rescued me from Martin. She had rescued him from me.

What the hell was going on? D'Agostino had violated about twenty different police regulations since I'd met her. The deeper I got into this thing, the more confused I got.

Was D'Agostino bent? That would explain why she was playing fast and loose here. But she seemed like such a straight arrow. Maybe not a by-the-book detective, but there are a lot of people who bend a rule or two at their job. Maybe she was on Carlton Doyle's payroll and was supposed to make sure I didn't fuck up too badly. Maybe she owed Martin James a favor. Or maybe she was playing a game I couldn't see, hoping to reel in a big fish like Doyle. Maybe it was just about the murder of Britt Parker. I didn't know, and the more I thought about it the more it made my head hurt.

"Here comes Wonder Woman now."

I turned and watched D'Agostino swagger toward us with her confident cop walk. Her hands were hanging loose at her sides, and her shoulders were relaxed. Her arms swung naturally at her sides, and there was nothing there that told me anything at all.

"Hey," she said. "I see you found her."

There was a steady hard thumping coming from the trunk of the Lincoln, and D'Agostino slapped her palm against the lid.

"Shut up before I shoot you idiots," she said, and the sound immediately stilled. Whatever D'Agostino had done, it had scared the hell out of those two. She drew a weapon from her waistband and I saw that it was mine. She reversed it and handed it to me butt-first.

"Thanks," I said, and checked the cylinder to make sure it was loaded. I was careful not to point it anywhere specific. Instead, I held the weapon along the length of my thigh. It was a double-action revolver. No need to pull the hammer back. Just point and pull the trigger. I didn't put the gun away. Not yet. D'Agostino's eyes narrowed, and Abby moved discreetly away from us, out of the potential line of fire.

"Now," I said. "Are you going to tell me what's going on?"

"What are you talking about?"

"Two guys kidnapped you."

"Yeah."

"You got away from them, overpowered them, stuck 'em in the trunk. Then came here."

"That's right."

There was no tremor in her voice that betrayed emotion of any kind. She didn't care if I believed her or not. In my experience, that was the voice of a person who had nothing to hide, a person telling the truth. But my experience with innocent people *was* limited. Almost everyone I knew was guilty of something.

"Why here?"

"Same reason you did," she said. "Martin James pops up in an investigation, I want to know why. By the time I got here, you'd already busted open the door."

"You thought he'd sent the kidnappers?"

"Yes," she said, but there was hesitation, and she wouldn't meet my eyes when she answered. It was the first time I'd caught her in a lie.

I looked over at Abby, but she wouldn't meet my eyes, so I took a deep breath and holstered my weapon. Then I slapped the trunk of the car.

"What do we do with these two?"

"The proper thing would be to haul them in and charge them with kidnapping, assault on an officer, whatever else I could think up."

"Yeah, you been wanting to arrest somebody since this whole thing started. But you do that, you're in trouble with the job."

D'Agostino nodded. Abby was very carefully not looking at us as we talked.

"All right," I said. "We know what's proper. Now let's talk about what we're going to do instead."

Abby's eyes were very wide, and D'Agostino smirked at me a little.

"Something I've always wanted to do," she said.

"Yeah?"

She told me, and about halfway through I started to laugh, really laugh. Finally I held up a hand to stop her.

"Okay, I get it. Let's do it." I shook my head. "Jesus Christ, remind me to never piss you off."

Twenty minutes later, D'Agostino had the Lincoln parked in long-term parking at Birmingham-Shuttlesworth International Airport. She pocketed the parking slip and slid out of the car, locking the doors behind her. Abby and I waited in the Mustang, watching as the detective walked toward us.

"This is so mean," Abby said.

"Yeah, I would've just shot them in the head."

"Jesus, Kincaid."

My left hand gripped the steering wheel loosely and my right fiddled with the gearshift. When D'Agostino hopped in the Mustang, I held out my hand for the keys. She looked at me quizzically for a moment, but handed them over. I put the emergency brake on and left the car running while I moved to the trunk of the Lincoln.

I popped the trunk and peered inside. There were two burly-going-to-seed white guys each laid on their sides in the trunk. Their hands were indeed pinned behind their backs with zip ties. I grinned down at them, chuckling to myself.

"Hey—" one said, and I shut the lid. His voice sounded muffled and far away.

When I got back in the Mustang, Abby asked me why I'd gone to look at the men who had taken them.

"Studying to be a proctologist," I said. "I never pass up a chance to look at a couple of assholes up close."

On our way out of the parking area, I tossed the keys into a garbage can.

"Are we just going to leave them there?" Abby asked. "It's really hot."

D'Agostino was quiet for a moment as she thought.

"It would serve them right," she said, "the assholes. But no, I'll call somebody from the airport police and give them the plate number. They'll sweat a little, but they'll be fine. I think."

I concentrated on my driving. I had to find a place to stash Abby while I looked for Becks Towson. I needed more information. I wasn't a detective—not in the least—but if I wanted to keep Abby safe, I had to know what was going on.

One thing I was sure of: If Towson had anything to do with this, things were about to get a lot more dangerous. So whatever I did with Abby, she had to be one hundred percent safe. Times like this were when it was a real pain in the ass to be an independent operator. I didn't have a network of safe houses, no friends on the cops I could go to—well, maybe one—to keep my charge alive in my stead.

"So how do you feel about babysitting?" I said. D'Agostino looked at me while I watched Abby in the Mustang's rear-view mirror for a moment. We were stopped at a train crossing on 41st Street South, about two blocks away from the Avondale Common House and Distillery, watching the freight trains pass by with the speed of arthritic turtles.

"You want me to watch Abby while you go off and perform some thrilling heroics?"

I ran my hand through my hair, flinching a little when my fingers brushed the swollen side of my face.

"Becks Towson is more likely to talk to me than you," I said. "Not because you're a woman."

"Because I'm a cop."

"Yes," I said. I put the Mustang back in gear as the last freight car passed. We moved down the block past the brewery on one side and the 41st Street Pub on the other.

"Saw's is up here, isn't it?"

"Wanna grab lunch?" I asked. "I'm starving."

"Me too," Abby said.

Saw's Soul Kitchen is a part of the Avondale neighborhood's gentrification, but I'll be damned if it isn't some of the best barbecue in the world. The building isn't much more than a pile of bricks stained black by time and smoke. Freshly chopped wood is stacked in the back of the building, and they smoke their pork slowly, starting at some ungodly hour of the morning to be ready for their lunch rush. I pulled over at the curb, and the women got out. The line was out the door and probably had been since they opened that morning. I put some cash in D'Agostino's hand and told her to order for all three of us. I found a parking spot about three blocks away, and by the time I joined them, D'Agostino and Abby had already ordered. They were sitting together, laughing at something—I had a feeling it was me—and D'Agostino looked up when I arrived at the table.

She looked from me to Abby, who was still smiling a little.

"Yeah," D'Agostino said finally, "I think I can pull babysitting duty. For a little while."

FOURTEEN

BECKS TOWSON WASN'T an easy man to find, but I kept at it for a while. I started at the Gable Square Saloon at the corner of 8th Street South and 10th Street South, a location you wouldn't think could exist in a major modern city. But this was Birmingham. With its location, the bar should have been a favorite of the college kids. Instead, its clientele skewed older, mostly Black with a few working-class white folks mixed in. The place didn't have a bad reputation—or a reputation of any kind, really—and so it was a perfect place for a guy like Towson, who didn't care to attract attention.

He also happened to own the place, as well as Giuseppe's, the little Italian restaurant next door. I was pretty sure that Towson's name wasn't recorded on a deed anywhere, but in the parts of the city where gentrification hadn't reached its lily-white hands yet, Becks Towson was very much the Man.

I hung out at the bar for a little while, making a draft Coors Light last longer than it should have. The bartender, a lean and tall black man with a neat mustache and hair cropped close to his head, wandered down toward me during a slow moment and squinted through the dark.

"You waiting for somebody?" He asked. His voice was carefully neutral.

"Yes," I said. "I'm looking for Becks."

The bartender's hands hung below the bar. I wasn't sure what was down there below eye level, whether it was a baseball bat or a scatter-gun. What I did know was that the guy looked like he could handle himself.

"I don't know anybody by that name," he said, and I grinned at him. It was a real grin, there and gone, blinking on and off like a truncated caution light.

"You lie to your friends, and I'll lie to mine," I said. "But let's not lie to each other." I finished the beer and pushed the empty glass toward the bartender. He rinsed it and put it aside in a rack meant for an industrial dishwasher, pulled a clean, frosted glass from the cooler, and drew me another beer.

"So when is Becks usually in?"

For a moment the bartender didn't say anything. Behind me there were a few quiet, solitary drinkers scattered at tables around the room. In another part of the bar, I could hear the click of billiard balls rolling and ricocheting on green felt. Then he leaned across the bar and whispered.

"Fuck you, sow belly."

It went like that all over metro Birmingham. I bought overpriced beer while suburban white boys ogled doughy strippers at Sammy's, then questioned supposedly ignorant bartenders at both the Furnace and Platinum until I couldn't take it anymore. The bouncer at the Palace had already heard about me and wouldn't let me in. At Mike's Crossroads, I was told to take a hike after my first drink. At each place, I left a business card with my name and number on it.

No one would admit to knowing Becks Towson.

Out in Ensley, in the western part of Birmingham, Club Volcano was the closest I came to getting into a physical altercation. As soon as I got out of the Mustang, a group of men began to drift toward the front door of the bar, blocking my way. I paced forward until I was about twenty feet away.

"Nice night for a beer," I said. "I'm buying, if y'all are interested."

The men—each of them six feet tall or more—glanced at one another. Some wore T-shirts and jeans. Others wore wind pants and the scrappy kind of sleeveless undershirts we used to call wifebeaters in a less-enlightened age. The air was redolent with the smell of cheap beer and expensive weed.

"Appreciate the offer," one of them said. He was narrow through the waist and hips, wearing a tight-fitting shirt that showed well-defined ridges of muscle in his shoulders and chest. His goatee was trimmed neatly, and his teeth were very white underneath the sodium-arc lights of the parking lot. "But we got the word, and the word is to keep you out."

"I'm looking for someone," I said.

"I know," he looked around at his companions. "Everybody knows who you looking for, man. He ain't here. He ain't ever gonna be here, either. You get it?"

I looked into their faces. There was nothing there for me. Each man was closed off, sullen-looking, ready to pound someone's head in. And unfortunately, right now that someone was me.

"Yeah, I get it," I said. "Becks wants me to lay off. But why? All I want to do is talk to him."

The spokesman of the group shrugged.

"Nobody say. I don't care 'bout *why*. I'm the gun, you know. The man points me at a problem and I go bang. The problem goes away."

I ran a hand through my hair and risked a look up at the velvet night sky. Then I blew a breath out.

"You're that good, huh?"

He flashed a broad grin, and then suddenly affected the accent of a bored British lord. "My fellow, you simply have no idea."

Our eyes locked for a moment, and I saw that he was serious.

Whatever else this man was, he was dangerous. I looked carefully from him to the others who stood, I saw now, a little apart from him.

"Then why do you need all the backup?"

He raised an eyebrow at me and then cast a look back at the men standing behind him.

"The man say beat you real good if you don't leave. Say not to kill you if I can help it."

"So?"

"So they for you," he said. "They here to keep me from it."

He paused, thinking about it carefully, then lifted his hands to his shoulders in a dramatic shrug.

"If they can."

I thought about it for a long second. On the one hand, I was pretty dangerous in my own right. I'd hurt people—killed some, too—so I wasn't really worried about this guy. Still, it paid to be wary. I was on my own in Ensley, an area considered by many to be one of the most dangerous parts of Birmingham. And no matter what he said, there were eight of them and only one of me. Inside, there was a wild flame of anger that burned, screaming at me to fight, to bust some heads, to roll through all of Becks Towson's people until he had no other choice but to talk to me or kill me.

But even though that flame was hot and loud in my soul, my brain won the day. I put my hands up, making sure they could all see that they were empty.

"I'll go," I said. "But pass a message on for me, if you would."

The muscular black man never moved.

"All I want to do is talk to Becks. Fifteen minutes of his time, that's it. I'm not going to quit until I find out what I want to know."

He nodded at me finally, and I got back into my car and left.

In rapid succession, I hit the Tutwiler Pub, the Seven Lounge, the Owl, and the House of Cognac. In each place, I got the same thing: stonewalled. No one had seen Becks Towson. No one would even admit to knowing his name. In every bar, I seemed to be the only white face. If I wasn't so intrepid, I might have felt a little nervous. I went through the western side of Birmingham, the area they called Dynamite Hill in the 1960s as the racist white people began setting bombs to drive the Black people out, to frighten or kill them. It got so bad that they started calling the city 'Bombingam' after a while.

I moved along the streets of Midfield and Fairfield, driving along the burned-out husks of Brighton and Roosevelt City. The whores on the streetcorners were brazen. If you slowed for a stop sign or traffic light, they'd reach out and slap the hood of your car to try to make you stop.

I was an alien in this place, a being with only a passing knowledge of the landscape and customs of the human beings who lived in the tract houses huddled close together like survivors of a long-forgotten war. And then I was in Bessemer, that odd appendage twenty miles outside of the city. You won't see it on the 'Welcome to Bessemer' signs, but this place is the murder capital of Alabama, and one of the top 10 cities in the country for murders per capita.

It was also home to one of the only authentic juke joints left, a place called Gip's. It's a little roadhouse tucked into a residential street—Avenue C—and it's hard to find. You'll hear it before you see it, sweet blues played low down, dirty and mean, the way it was meant to be played. There's no sign out front, but you can find the place marked with a string of white Christmas lights around the door.

Henry Gipson ran the place for years. He was a large, heavy black man whose smile was wide. When he shook your hand, he shook the whole thing, his mitts enveloping yours in a warm, tender grip. Grip wore bright clothes and fedoras with wide brims. And if you could find his place—and if you were very lucky—you'd get to hear him take the stage and play.

Nobody would hear him play anymore. Gip had gone down

suddenly and permanently a few weeks before my visit. You could say it was expected—Gip had celebrated his eighty-sixth birthday at least nine times that I knew of—but the man had seemed like a permanent fixture at the bar, his big brown hand cupping a crinkled can of Budweiser.

The folks who loved Gip were trying their best to keep the tradition alive, but once I paid the customary ten-dollar cover and stepped inside, I could tell the air of the place was funereal. A shoulder wedged into the crowd at the bar bought me a little space, and I ordered a beer and let the atmosphere of the blues soak into my soul. The bartender, a thin older black man with white hair and a bar towel tucked into his belt for an apron, came back with a tall glass full of amber liquid, and I gulped down nearly a third of it in one swallow.

Officially, Gip's had air-conditioning, but when the bodies were packed in the place and swaying to the music from the tiny postage-stamp of a stage, the sweat began to glow on the faces of the audience and drip from the foreheads of the performers.

My beer went down quickly, and I ordered another. I didn't bother to ask anyone about Becks Towson. It would have been useless. Between the pounding bass and the wailing guitar, no one could have understood me anyway. So I settled in and drank my beer and listened to the musical wake for Gip and his juke joint.

A little after one a.m.—not last call, but not too far from it, either—the band took a break. They left their instruments onstage and stepped outside for a breath of air or a smoke. I was nearly done with my third beer by then, and the bartender tapped me on the arm to get my attention.

"Excuse me," he said, leaning forward so I could hear him. My ears were still ringing from the music. "There's a gentleman on the phone who'd like to speak to you."

He slid a cracked phone straight out of the 1970s toward me, with a rotary dial and everything, and gave me the handset. I looked at the black plastic relic and wiped off the earpiece. When

I spoke into the handset, I was aware that my own voice sounded alien to my ears.

"You don't quit, sowbelly, I give you that." I'd heard the voice a few hours before outside the Club Volcano. This time it wasn't quite as playful. The hard steel edge of the man's voice came through in a more concrete way over the phone, and it sent a shiver down my spine.

"Don't know how," I said. There was a pause on the line as he considered this.

"Maybe somebody will teach you one day," he said. "That don't matter. What matters for you is that Becks say he'll meet you. This morning, ten a.m., Vulcan Park. Come alone."

"I'll be there," I said, but by the time I got the words out, he had already hung up.

Hot damn.

FIFTEEN

VULCAN PARK IS AT THE TOP of Red Mountain, straddling the boundary between Birmingham proper and Homewood. The centerpiece of the park is the statue of the Roman god of forge and fire, some fifty-six feet tall in its own right, perched atop a sandstone pedestal measuring one-hundred-and-twenty-six feet. Vulcan's face peers toward the sky, and the statue towers over downtown Birmingham. In one hand, a hammer rests on an anvil; the other hand holds a spear aloft toward the heavens. On the back side of the statue, as it were, his naked hind parts wave cheekily at the suburbs.

The park is one of the more public spaces in Birmingham, so I felt at ease meeting Becks Towson there.

"This is bullshit," D'Agostino told me as I checked myself in the motel room mirror at the Tourway Inn just off the interstate on Third Ave. We were on the first floor, and there was a DO NOT DISTURB sign on the door. "He can't just order you to meet him with no backup."

"I prefer to think of it as a request," I said. My suit looked okay, and if I tucked the tee-shirt in tight, it didn't look too wrinkled.

I wet my fingers in the sink and ran my hands through my hair, trying to get it in some semblance of order. I almost succeeded. I'd showered and toweled dry, but I needed a toothbrush and some deodorant in the worst way. That would have to wait. My face was still swollen and bruised, and a couple of molars still felt loose from my run-in with Ralph the walking mountain, but that couldn't be helped.

Abby sat on one of the twin beds in the room, watching D'Agostino and me. She hadn't said much to me since she'd been taken, preferring to stick close to D'Agostino. I couldn't blame her. Laura was doing a much better job of actually keeping her safe than I was.

"I still think we should put her in protective custody," D'Agostino said. "She'll be safer, and then you can have some backup."

I thought about it for a couple of minutes. Finally, I shook my head.

"Nothing has changed. I still don't know which of your cop buddies I can trust."

"God damn it."

"I know," I said. "I don't like it much, either." And there's the fact that I still don't know whether I can trust you, I thought but did not say.

I arrived an hour ahead of time, driving around the parking lot first to make sure that no one was set up early to make life difficult—and possibly short—for me. Barely a quarter of the spaces were taken, and there didn't appear to be anyone waiting around to do me harm.

Still, there was no point in being sloppy about it. I parked the Mustang and trudged around the park, to the base of the Vulcan and then over to the gift shop. There were some tourists taking photos from the scenic overlook, but overall the place was sparse. So I did what you do when you show up early: I waited.

Waiting is an art. When I was in the service, it was the hardest thing of all. You'd be keyed up and ready to go, wearing every piece of equipment you might never need, all your battle rattle intact and perfect, understanding that your shit would never quite be this tight again. Not knowing when the order would come. Some guys banter, using humor to burn off nervous energy, their laughter shrill and annoying. They'd shift their weight from foot to foot like high-strung thoroughbreds in a racing paddock.

I was never like that. When I was a kid, I read a bunch of Louis L'Amour novels, plowing through each one in turn until I'd read everything the man ever wrote. And if his depiction of Native Americans was flawed—it was—it was also clear that he had a great appreciation and admiration for their culture, and he described their warriors' powers of patience as nearly supernatural in nature.

So I sat down on one of the benches in full view of the parking lot and got to it. Both feet flat on the ground, back straight, hands on my knees. Above, the sky was the kind of flawless blue you get on some September mornings when planes crash into buildings and your life changes forever. I tried to keep my mind mostly blank, although I knew my subconscious was working like a madman down there beneath the silent waves of my front brain. There were things I didn't know yet, but I would know them eventually, when that hard-hatted sewer worker in my imagination finally came up from the depths and called it a day.

Some folks call it intuition, and I guess that's as good a word as any. I knew that I was into something that was going to change my world again, and I was just as sure that I wasn't ready for it. If my conscious mind thought of anything, it was the wide soft smile and the pleasant little crinkles around the eyes on D'Agostino's face and how much I had wanted to lean forward and kiss her that morning before I left the motel.

Somewhere nearby in the artfully arranged landscaping of the park, a bee buzzed. Birds called to one another. And eventually the loitering tourists slowly departed. When a white Infiniti SUV pulled into the parking lot at five minutes until ten, the place was nearly deserted. I didn't move, just watched the big glossy vehicle make a similar circuit to the one I'd made around the blacktop earlier. The car was parked in one of the handicap-accessible spaces in the front row, and the dangerous-looking young man I'd met the night before got out on the driver's side. He went around to the passenger-side rear door and opened it.

I breathed out a little, feeling a shiver run down my spine as I got my first look at the legendary Becks Towson.

He was tall and wide-shouldered, and even in the direct sunlight, his skin was so black that his features defied description. He wore his gray hair in a medium-length natural, and his mustache was neatly trimmed. He leaned heavily on a crutch, the kind that clasps around the forearm, and his right foot dragged a little.

Becks was dressed in a pearl-pink suit with a gray pinstripe. His shoes were a deep and soft brown, shined to a mirrored gloss. He was heavy, his chin and jawline blurred a little from either age or over-indulgence.

He and his driver walked slowly toward me, and I stood up from my seat in order to show the old man the respect he deserved. When they got to the bench, Becks was perspiring a little, but his breathing was normal. Neither of us made a move to shake hands.

"People who should know say it's easier to talk to you than kill you."

His voice was like the rumble of an oncoming train heard from a distance. It was soft, but there was a gravelly tone of malevolent import in his raspy bass. I stood quietly and said nothing.

"Let's sit down," Becks said. "I ain't got my strength back yet."

I moved aside and let Becks pick his seat. He sat heavily and shifted over to ease his bad leg, and then moved further still until I had room to sit beside him without either of us touching. When we were settled, Becks Towson looked up at his driver.

"Wait in the car, Thomas."

I saw the young man draw in a quick breath, and he made as if to protest, but a quick look from Becks made him stop and say

"Yes, Mr. Towson." He walked quickly away from us, got in the Infiniti, and cranked it to let the air-conditioner continue the good fight against the Alabama heat. When Becks was satisfied, he turned to me.

"This is your meeting, white boy. You want to open the ball?"

"I need to know some things," I said, and Becks laughed.

"Like every other white man I ever met. What you boys don't know could fill the Encyclopedia Britannica, if they still made those things."

"I heard you were interested in the Carraway Hospital deal."

Becks was very still on the bench beside me. His eyes surveyed the parking lot in front of us, and I was aware that the park was quiet and nearly devoid of life. A droplet of sweat ran down the center of my back. I didn't dare shiver. Becks was a predator, and you don't show weakness to predators.

"I'm interested in everything that happens in north Birmingham," he said. "That's Black folks' business, and that makes it my business."

"So when Carlton Doyle put together a deal to buy the hospital, you wanted to cut in?"

Becks snorted. The sunlight glanced off the small gold rings he wore on each finger of his right hand.

"A cut? Who do you think I am? You think I'm gonna share with Doyle?"

I didn't quite know what to say. But he waited, obviously waiting for my answer. I thought about it for a little while.

"You would if you wanted to," I said. "If it served your purpose. You run the parts of Birmingham that Doyle doesn't."

"Say you're right," Towson said in his quiet rumble. "Say I wanted to get into bed with Doyle. Why should I tell you anything? Give me a reason not to get up and drag my ass outta here."

"You already said it. I'm easier to talk to than kill. I've already proved that I can be very annoying, very persistent. I can get worse."

"Can get dead, too. Just 'cause it hard to do don't mean it's impossible."

The words were there and full of menace, but strangely without heat. He was considering his options, that's all. He turned the heat of his gaze away from the dark asphalt parking lot and let its weight bear full and pitiless on me.

"You think you know something? You don't know anything. Doyle buys the boodle, he don't know nothing about the neighborhood or the people in it. First thing you people did was run off from the city when you thought the Blacks would ruin it, now y'all back and you want to take it away from us."

"Becks," I said. "You don't believe in us versus them. You don't believe in black and white, none of it. You believe in money. You believe in power. Why else would you even care about this? There's money to be made, and Doyle snubbed you in a part of the city that everyone recognizes is yours."

Becks was quiet for a time, thinking. Or maybe he just liked the sunshine.

"Shit," he said. "I'm getting old. I used to be able to put the fear of God into white boys like you."

"You still do," I said. "I'm scared as hell. People who cross Becks Towson tend to live short and depressing lives. I'm trying very hard to give you the respect you deserve while still doing my job."

Becks chuckled low in his throat, and I could feel my bowels shrink. My bladder didn't let go automatically, so score a point for me.

"You wanna know who got it out for Doyle," he said. "Be just about anybody in this city. But you think I got something to do with it."

"Because of the Carraway deal."

Becks shrugged.

"That deal be dead before next month. They ain't never gonna put in one foundation, not a single brick, without me. You ever been on a construction site before?"

"A couple times."

"Then you know how it is. Stuff laying around everywhere. Supplies disappear. You get a good price these days for shingles, copper, masonry, whatever, and folks don't ask where it came from as long as you can deliver. Tools and vehicles go missing or get burned up. Somebody mixes concrete wrong so the foundation won't set. Maybe the union guys go on strike."

I grinned suddenly, stifling a laugh.

"You're gonna have his tit in the wringer."

Becks cackled along with me.

"And squeezin' harder every day. You think them union boys let a scab cross the picket line? No sir. So I'm not just in the Carraway deal, I *am* the deal, whether Doyle likes it or not. He just don't know it yet."

I thought for a minute until Becks shifted on the bench and grimaced in pain.

"You got anything else? This goddamn leg."

"Who the hell wants Abby Doyle? If everything you're saying is true—"

"If?"

I shook my head and plowed on.

"—then who's after the girl?"

Becks hauled himself up from his seat and got his crutch situated to his liking.

"Now you asking about stuff that falls into two categories: a) I don't know; and b) I don't care."

I watched Becks's peculiar shuffling gait as he walked to the Infiniti. Thomas was there immediately, hopping out of the driver's side and racing around to open the door for Becks. The older man put his hand on Thomas's waist and leaned forward to kiss him gently on the lips, while the younger man cupped the back of Becks's head. It was a moment of real tenderness, and it made me consider Becks Towson a little more human. He was a monster, for sure, and if I thought of him as anything else, it would be to my own detriment. But he was a person. He didn't just care about himself.

Thomas helped Becks into the back seat and then shot a look at me, wondering if I'd noticed the intimacy between the two.

I kept my gaze level. As Thomas walked around the front of the car to the driver's side he looked at me and pointed his forefinger at me, dropping the thumb like the hammer of a gun.

SIXTEEN

D'AGOSTINO AND I had decided that moving Abby into the detective's apartment was easier—to say nothing of cheaper—than moving her from motel to motel around the city. I went back to my own semi-permanent home and grabbed a shower and changed into a pair of broken-in blue jeans, a black tee-shirt, and hard-soled, well-sprung cowboy boots. I hadn't shaved in a couple of days, and the stubble itched a little. I didn't want to take the time to shave. Instead, I packed a Dopp kit with my toiletries. After a second's hesitation, I added a small bottle of cologne.

Under my bed was a small nylon duffle bag with a change of clothes, spare ammo, and a small bundle of cash. I checked it to make sure everything was there and then slung it over my shoulder on the way out. Before I shut the door, I looked at the spare, neat room. There wasn't much to mark my life there, and if I never saw the place again, no one would care. If our lives are like concentric circles on the surface of a pond, would mine make any contact—any difference at all—with anyone else? I didn't want to think about that. Instead, I drew the door closed behind me, stowed my gear in the Mustang and headed across town.

It was an easy drive to D'Agostino's place. Like Abby, she lived in a gentrified part of downtown. But unlike the Pizitz, the security on her building was tight. Not only was there a security code that I had to punch in to get to the parking deck, but there were off-duty cops stationed at each entrance and exit. I had to show my ID to one of them, give D'Agostino's name and apartment number, and then the guard called ahead to make sure I was okay. Not bad. Not impossible to get around, but not bad.

D'Agostino was waiting for me in the doorway of her apartment, leaning one shoulder against the jamb, one hand cocked on her hip. She was wearing a dark blue BPD tee shirt with 'Protect and Serve' in script below the gold-colored shield that decorated the center of the shirt and a pair of yoga pants that accentuated her shape. She was barefoot, her toenails gleaming with the same shade of polish as the tips of her fingers, and she had scrubbed her face clean of makeup so that I could tell what she had looked like as a little girl.

That wasn't too bad, either.

"Hey," I said. That's me, Mr. Smooth. Never at a loss for words.

"Come on in," D'Agostino said, and shrugged away from the door. "Be quiet, though. Abby's asleep in the guest room."

The apartment was big, with an open living space that encompassed living and dining spaces. Between those two areas was a large bay window that looked out over the city. D'Agostino had placed a heavy cherry-wood desk in front of the window, and her laptop glowed atop the desk. The place was clean and orderly, and the only photo on the wall was of D'Agostino in her patrol uniform with a furled American flag behind her right shoulder. Graduation from the police academy, I guessed.

On one wall above the dining room table there was a framed American flag folded in a traditional triangle. There was a brass plaque on the front of the frame that read *Captain Richard D'Agostino, US Army* followed by his dates of birth and death. After that, on a second line: *He served with distinction.*

D'Agostino finished locking her door, which was a process. She engaged a police lock, one end set into a small metal hole in the floor and the other locked against the door just below the door-knob. The apartment was just about as secure as it could be. She saw me looking at the folded flag and glanced away from me.

"My brother," she said. "Afghanistan. We don't have to talk about it, do we?"

We didn't. I had seen too many of those flags over the years. I didn't want to talk about it either. What the hell was there to say?

The kitchen area was an alcove separated from the main body of the apartment by a waist-high bar and low, heavy wooden stools. I pulled one out and settled down, putting my elbows on the bar. D'Agostino looked around as if she were unsure of herself here in her own place. It was odd to see her that way. Normally she was sure of herself to the point of being cocky.

Game recognize game.

"I'm really bad at being a host," she said. "There's beer in the fridge. You want one?"

I did, and told her not to worry, that I'd get it myself. D'Agostino's fridge was sparse, with some cold cuts, eggs, and a few vegetables that looked close to wilting. On the bottom shelf was a row of Good People brown ale. I grabbed two cans and tossed her one, nudging the fridge door closed with my hip.

We cracked our beers, and I noticed that our positions were now flipped. D'Agostino was seated at the bar, while I was stand-ing in the kitchen. So much for gender roles.

"What?" She asked.

I shook my head.

"Amusing myself," I said. "It's nothing. Have you eaten?"

"I was thinking about sending out for pizza."

I rested my hands on the bar. "I can cook."

D'Agostino's eyes narrowed. I raised my right hand in the Boy Scout salute and crossed my heart with my left hand. "I swear I won't poison you."

I rummaged through the kitchen cabinets, being careful to stay quiet, and found a medium-sized sautée pan that looked like it had never been used. Then I set to work with the eggs, cracking four of them into a cheap plastic mixing bowl. D'Agostino didn't have a whisk, so I used a fork to scramble the eggs, then added a dash of cold water.

"I've never seen anyone do that before," she said. I added salt and kept whisking away until the eggs were a uniform golden yellow.

"Little trick Alton Brown uses," I said.

"Really."

"Well, that's what he said on TV."

I cut up a quarter of an onion that was moldering in the fridge, and while I was getting my second beer I found some mushrooms that didn't smell too bad. D'Agostino had a knife block on her counter that held knives whose blades looked like they'd never been used. I sharpened the biggest of them and then set about chopping the veggies fine. Over medium heat, I melted some butter in the pan and then added the mushrooms. Once they'd cooked, I added the little pile of onions. Soon the smell of the food filled the apartment, and my stomach moaned its hunger.

While I was working in the kitchen, D'Agostino didn't say anything. She watched me work, and I tried to look competent as I moved.

I put the mushrooms and onions aside into a small bowl and made sure the butter still coated the bottom of the pan. Then I added about half the eggs. I wasn't classically trained, so I couldn't do the traditional French rolled omelet, but I paid attention and added some shredded cheddar cheese and some of the sauteed vegetables. When I was satisfied, I ran a spatula under one side of the omelet and flipped it. Then I slid the whole thing onto a clean white plate D'Agostino had taken down from an overhead cabinet.

I repeated the process while D'Agostino ate her omelet. By the time I sat down with my own plate, hers was empty.

"Oh my God," she said. "That was incredible. Where did you learn to do that?"

I shrugged.

"I like to eat," I said, and she laughed a little.

"I never learned. The way I grew up—it was just my Dad and us—he was a cop, too. And I'm sure you know how a cop's life is. You do your tour, you're tired but you can't come down off the nervous energy. Your guard's been up for ten, twelve hours, ever since you left your house. Dad would stop at a diner, have a cup of coffee, steak and eggs, whatever. He'd swing by the babysitter's house and pick us up, take us with him."

She finished her beer and got two more out of the fridge. Bless that woman. She cracked them both and handed me one. A third beer in this pleasant apartment with an attractive woman felt just about right. I finished the one I was drinking and watched the condensation bead on the new can next to me. It made talking about myself easier.

"I never knew my parents," I said. "I grew up mostly in foster homes."

"I'm sorry," she said.

"Don't be," I said, and silence spun out between us like a fine spider's web, catching any words I might have said before they could leave my mouth.

Shit.

I cleared my throat and tried again.

"You're a cop. You know what the foster system is like. There are a lot of good families out there, and I finally landed in one when I was twelve. Before that, it was ... bad. I remember a lot of group homes, but a lot of times the details are hazy. Other kids would steal my clothes. I was always the smallest one. By the time I fought my way to the dinner table, everything would be gone."

I hadn't meant to let that out, never intended for the scared little kid I had once been to peek his way out of the cage in my soul where I kept him safely locked. It felt like there wasn't enough oxygen in the room. I breathed in, I knew I had air in my lungs, but the flow of it had constricted and my chest felt like there was a wide iron bar lying atop it. At some point I realized D'Agostino had reached across the table and taken my hand in hers.

"Things change when you get in a good place," I said. "But the thing is that you don't change. Not at first. I was a scrapper from way back. When I got in with the Skinners, I didn't have to fight for a place at the table. I started eating regularly. I put on size. Mike, the father, put me in karate. Figured if I was going to fight, I ought to know what I was doing."

D'Agostino smiled a sad, knowing smile.

"It's more, though," she said. "You learn a lot of other things, too."

I drank some beer. "Sure you do. You learn to follow through on a punch or a kick. You learn what hurts. You learn *how*. But you also learn self-control. It was probably the best thing Mike could have done for me."

"What happened to him?"

"Car accident, coming back from Huntsville. The other driver was drunk, going the wrong way on I-65. They collided head-on. Mike died. The other guy was just scratched up and bruised, so he lived."

D'Agostino didn't say anything. Her hand was warm and dry on my own, and the beers had worked their way down into me so that I felt integrated and whole, and I said the rest of it.

"For a little while," I said, and D'Agostino squeezed my hand hard. I looked at her face-to-face then, and her green eyes were soft and full with unspilled tears.

"Jesus," she breathed, and looked away. But she didn't move her hand.

"It was cancer for my Dad," she said. "He was always a big guy, an Italian cop who liked huge meals, spaghetti with a lot of gravy—not the Southern kind, either, you know what I mean?— lots of red sauce. And a couple of cigarettes after, too. Toward the end of his career, he had packed on some pounds. By then he'd moved to a desk job and become more and more sedentary. And then he started losing weight. A lot of it. His uniform didn't fit right anymore, and his equipment belt was down to its last loop within about three months. I finally got him to go to a doctor.

"By the time he got checked, it had, you know, metastasized. It was in his spinal cord, his brain."

D'Agostino looked at me hard. "Cancer can let you last a long time. And it doesn't just hurt you. It hurts everybody who ever loved you. And by then, Richard was in Iraq. First tour. He wasn't—he couldn't be here to help."

Now I held her hand. The skin was soft, and I used my thumb to trace the narrow trail of veins along the back.

"I prayed," she said. "I begged God to let him go. And then, you know, nothing happened. He just kept suffering. So we kept suffering. Richie was half a world away, so it was all on me. I was right there, I got the brunt of it."

There was another long pause, and I swear that her soul looked into mine and found something there that was the same. Now her tears really did come, splashing onto the bar top. I looked away. D'Agostino was a tough-as-nails cop. If she knew that I saw her crying, I wasn't sure she'd ever forgive me.

"The thing about cancer patients that are so far gone … they don't do an autopsy."

I squeezed her hand hard, the same way she'd squeezed mine. Around us the apartment was quiet, its stillness broken infrequently by the muted rumble of the refrigerator's ice maker. Only the overhead light in the kitchen shone. I chanced a look at D'Agostino; she had her head turned away from me. I don't know what she felt, but I guessed it was the same emotions that were running through me: shame and guilt mixed with relief at having told someone the awful thing that weighted down our souls like a millstone around our necks.

She turned to me, tilting her face up to meet my gaze. Her cheeks were streaked with tears, and her lips were parted slightly so that I could barely see her even white teeth. I leaned down without thinking about it—or at least not thinking much—and kissed her. She froze for just a second, and then she returned the kiss. Our bodies turned toward one another, hands scrabbling for purchase, bodies brushing against one another with the bursting energy of falling stars. I felt myself moan into her mouth, and she pulled away for a bare moment.

"Shhhhh," she whispered. "Be quiet."

"Make me," I hissed, and her mouth was on mine again. We left the dishes on the counter unwashed and barely made it to her bedroom, stumbling a couple of times along the way. But we never broke the kiss. D'Agostino locked the door behind us and put her gun carefully into the small safe she kept on a shelf in her closet and turned to me.

I shucked out of my boots and tee-shirt. Barefoot, I was only a little taller than her. She ran her hands over the broad muscles of my chest, her slender fingers hesitating when they found the scars I carried there. But if her hands hesitated, her mouth never did. We broke the kiss once, when we moved from our feet to the bed. After that, everything was wanton need and desire, and when she reached her climax she dug her nails into my shoulders so hard that she drew blood.

Afterward, it took both of us a long time to come back to Earth from wherever the hell our lovemaking had taken us. I wasn't asleep—not quite—sated, pleasantly satisfied and floating on the cloud of endorphins that were still hanging around. Laura—how could I think of her as D'Agostino anymore?—was saying something, and it took an effort of will to concentrate on what she was saying.

"Hmm?"

"Were you asleep?"

"No," I said, and paused. "Not quite."

She giggled, then grew more serious.

"Did we just make a mistake here?"

I thought about it for a little bit, reaching down to twine my fingers with hers so that she'd know I wasn't falling asleep again.

"Maybe," I said at last. "I don't know."

Laura nestled her head against my shoulder. I could feel her breath gently brushing the hairs on my chest.

"If it was, it's a mistake I'd be happy to make again." Her mouth reached for mine, this time her kiss was gentle. We'd left ferocity behind, and now we were two people reaching for tenderness in the dark. I turned toward her and put my arms around her, letting my hands trail along the line of her spine and down to her buttocks. She shifted one leg over me, hooking her ankle behind my knee, and leveraged us both into a half-roll so that she ended up on top. I broke the kiss with a groan.

"Laura," I said. "I'm nearly fifty years old."

She propped herself up so that she could look down at me in the dim light streaming from her closet door. She moved her hips back and forth gently, and I felt myself beginning to respond.

"You're only as young as you feel," she said, rotating her pelvis in small circles above me. I brought my thighs up to support her hips, and she leaned forward again to kiss me as we found our rhythm and began again.

The second time was better than the first, sweeter, with less urgency. And when we were done, we were no less spent than the first time, and I felt like I could sleep for a week afterward. I kissed the top of Laura's head and felt her snuggle in beside me. Her breathing became deeper and more regular as sleep claimed her.

And then I closed my eyes, feeling the gentle susurration of her breathing, and let sleep take me, too.

SEVENTEEN

"HERE'S WHAT I DON'T UNDERSTAND," Abby said. "Why would anyone want to hurt Britt?"

We were eating scrambled eggs with toasted rye and drinking Wild Roast coffee from thick china mugs, none of us talking about the fact that when D'Agostino and I came out of her bedroom that morning that Abby was waiting on one of the couches with a kind of triumphant, gloating grin on her face, as though we had confirmed something that she'd known long before either of Laura or I had understood it.

Laura chewed her toast thoughtfully, nodding along.

"We've been thinking that Britt had walked in on someone waiting for you," she said. "Wrong place, wrong time. But what if he was the target? Who has reason to hate him?"

Abby put her fork down on her empty plate, then rose from the table. She crossed to the cabinet above D'Agostino's sink and took down a nearly full bottle of Richland Rum and poured a liberal shot into her coffee mug, then freshened her cup from the pot. She left the cabinet door open, the bottle of rum on the counter.

"I'm sure I don't know," she said, retaking her seat. "I mean, no one at the tennis club likes him, but that's because he's a really good player. I mean he was, anyway."

Abby looked away from us, mourning her fiancé, but her eyes were dry. She sipped at the fortified coffee in her mug and seemed to become a little calmer, as though the alcohol had reached a place deep inside her where love and need were one. I'd met Britt only once, and he'd been so much of a tool then that I couldn't imagine anyone being truly broken up about his passing. Abby knew she should feel badly about his murder, but what we were mostly seeing was relief, I think. She wouldn't have to marry him after all.

I couldn't blame her for feeling that way. I also didn't like myself very much for thinking about it.

Abby had asked a good question, though. We'd been going on the assumption that Abby had been the target. I'd been hired earlier in the day to protect her, and then Britt ends up dead in her apartment that night. It had seemed like the two things must be related. But if they weren't, then Britt had been the target all along. We had to consider that possibility.

So that begged the question: Why?

When we'd tried to look through Britt's house, we'd been stopped. Laura and Abby had been taken, and that had put us on the run. My instincts weren't an investigator's. My first thought had been to protect the women, to get them out of the way of harm and then backtrack. Of course, D'Agostino didn't need me to rescue her. She wasn't a damsel who waited around in need of a big, strong man to help her. But even so, what if there were answers in Britt's house that we could have found? Going back to his house would give us a next step to take, and in my experience it was better to do something rather than nothing at all.

"We have to stop reacting," I said slowly, and the women looked at me. "I think we've been looking at this all wrong. My job has been to protect Abby. But you—" I looked directly at Laura—"should be investigating. Our strengths are different. If we're going to find out who killed Britt, you've got the best chance of doing it."

D'Agostino took a deep breath and blew it out through her mouth like a powerlifter getting ready to snatch a heavy weight. She turned her face to the ceiling and rubbed at her chin, thinking hard. I went to the coffeemaker and refilled my cup, eyeing the bottle of rum still on the counter. I added sugar and cream, and then went back for D'Agostino's cup. I refilled it for her and brought both cups to the table. Abby held her empty cup out to me, a silent request for a refill. I went back to the kitchen, poured black coffee into her cup, and then set it down in front of her at the table.

She looked at the steaming mug, huffed softly, and hauled herself from her chair. She went to the counter for the bottle of rum and brought it back to the table. She drank a little coffee to make room, then poured in a dose of the liquor.

"I hate it black," she said. "Abbadoo's got to have a little something-something."

I drank my coffee and reminded myself that Abby's personal habits were none of my business, and that keeping my mouth closed was a technique of adulthood that I should work on. D'Agostino eyed the bottle of rum and cut her eyes to me.

"Okay, let's talk about what we know: Carlton Doyle hired you to watch Abby. Later that same night, Britt Parker is killed in Abby's apartment."

"Right," I said. "And we've been thinking that those two things are related, because Abby is supposedly in danger."

"But maybe we're wrong. Correlation isn't necessarily causation. Britt was a lawyer, is that right?"

"Yes," Abby said, and nothing more. She seemed uninterested in the conversation.

"So you have Doyle and Martin James—"

"And Becks Towson, don't forget him."

D'Agostino shivered. "I'd like to, but that would be really dumb. He's too dangerous."

We thought for a while. I got up from the table and refilled our coffee cups. Abby declined a refill, instead filling the cup nearly halfway with straight rum. She moved away from us to go sit on one of D'Agostino's well-worn leather couches and sipped contentedly from the mug. When I took my seat again, my knee brushed against Laura's, and she pressed her leg against me. She was wearing a pair of boxer shorts and a green and gold UAB tee and nothing else. It looked great on her. It felt good to be there in her space, feeling her move gently against me.

"Towson said he didn't know anything about it," I said. "But there's too much money around. I don't think he lied to me, but maybe there's something he doesn't know."

"Becks? You're kidding. He knows everything when it comes to his territory."

"You didn't see him like I did. He's gotten old. And besides, he's an executive now. He doesn't have to know everything that goes on at street-level. He's got guys that handle that for him. Probably, anyway."

I thought about Thomas, Beck's driver and muscle—and whatever else he was. The last part was none of my business, but what I'd seen had suggested a level of intimacy that I hadn't known about before.

"What about Ralph?" D'Agostino said. "The skyscraper that walks."

"What about him?"

"He was keeping Abby before you were. So was this a new threat? I mean, think about the size of the man. What kind of trouble couldn't he handle? Why bring you in?"

I started to say something and then stopped. Why, indeed? Ralph wasn't smart, but he was exactly what you thought of when someone said the word bodyguard. He was enormous, with a scowl that could turn away almost anyone. And speaking from experience, the man hit hard, and he was faster than anyone that size had a right to be.

Why move Abby's protection from Ralph to me?

"Abby," I called. "Do you have any idea why your father wanted to hire me, specifically?"

"What? No. He just told me that Ralph was needed on something else."

She concentrated on the brown liquid in her cup, her brow furrowed.

"Did he say what it was?"

Abby hesitated. "No."

She drained the rum and settled back on the couch, laying her head against the backrest, her eyes closed. Out of the corner of my eye, I saw Laura purse her lips. So she knew Abby was lying, too. Now we had to decide whether or not to pursue the lie. D'Agostino was the detective, so I decided to let her make the play.

"Abby," she said gently, and the young woman's eyes opened. "You're lying."

Abby Doyle refused to look at us. I took my half-empty coffee cup with me and crossed the room to sit in the glider rocker near the couch.

"I was there for you," I said. "I helped you after Britt died. And remember, you called Laura 'Wonder Woman' after she got the two of you away from those two mooks who tried to kidnap you.

"Look at me. *Look at me.* Maybe you don't owe me anything, but you owe *her.* And you know it. They would have killed you."

D'Agostino came over and put her hand on Abby's shoulder.

"They would have killed us both."

Abby put her head in her hands and bent forward on the couch. Her shoulders shook, and she began to cry—big, wracking sobs that came from deep in her gut—as if all of the affectation she wore had slipped off her shoulders like a coat falling to the floor.

"I—I don't know," she moaned. "I don't know what's going on. Daddy said it would all be okay, that no one would know. But

Britt's dead and now people really are trying to maybe kill me too, and I don't know why.

"God, I need a drink."

Now D'Agostino was gentle. She moved her hand from Abby's shoulder to her back, rubbing small circles and patting occasionally.

"It's going to be all right," she said, and looked past Abby at me. Her eyes were steady. "It really will. But we need to know what's going on."

Abby kept her face in her hands, so her voice was muffled when she spoke.

"I can't," she said. "I can't. I won't."

"Why not?"

"I can't talk about it, you know, with *him* here."

D'Agostino raised her eyebrows at me, and I shrugged back. I rose from the glider, my knees popping audibly as I got my feet under me.

"I think I'm going to shower," I said, and went into D'Agostino's bedroom. The attached bathroom was small, with a toilet, vanity, and a stall shower. I ran the water as hot as I could get it and used some of D'Agostino's cherry-blossom shampoo, working the lather through my hair and letting it rinse off. I scrubbed myself down with her loofah and some vanilla-scented soap. When I got out of the shower, I toweled off and put on a blue T-shirt that read The Drive-By Truckers on the front and listed their 2004 tour dates on the back. I didn't want to think about how long ago that was.

I was just tucking into my blue jeans when D'Agostino opened the door to the bedroom. She looked me up and down, smiling a little. Then her face grew serious and she crossed the soft nubby carpet. I took her in my arms, and she rested her head against my chest for a moment.

"You're not going to like this."

I waited.

"She's pregnant."

"Oh."

"She's not very far along. Only about ten weeks, she says."

"I don't understand what the big deal is," I said. "It happens. It's not even that uncommon. Is it because she's not married yet?"

"No, it's not that. But it's not Britt's," she said. "That's why she had Ralph with her, to keep Britt away, to keep him from finding out."

"But if it's not him, then—"

D'Agostino took a deep breath. She dropped her eyes away from mine and twined her fingers with mine, squeezing hard.

"She doesn't know. She thinks it could be her father's."

For once, I was speechless.

EIGHTEEN

D'AGOSTINO AND I left Abby in Laura's apartment, where she was under strict orders to stay put. Now that the secret was out, now that we knew the Terrible Thing, Abby seemed spent, as though the last breath of wind was spent in her sails.

We were in Laura's car, deking through the downtown traffic, heading to St. Vincent's Hospital. She was driving. A quick phone call to one of her cop buddies had located Ralph, who had been admitted with serious but— sadly— not life-threatening injuries. When we got to the hospital, D'Agostino parked on a hydrant, secure in the knowledge that the nearly rabid meter-readers that patrolled downtown wouldn't ticket a cop car. We took the elevator up to the fifth floor and found Ralph in bed in a private room, his right leg hoisted to nearly forty-five degrees by a pulley and sling contraption. The left leg was immobilized in a cast. His nose was bandaged and both eyes were black. Bruises ran down his arms like streams heading toward the sea. I tried not to look too pleased with myself.

Bolted into the far wall near the ceiling was a flat-screen TV tuned to ESPN. It played without sound, highlights of professional basketball players I'd never heard of. Where had Larry and Magic gone? There was a table beside the bed with a plastic pitcher and Styrofoam cup, as well as a black smartphone. Pushed away into the far corner of the room was a small table that held the remains of Ralph's lunch. It looked like it had been meatloaf, and from the state of the leftovers, it hadn't been very good.

It took a moment for Ralph to register who we were, and then he shifted in the hospital bed and the whole thing almost went over. The setup was nearly too small for him, and I had a moment's pity. He was a large man in just about every way. Yes, he was fat, but that was just one layer on top of heaps of muscle. None of it was pretty, but Ralph was as tall as an NBA player, and he was wide-shouldered and thick-bodied, a man of immense mass who could still move quickly enough to be dangerous to just about anyone.

And here he was, flat on his back. Helpless. I tried not to grin about it too much.

"What the fuck are you doing here," he said. It wasn't a question. Instead he seemed to be musing to himself. He never looked at D'Agostino, instead staring beady eyes at me, shooting daggers at the man who had put him in traction.

"Ralph, how's it going?" I asked. He didn't answer, so I plowed on. "The time has come for us to put aside our differences and apply sweet reason."

"I don't know what the hell you're talking about." He finally dared a glance at D'Agostino. "What's with the cop? You think she's gonna protect you when I get outta here?"

Laura laughed and stepped toward the hospital bed.

"You think I'm going to protect him from you? He's going to have to protect you from me, you asshole. You and your boss got me thrown off my goddamn case. I'll—"

I caught her arm as she swung it back. We were putting on a little for Ralph, sure, but I knew exactly how angry she was at being pressured off the case. That Carlton Doyle's reach could extend to her own job had not just pissed her off; it had scared her as well.

"Trust me, Ralphie-boy, I'm much easier to deal with than our friendly police detective," I said.

Ralph leaned back in bed and looked at the ceiling.

"All right, you ain't come to rough me up. So whaddaya want?"

Beside me, D'Agostino had dropped her hand. Now she moved back, letting me take the lead. We hadn't discussed how we'd approach Ralph, instead relying on our instincts. Since I was the one who had put Ralph in traction, it would make sense if he were more afraid of me than D'Agostino.

"Did you know Abby's pregnant?"

Ralph stared out the window of his hospital room and didn't say anything. I moved closer, keeping an eye on those big hands the size of canned hams. Even from a hospital bed and short a couple of working limbs, Ralph was dangerous enough to deserve some respect.

"So what if she is?" He said finally. He still faced the window. "Don't make no difference to me, man. It ain't my baby."

"Not what I asked," I said, keeping my voice soft. "Did you know?"

"Man, I was with her every day for nearly two years. Of course I knew. You think I don't pay attention to my job?"

"Do you know who the father is?"

Now Ralph turned back to me, his gaze level.

"Do you?"

I glanced askance at D'Agostino, but she was no help. She didn't want to give away anything, and I didn't blame her. I saw no reason to lie to the big man, so I decided to play it straight.

"Yeah," I said. "We think we do."

Ralph closed his eyes and turned his head away again. When he opened his eyes, he wouldn't look at us.

"That girl. You don't know her, what she's really like," he said. "She told me it could be mine, but no way. We only did it the one time, and I was careful. It can't be mine, anyway. It's been too long."

D'Agostino went very still. So did I. I could feel the hairs on my arms rising as gooseflesh prickled my skin.

"What?" She asked. "You and Abby?"

Ralph looked at her and flashed a mean little smile at us.

"Like I said, you don't know her. Girl would fuck a snake if only it'd stay stiff, you know? She didn't even like me. It's just that I was always around, so eventually she put the moves on me. I'm not proud of it, I guess, but am I gonna turn down a piece that looks like that? Come on. Where am I gonna get another chance for something that sweet?"

Ralph's words held the ring of truth, but D'Agostino wasn't so easily convinced.

"No way," she said. "I don't believe it."

Ralph shot me a look, sly and pleased with himself.

"You want proof? Gimme my phone. It's on the table over there, they keep moving the goddamn thing."

Laura handed Ralph the phone, which he opened via thumbprint. The home screen came to life, and he thumbed to the photo library, clicking on a picture so that it filled the viewable area.

The photo showed Abby Doyle, naked. She was on her knees, the coral-colored tips of her breasts just barely visible. She was fellating someone in the picture, though we couldn't tell who from the angle of the camera. Whoever he was had a large, elaborate tattoo of the ace of spades on the front of his thigh. D'Agostino looked away.

"Jesus Christ," she said. "Put that away."

Ralph minimized the photo, but kept scrolling through.

"I got about twenty pics from that night. You wanna see?"

D'Agostino shook her head.

"That's you with her?" I asked.

"Accourse," Ralph answered. "You saw the tattoo, right? Look on my left quad. That enough proof for you two assholes?"

It was.

"Shit," D'Agostino said.

"Is that why Doyle wanted you away from his daughter?" I asked.

Ralph shrugged his massive shoulders.

"I don't know, man. I don't think he cared. He was getting his piece off her, too, you know? Didn't care that she was his daughter. Why would he care what I did with her?"

D'Agostino crossed her arms over her chest. Now she was the one who wouldn't look at Ralph. Or me.

"Maybe he didn't care," I said. "But why hire me otherwise?"

"I don't know, man. First thing I knew about you was an hour before I handed her over. She give you a little bop yet?"

I think I actually blushed.

"She hasn't worked her way up to it yet," I said. "But I think things were heading that way before her fiancé got himself killed."

"Yeah? You missed out, man."

"I don't think so."

Ralph looked from me to D'Agostino, sudden realization dawning on his face.

"Oh," he said. "That explains it. That's gotta be a tiger in the rack, am I right? I noticed the other night, you watching her walk away. That is one nice-looking ass, I bet I could—"

I stepped forward, and buried each of my middle fingers behind Ralph's massive jaw on either side of his face. I pushed the fingers toward each other and then pulled toward me. Ralph let out a surprised gurgle and then a high whine of pain as I found the pressure points that ran there. Ralph's eyes widened in panic when I didn't let off the pressure but instead pushed my fingers further into the deep nest of flesh there. Unrelenting pressure in certain areas is disabling, at least momentarily, and there are pressure points in the neck, arm, and under the nose that can make even a tough man scream like an infant in need of a new diaper.

"You will not talk about Detective D'Agostino that way," I said.

"She is a person. She is not a piece of meat. And if you do it again, this will be the least of your pain. Do you understand me?"

"Yes," he hissed, straining to shake me loose. But he was on his back, nearly as immobile as a turtle overturned on its shell, and he had no leverage. I bore down on him with all my weight, pressing my fingers deeper and deeper onto that raw, hot nerve until D'Agostino laid her hand on my forearm.

"Enough," she said quietly, and I let Ralph go. He lay back against the bed, sweat darkening his lank hair and snot leaking freely from his nose. He shifted away from me on the hospital bed, getting as far away as possible. I stared at him, my eyes hard. I didn't want to, didn't want or need to see the big goddamn fool cry. But I couldn't look away. I knew he was hurting, and I took no pride—okay, maybe a little in being the cause of it, but I would not allow myself to look away.

"You son of a bitch," he said. "I'm going to kill you. If it's the last thing I do, I'm going to put a fucking bullet in your brain. You won't always be looking, Kincaid. One day I'm gonna put you in the ground."

One day someone would. And I knew that I'd made a dangerous enemy. From now on I'd have to go around looking over my shoulder until one of us was gone. I was fairly certain I could take Ralph. After all, I'd already done it once, in a dark alley, when he had the advantage of sucker-punching me. We stared at one another, and every instinct told me to go after him right then. He was about as helpless as he was likely to get. But I couldn't bring myself to do it.

D'Agostino told him to shut up. She got him some water from the little plastic pitcher on the bedside table, getting him to drink a little. He dabbed at his eyes with bratwurst-sized fingers and said, "Why don't you go ask Mr. Doyle, see where that gets you. Leave me out of it."

"We will ask him," I said. "And if we don't like his answers, we'll be back."

NINETEEN

"I DON'T WANT to slut-shame anybody," D'Agostino said, "but Ralph? *Ralph*? There has got to be some deep-seated neuroses going on inside that girl's head."

She was driving again, taking us away from the hospital, ignoring the occasional bursts of static and cop-talk that came over the radio. I was trying not to watch the traffic. If D'Agostino made one mistake, Ralph would never have to come looking for me, because I'd be a casualty of bad driving. I held onto the oh-shit handle, closed my eyes, and pondered why in the world a girl who looked like Abby Doyle would sleep with Ralph.

"I don't know," I said, keeping my eyes closed. "There are lots of people who go to bed with someone you wouldn't expect them to. Even some cops fall for professional thugs."

"Ha."

"I'm just saying that's not the part that bothers me."

"So what does?"

"Pick one: the drinking, the lies. There's no way we can trust her," I said. I chanced a look at D'Agostino, who was concentrating on detouring around some of the diverted I-59/20 traffic.

"Clearly."

"Would you stop? You know I'm right. If she's tried to tell Ralph that he was the father of her unborn child, and now she's blamed it on her father—watch out—"

"Oh, fuck you," D'Agostino said cheerily and blatted the car horn at a pedestrian who had dared to try to cross the street. In the crosswalk, no less. "You want to really be suspicious, think about this: We don't even know for sure that she's pregnant."

I closed my eyes again and leaned my head against the seat rest. She was right.

"I'd prefer it if she weren't," I said.

"Me too," she said. "Everything about this is awful. I can't imagine going to bed with Ralph. Ick."

"Yeah, but the alternative is even worse to consider."

"I know, I know."

Everything I thought I knew about Abby felt slick and slippery, like water through my fingers. I didn't want to think that she would lie to me, but I couldn't discount the idea, either. It seemed like she was lying to everyone else.

"Hey," D'Agostino said, "are you in a hurry to see Doyle?"

"No, why?"

"I want to go by and look at Carraway."

"Fine by me," I said, and then whispered, "if you don't kill us first."

"What was that?"

"Nothing."

"Asshole, my driving is not that bad." She paused to swerve around a series of traffic cones, turning right onto Carraway Boulevard. The car rocked toward the driver's side so that we were nearly on two wheels. When the weight of the big Charger settled, the car was very quiet. "I mean, I haven't killed anyone."

"Yet," I said, and she took one hand off the wheel to punch me in the shoulder playfully, or as playful as D'Agostino got.

Carraway Hospital—officially named Carraway Methodist

Medical Center—had been a fixture in Birmingham's Black community since it opened in 1908. Since its closing, the ownership—and the city—had let it slip into ruin, and the shadow of the 10-story building and the surrounding property loomed over the Norwood neighborhood like a giant who has already died but not yet fallen down.

D'Agostino slowed as we approached the property. She drove around, taking a quick turn into the street that ran between the parking deck and the hospital proper. Broken glass from the hospital's doors and windows littered the ground and weeds grew everywhere. Graffiti was thick as kudzu on the lower levels of the buildings, and the place seemed to reek of despair and desolation. While much of the city was making a comeback, the neighborhoods in north Birmingham hadn't seen the same kind of recovery.

"It's not a bad thing, you know," D'Agostino said.

"What?"

"Making this place into something new, something usable."

I didn't disagree with her on that point. The area was too historically valuable to the city to continue to go to waste. What I disagreed with was that gentrification was the way to go. Property values would rise and the poor black people who lived in the neighborhood would soon flee increased property taxes or rental fees. The place would become increasingly white and homogenized. The neighborhood—and Birmingham at large—would lose a little more of what made it a unique metropolitan, urban center. The poor would get pushed around again, and nobody would complain much. Or if they did, it wouldn't matter.

In other words, business as usual in the Magic City.

There were already parts of the gentrification process that had pushed into the area, like the TopGolf complex that stood out in gaudy juxtaposition to the poorer neighborhoods surrounding it. White kids from the suburbs came through with the late-model luxury cars, hoisting oversized golf bags into the facility and playing at some weird golf-like game that didn't require anyone to walk around a course or tip a caddy at the end of the round.

I had always viewed golf suspiciously. In the homes where I grew up, sports ran to baseball and football—sometimes basketball if a kid had a little bit of a vertical leap and a good eye—and golf was something reserved for the rich folks in town. But the place in north Birmingham was a sign of things to come, and I wondered if Becks Towson understood that. He was getting old, somewhere near seventy, maybe older. He'd gone through the Civil Rights wars when he was just a kid, and as a teenager he'd seen opportunity in neighborhoods like Norwood, East Lake, Crestwood, Avondale, Ensley, and Midfield.

Becks must have wondered what the hell was going on when the bearded white hipsters with their black, plastic-framed glasses and tallboy cans of PBR started to infiltrate his part of the city like advance scouts in a mostly bloodless war. Now Avondale and Crestwood were a couple of the most-sought neighborhoods in Birmingham, with breweries and bars, Zagat-rated restaurants, and mostly crime-free streets. Weed was in plentiful supply, but if you wanted to buy a baggie of coke or skag, East Lake or Glen Iris would be a better bet.

And even there, time seemed short for guys like Becks. In some ways, when he was gone, a part of Birmingham's past would go with him. He had been around a long time, and despite the BPD's best efforts, no one had taken him down yet. I kind of liked him, just for the pure ballsy guts of the old man, even though I knew that he was a stone killer who would just as soon pull a trigger as look at you.

"What are you thinking?" Laura asked, and I told her.

"Sentimental," she said. "I wouldn't have thought it of a tough guy like you."

I laughed and recited a line I'd heard somewhere—maybe on TV, maybe in a book—"Tough, but oh so gentle."

Laura took my hand in hers and dared a look in my direction.

"I'm familiar," she said, and flashed me her even white teeth.

We circled the dilapidated old hospital a couple of times, then looped around the property in ever-widening circles. The Norwood neighborhood was predominantly Black, like most of the city proper, and most of the houses were crowded close together, their clapboard siding fraying and deteriorating over time. There were few garages. Some of the larger homes—these made of brick—had carports. Narrow, rutted, and nearly forgotten alleys wriggled like diseased worms behind many streets. We drove down them, not seeing much. Occasionally there were dogs that moved in packs, canines that had filtered down through the litters of so many years that they no longer appeared to be of any specific breed and were merely the apotheosis of Dog. They rummaged through trash and refuse that lined the gutters of the back alleys, and they raised their muzzles at us as we passed, their teeth bared in a silent warning snarl. But they didn't bark.

"I hate this," D'Agostino said.

"What?"

She gestured around us with the hand that occasionally worked the steering wheel.

"All of this."

A lot of the houses were one- and two-bedroom bungalows, small affairs that had probably been owned by Black people for generations. In many driveways, newer cars and SUVs were parked. At first glance, it looked incongruous.

"This is a working neighborhood," I said. "These people go out to a job where they make ten bucks an hour, maybe a little more. The houses have probably been in their families for a couple generations, maybe longer. In some cases, it's all they have. Whole families are crowded together in these little one-bedroom houses. I mean, I don't know what to tell you."

"I know," D'Agostino said. "I'm not judging, I swear. I just wish—I don't know what I wish."

"Life is hard here, babe," I said.

"It's hard everywhere."

In truth, much of Birmingham had been in decline since before the Civil Rights era. The city, which was once considered the steel city of the Confederacy, lost a lot of its economic momentum when Sloss Furnace closed in 1971. It had taken more than forty years and the place was making a comeback. While iron ore, steel, and coke continued to play a part in the economics of Birmingham and the surrounding areas, there were new industries making headway. Software developers had discovered the South; media companies were taking advantage of cheap, well-trained labor; and Birmingham had changed from a place where people made things that were meant to last, to strengthen the industry and infrastructure of a vast nation. Now it was no longer a place for concrete creations. Now it was a place for creating ideas.

I looked at the neighborhood around us as the blasted-out hulk of Carraway Hospital receded in D'Agostino's rear-view mirror. If Birmingham was indeed looking forward—as the city fathers always assured us that it was—then what would happen to these people who were being left behind?

"Are you ready to go talk with Doyle?"

I thought about it for a long minute, feeling the seconds tick by in my head.

"No," I said finally.

"What?"

"We don't know enough. We know what Abby says—what you cops would say she *alleges*—"

D'Agostino shot me an amused look, then turned her attention back to the road. Thank God.

"But I don't think we have enough information. We don't know what happened with Britt. Was he a target? Or just in the wrong place at the wrong time?"

Laura drummed her fingers on the steering wheel.

"I've been thinking about that," she said. "Doyle and Martin James put together the Carraway deal, right? So just spit-balling here, there's a lot of money involved in developing this project, yes?"

"Millions."

"So if you're dealing with a lot of money, putting together a deal like this, what would you do?"

"Me? I have no idea. I keep all of my money in my mattress."

"Yeah," D'Agostino said. "If you're a regular person, like me, you put it in a bank somewhere, let it draw interest. If you're really daring, maybe you get a money market account, some CDs, something."

"I buried some in a jar in the yard once, when I was a kid."

D'Agostino revved the engine on the Charger and sped past a school bus that was just pulling to a stop. My heart leapt in my chest, and I closed my eyes again. She continued to talk as if she hadn't noticed the school bus or my myocardial infarction.

"If you're rich, you don't do that," D'Agostino said. "You have people to manage your money. You have advisors, you know, people who tell you what to do with your money, where to move it around. You have accountants."

I opened my eyes and looked at her steadily.

"Britt was a lawyer."

D'Agostino started to grin.

"He was, wasn't he?"

"Lawyers and accountants, they find out where the money is, and then they go there."

Carlton Doyle and Martin James were doing a deal to buy and develop one of the largest pieces of private property in the city. Of course they'd have at least one lawyer on hand—maybe a team of them—looking at the deal. It made sense. And if Britt had been involved in that deal, then it meant that he was more than a man who was in the wrong place at the wrong time.

It meant that he was a target, too. Things were clicking into place, or at least that's what it felt like at the time. Finally, some forward momentum.

Laura laughed, and she turned the car South, toward Britt's place. The way she drove, it didn't take long.

TWENTY

"I DON'T QUITE KNOW what we're looking for," I said. We had let ourselves into Britt Parker's home using Abby's key. This time, since we didn't have to worry about her, D'Agostino went through the place properly, making sure each room was clear as we went. When we reached the office on the top floor, we knew we were alone. D'Agostino had taken out her phone and shot photos of the office from every angle possible.

"We'll know it when we see it," Laura said. She picked up a long accordion-style box from the floor and started riffling through the folders it contained. "Lots of records here, going back, good God, fourteen years? I hate you a little bit for this, Kincaid."

I looked around the office, trying to think of a place to start. There was a big calendar-at-a-glance blotter on the desk surface, but nothing seemed out of the ordinary. Client meetings, tennis matches. Britt looked like he lived the ordinary life of the young and upwardly mobile. The big cherry-wood desk was unlocked, so I started with the middle drawer. There wasn't much there, just the normal detritus of any home office, including paper clips, extra staples, a roll of stamps, spare pens and worn-down nubs of

Berol Black Beauty pencils. The drawer to the left held a couple of reams of white copy paper, a box of blank thank-you notes and envelopes, as well as various other envelopes ranging from business-sized to 11-by-14 manila-colored mailers. The top left-hand drawer held a lined yellow notepad, undated, with figures lined neatly along the left side of the page. There was no notation to indicate what the figures meant, so it was useless to us.

The right-hand drawer wasn't really a drawer at all. It looked exactly like the left-hand side, but instead of a set of drawers, it was one large door that opened outward to reveal a safe that had been custom-fitted to the space. A recessed space in the door served as a handle, and I slipped my fingers into it, pulling gently.

Locked, of course.

"Shit."

D'Agostino looked over, noting the presence of the safe, and continued walking her fingers through the folders in the accordioned case. She was methodical, not allowing my own discovery to derail her own work. I turned back to the safe. It was a combination lock, and instead of an old-fashioned mechanical combination that could potentially be manipulated by guys like me, it had a keypad and digital readout where a user could put in a passcode. Most people who owned a safe like this used a combination of numbers that was significant to them. For example, I always used the last four digits of my foster parents' phone number from the year I graduated high school: nine-four-seven-six.

Maybe Britt had used something similar.

I texted Abby, asking her for Britt's birth date. She sent me the information, and I entered it into the keypad. Nothing. Then I asked for hers. She sent a text back, and I entered the numbers. Again, the safe rejected the passcode.

"Try it backwards," D'Agostino said, and I nearly jumped out of my skin. She had finished her box and set it aside on the floor. I'd been so concentrated on what I was doing that I had never heard her come up behind me.

"Are you trying to give me an early coronary?"

"I don't know," she said. "Am I on your insurance policy yet?" One side of her mouth rose in her self-amused little smile, and she punched me gently in the arm. I bent back down to the safe and entered Britt's D.O.B. again, this time backward. Nothing. I looked at D'Agostino, and she raised an eyebrow at me.

"Might as well try," she said, and I bent back to it. This time I punched in Abby's numbers—backwards, naturally—and the keypad beeped at me. From somewhere inside, there was a soft click. I let out a little cry of triumph and pulled the door open before the damned thing could change its mind.

Inside the safe were stacks of cash. Fifties clotted the upper shelf, each banded with a brown strap and signed with what appeared to be Britt's initials in black Sharpie. I pulled the bundles out and counted them: twenty-five bundles, with one hundred bills each: a hundred and twenty-five grand, and that was just from the upper shelf.

The bottom shelf was piled high with neat rows of hundred-dollar bundles wrapped in gold bands and again apparently initialed by Britt Parker. I dug them out and counted. There were forty bundles of hundreds, for a cool four hundred thousand. D'Agostino's eyes were very large as she squatted beside me to inspect the money.

"Oh. My. God," D'Agostino said. I was glad she was able to say something, because all I could do was mentally stutter. I'd never seen that much cash before in my life. We looked at one another, neither of us sure what to do. I had visions of Aruba in my head, maybe a small boat to pilot from island to island down in the Caribbean while I worked on my tan. I pushed those thoughts away, but they came back.

Beside me, D'Agostino's breath seemed to have caught in her throat. She reached down and picked one of the bundles up. She flicked through it, then tossed it down on the floor again.

I watched her lick her lips, the pink tip of her tongue moving sensuously.

"This—" she cleared her throat, "—this is one of those times when I wish I was Elliot Ness."

I didn't say anything.

"Nobody knows about this money," she said. "We could—oh wow—"

Laura's voice trailed off as she wrestled with a temptation that I would never be familiar with. Had I been the only one there, the money would have already been stuffed into a trash bag and hauled down to my car to eventually be salted away somewhere. But Laura was better than me, and she made me want to be better.

Damn her.

She finally looked away from the big mound of cash, used her hands to push against her knees, and levered herself upright.

"Put it back," she said. "You have to put it back."

I was looking at the safe. Something didn't seem right with it. I swept the upper shelf with my hand and then ran my hand along the underside. There was something there.

"Wait," I said, and Laura turned back to me. I bent down to get a better look, and saw it: a manila envelope taped to the bottom of the shelf with duct tape. I used my Swiss Army knife to peel away the tape from the shelf and then handed the envelope to Laura. She got a fingernail under the little metal butterfly clasp and pulled the envelope open. She shook the envelope out onto the surface of Britt Parker's big desk. Several sheets of folded white paper as well as some kind of grainy, black-and-white images fluttered onto the desk.

"Is that—" I hesitated.

"An ultrasound," D'Agostino said, lifting them carefully by the edges so that she wouldn't leave fingerprints on any potential evidence. "Five of them."

She handed me one of the photos, and I held it the same way she had.

"I don't understand what I'm looking at.," I said.

"Look at the dates," she said, and used the back of one knuckle to spread the flimsy photos out so that I could see. When I leaned over them and really looked, it dawned on me. Each grainy black-and-white photo showed a small blob that looked something like a kidney bean. It was hard to believe that the bean was anything that would eventually become a real human being, but I knew D'Agostino had to be right. Each of the photos bore Abby's name, the name of the hospital, the gynecologist who had performed the procedure, and the date it was completed. From the date of the oldest one, Abby would have been about fourteen the first time she got pregnant.

None of the photos was recent enough to be from her current pregnancy.

I blew out a big breath that I'd been holding in. I wanted to hit someone. I wanted to find Carlton Doyle and pound him into dust, wanted to dig up Britt Parker and beat him back to life just so he could die at my hands. I want to go back to Ralph's room and put my hands over his mouth and bear down with all my weight so that I could watch the life fade slowly from his eyes.

I blinked back tears and worked to get ahold of my emotions. While I did that, Laura unfolded the sheaf of papers that had accompanied the ultrasound photos.

"Medical records," she said, shuffling through the loose sheets. "When she was younger, Abby had a bad habit of falling down stairs and running into doors."

I bet. And I'd bet that no one ever witnessed those things. She'd just show up at the hospital with bruises or sprains or the occasional cracked or broken bone.

"There's more here," she said. "She had at least one miscarriage, that one was the first. Oh, here's the second one, too. But the rest—" and she looked through the pages again "—all D&C's, pregnancy terminated."

Laura kept her voice neutral, but I saw her hands shake a little as she folded the records and slipped them back in the envelope, then stuffed the ultrasound photos in there, too. She couldn't seem to fold the clasp closed, so I took it from her and did it. I stuck the envelope into the back of my jeans and tucked it under my shirt.

"I need a shower," D'Agostino said, "or a drink. Maybe both at the same time."

I nodded. It seemed clear to me that the medical records were blackmail of some kind. Maybe Britt had been blackmailing Abby to stay with him? I didn't understand it, but why keep those kinds of records if not for leverage?

I thought about that for a little while, while I stacked money neatly back into the safe and closed it. An electronic beep told me the safe was locked again, but now I knew the way in. I smiled a little. It was a good thing to know, just in case things with Laura D'Agostino didn't work out. Always good to have an exit plan. The more I thought about it, the more I realized that the murder of Britt Parker may have been exactly the same thing: a way out.

I explained what I was thinking to Laura, and she began to nod along. I didn't know if that meant that she agreed with me, or if she just saw the logic of my thinking. Knowing what we knew, Carlton Doyle had to be the target of extortion—presumably by Britt Parker, and maybe by his daughter, too. The wads of cash in the safe seemed to indicate that the blackmail was ongoing.

"Follow me on this," I said, my voice rising in excitement. "Britt finds out about Abby's medical history—I don't know how—but something clicks and he realizes that Carlton is to blame. This is stuff that no one, not even a monster like Doyle, would want to come out, right?"

Laura nodded.

"So Britt blackmails him. It's successful, but he wants more. He gets greedy. Carlton stumbles onto him in Abby's apartment, alone," I said, and made a shooting motion with my right hand. "Too good of an opportunity to pass up."

D'Agostino rubbed her upper lip thoughtfully.

"It makes a kind of sense," she said, "but there are other things we have to consider here."

"Like what?"

"We came here thinking that Britt was involved in the money end of the Carraway deal," she said. "I don't think I'm ready to give up on that, and if Britt was in bed with Carlton, then there's really no need to kill him, is there?"

I didn't say anything. She wasn't wrong, her conclusion didn't fit with my own theory, and I wasn't ready to give it up yet. The envelope scratched a little at the small of my back, and another theory—maybe more in line with what D'Agostino was thinking—wormed its way into my head.

"Maybe it's insurance."

"How do you mean?"

I ran my hands over my face, feeling the stubble scratch gently against my fingers. My eyes felt like someone had poured ground glass behind them, and every time I thought about Carlton Doyle, I wanted a hot shower.

"I think Britt was mixed up in the whole Carraway deal. No way he couldn't have been. But let's give him the benefit of the doubt: he was an asshole, greedy, dissolute, crooked as a dog's hind leg—"

"Tell me what you really think of him."

"—but I think he may have loved Abby. I don't know if she really loved him or not—say she just thought he could take her away from her abuser—and it really doesn't matter. But if he did love her, we have to ask: What if the medical records were a way to ensure that Carlton stayed out of Abby's bed?"

D'Agostino thought about it. I could almost see her turning it over in her mind.

"Could be," she said, finally. "And if she turned up pregnant by Carlton ..."

She let the words trail off, and we both thought about it for a little while. Say Britt is waiting in Abby's apartment. He's hoping to talk to her alone, after that big ape—hey, that's me—her father hired has gone home for the night. So there he is, tie loosened, the top button of his shirt undone. His suit jacket is slung over the back of a kitchen chair. He's fixed himself a drink from the wet bar when he hears a key in the lock.

And Carlton Doyle comes in. Whatever happens next—and this part I couldn't see in my mind—Doyle shoots and kills his future son-in-law. He's lucky, of course. The apartments in the Pizitz building are thick-walled and nearly soundproof. But he's gotta get out of there. So what does he do? He runs. Would he throw the gun away? Of course he would. It was probably in the Cahaba River or at the bottom of Lake Logan Martin. Regardless, that gun wouldn't ever be seen again.

And here I come—that big ape again—and discover the body. I thought about all of the steps I had taken that night. If I had known then what I suspected now, would it have made any difference? I couldn't see how, but I also felt lousy about Britt's murder. I wasn't complicit, but I had been more than cavalier on the only occasion we'd met.

D'Agostino didn't have the same concerns I did. In fact, she didn't have any at all, as far as I could see. She'd been pulled from the case by her superiors, and that dovetailed with the idea that Carlton Doyle was the murderer. Only he and Becks Towson had the kind of pull it would take to get a detective reassigned to other duties, and I didn't think Becks was lying to me.

But Becks—by his own admission—was getting older. Maybe there were things going on that he didn't know. I'd have to think about that.

"Hey," D'Agostino said, and shoved my shoulder with one hand. "Get out of your own head, Kincaid. You gotta be in the game here."

I shook my head.

"I don't think I'm doing anyone any good," I said. D'Agostino sent me a smoldering look, and I felt my heart rate jump a couple of notches. It was the kind of look that stripped my clothes off and made electricity fire down every synapse in my body.

I pulled out my phone and checked the time. Well past lunch.

"Come on," I said, heading for the door. "You may be Wonder Woman, but even superheroes have to eat."

"Oh, good," D'Agostino said. "Let's find a place where you can order oysters. You're gonna need 'em later."

TWENTY ONE

THE LITTLE DONKEY didn't have oysters. But they did have brisket nachos and ramekins of salsa packed with enough chili peppers that it would kill or cure or whatever ails you. The place was upscale and expensive, having recently been relocated to a new brick-and-glass building in Homewood. We sat at an open table facing a floor-to-ceiling window and drank sweet tea and didn't talk very much. What was there to say? Every now and then, D'Agostino would lean a shoulder against me as if to reassure herself that I was still there. I wasn't planning on going anywhere. D'Agostino's presence made me feel peaceful, a feeling I wasn't too familiar with. I felt like a junkie chasing a high; whatever was going on with us, I wanted more of it.

"I don't think I've ever been here when it wasn't elbow-to-elbow," Laura said, and I agreed with her. The Little Donkey—and places like it—was the backbone of a restaurant explosion taking place in and around Birmingham. A dedicated foodie could go to a new restaurant every day of the year, with new ones popping up every day. It was impossible to keep up. Our food came, and we ate in an embarrassing frenzy, washing it down with cold iced tea.

"You've got some sauce on your chin," I said, and laughed as D'Agostino wiped it away with her linen napkin.

"I was saving that for later."

I leaned back in my chair, full and sleepy. Under the table, one of my booted feet was touching D'Agostino. I felt contented in a way that I'd rarely known. Laura leaned forward and put her elbows on the table.

"You look like you could use some rest."

"I always look like this."

"Sure, sure," she said. "You know what it looks like to me?"

"What?"

"A perfect time to interrogate you."

I groaned in mock protest. "Oh, God, no. Anything but that."

She nudged me under the table with one of her knees.

"Come on. I want to know about you. About who you really are, down there underneath all of that armor, when you're not busy being Kincaid."

I shrugged.

"Ask anything you want," I said. "I'm an open book."

D'Agostino snorted and somehow made it seem ladylike.

"If that's true, the pages have invisible ink."

Now it was my turn to laugh. I liked her, could feel myself getting dragged deeper into more than liking, and I didn't want to lie to her. I wasn't sure, though, that I wanted her to know who I really was. Always the heavy knowledge that she was a cop sat there with every word we passed between ourselves. There were things I couldn't tell her—that I wouldn't tell her.

"I dropped out of high school, got my GED," I said. "Joined the Army as a regular grunt, got my Ranger tab, got a Special Forces tab, too. Deployed in Iraq and Afghanistan. Caught some IED shrapnel outside Kabul—"

"Those were the scars on your chest?"

"Yeah," I said. I sat quiet for a little bit, letting lunch digest.

"I came back home, got the honorable discharge, used the GI

Bill to take some college courses. None of them seemed to have much effect."

D'Agostino's mouth was open slightly. She had on very little makeup, or she was so expert with whatever she'd applied that it appeared so. Her chestnut hair was soft and wavy, and I wanted to reach out and stroke it. Her emerald eyes were soft and fixed on me while I talked. To be the center of her attention made me feel fully whole, maybe for the first time in my life. That was a shocking thought, and I sat with it for a bit, searching for a way to continue, to say the things I wanted to say.

"I don't know if I can explain it," I said. "You come home after sleeping on the ground, after every moment of your life you live in fear that some asshole is going to come up out of the rocks like a snake and strike. You see guys next to you buy it, wonder why it wasn't you. You're home, driving on nice roads, but you see a garbage can set too close to the street and you drive two blocks around that street just in case."

D'Agostino reached for my hand, and I let our fingers intertwine for the briefest of moments before pulling away.

"Don't," I said. "Let me finish, okay?"

She didn't say anything, just nodded.

"So you come home, and there's nothing that, you know, interests me. I read Hemingway and it's close, but it's still bullshit, you know? Things don't heal stronger at the break. Sometimes they don't heal at all. So I started going to the bars. I was drinking, but it wasn't too much, you know? I wanted to be around people, but I didn't want to be close to anyone. I got in some scraps, Word got around that I was a guy who could handle trouble, and I got hired to do just that. And then again, and again. It became what I did."

I took in a little air through my nose. Around us, the restaurant had mostly emptied out. I'd told her the whole thing, almost. Nearly everything that mattered. But D'Agostino was a good cop. She'd interviewed suspects before, and even though I wasn't a suspect, she knew I was holding something back.

"What aren't you telling me?"

I didn't say anything. Instead, I grabbed our Styrofoam cups from the table and went to nab refills for our tea from the big silver urns near the counter where the cash register sat. When I got back, D'Agostino's face was carefully blank.

"I guarantee you I've heard worse," she said.

"I know," I said. "I'm not a cop, but we're kind of alike. We look straight at the world, see what's there. And we don't look away."

"That's right."

"And what do you see when you look at me?"

D'Agostino drew in a short breath. "I don't know," she said. "I think you're a good man, but sometimes people fool me. I think you almost certainly have PTSD."

I was shaking my head before she even got the words out.

"Nope," I said. "I saw a therapist for a little while after the Army shipped me home. Negative diagnosis on post-traumatic stress."

"Huh."

"Yeah, I was surprised, too. But I don't hear gunfire in my sleep, and I don't break down in fear and shock when I hear a car backfire."

"That's good, I guess."

"And I can tell the difference between the two. So maybe I'm not as fucked up as I think I am. But some people got the idea that I was a tough guy, so they keep hiring me to do tough guy shit. And paying me for it."

"So that's why you do what you do? Because you can?"

I spread my hands. It was as good an explanation as any. I could tell her about Rocky Marciano, who went on tour after his boxing days, doing one-man shows. People came, but they were never sure what to expect. Rocky told 'em that he couldn't sing or dance, but he could whip any man in the house. It was how I felt. I'd called it tough-guy shit, and that's what it was.

"What about you?" I asked. "Why are you a cop?"

"Oh, sure. Turn it around on me, why don't you?

"The truth is that I never thought about doing anything else. This was what my Dad did, and I can't ever remember wanting to be anything else. You know how on Halloween, lots of little girls dress up as princesses, queens, fairies, whatever? I was always a cop, one time even an Old West sheriff."

I laughed, picturing Laura D'Agostino as a small child in a police uniform. I could almost see it. And then I did see something outside the plate glass window of the restaurant, my eyes going wide. I grabbed D'Agostino's shoulder hard and yanked her toward me, then used my right hand against her elbow to turn the arm in and force her down, down, down to the floor. I was a second behind her, covering her with my body and screaming a warning to the others who were still in the restaurant as the plate glass window in front of us blew inward and the air was rent by the sound of shattering glass and an automatic weapon firing.

It was over in a second, and once the gunfire had ceased to bark, the silence was eerie. I pushed myself up off of D'Agostino, and slivered glass cut my palms. It was only superficial, but it still hurt. I was going to help Laura up, but she came off the floor like a coiled spring. She looked around the open dining room. There were some people down under tables, but none of them were hurt. In the wall behind us, a line of bullets had stitched an unsteady line.

D'Agostino and I stared at one another. Whatever else we were doing, we'd succeeded at making targets of ourselves.

TWENTY TWO

THE FIRST COPS on the scene had separated D'Agostino and me. I'd called Abby to make sure she was all right—and to make sure she was staying put at Laura's—and waited with my backside leaned against one of the all-black Homewood police cruisers while officers talked to the other witnesses. They had already taken a look at my ID and recorded it. I started to tell them what happened, but a tall black patrolman said "Save it for the lieutenant," so I shut up. They cordoned off the area with yellow crime scene tape and big plastic sawhorses they pulled from the trunks of their vehicles. A lone officer at each end of the block directed traffic away from the scene.

Around us, there wasn't much damage other than the big picture window being blown out, and the manslaughter of a cash register. A big white Ford Expedition pulled up, telltale blue lights flashing in its grillwork and taillights. A tall, rail-thin man with an aggressive posture and assertive jaw stepped out of the passenger side, while the driver of the Expedition stayed put. The man wore a seersucker suit with a blue tie and white shirt, and he wore his gold detective's shield on a black leather case clipped to his lapel.

Uh-oh. This had to be the lieutenant.

While Homewood had its own police department, those cops worked hand-in-glove with the BPD, so once the cops had called it in that a Birmingham cop had been involved in a shooting—even as a potential victim or witness—BPD was notified. So now the brass was on the scene, and it probably wasn't going to go well for D'Agostino and me.

The tall detective stalked over to D'Agostino. He towered above her, leaning down into her face as they talked. She didn't shy away from him, and that made me smile. But I could also see shards of glass still in her hair, glinting in the late summer sun. They spoke for less than five minutes, and then the jerk jerked his head around, found me with a gaze that could have melted steel, and inclined his head. I shrugged off the cruiser and walked over. The whole time, he looked at me as if I should have come on the run. I stood in front of him with my hands in my hip pockets, at ease.

"Lieutenant Mark Davies," he said. He made no move to shake hands. "I've heard her story. What's yours?"

"Just a man who was in the right place at the right time," I said. "No need to thank me."

He huffed.

"I know who you are," he said, "and I know you think you're funny. But right now one of my detectives just got shot at, and I want to know everything you know. Save the funny lines for someone else."

His attention wasn't fully on me when he said it. He was looking at the crime scene, the recently ventilated restaurant where Laura and I had lately sat. No cars in the lot had been damaged. No shop near the restaurant bore any damage. It was a hit, and one that had failed only because I had noticed movement at the right time.

"Sir, yes sir," I murmured under my breath, and D'Agostino shot me a look.

"Detective D'Agostino and I were in the middle of a

conversation," I said. "We were sitting facing the street. I noticed a red car drive down the block, and its rear window lowered. I saw the barrel of the gun come out, and that's when I grabbed her and pushed us both to the floor."

Davies nodded once, a clipped and precise motion.

"Why was she hanging out with you, a known criminal?"

"Hey," I said, throwing up my hands, palms out, "no convictions."

"You two seeing one another socially?"

"None of your business."

Davies cocked his head at me, and his stone-cold blue eyes never wavered. If a look could say "We'll see about that," this one was it. If I hadn't been so tough, I might have shivered a little. Beside us, D'Agostino cleared her throat and that seemed to break the tension for a moment. Davies remembered why he was here: one of his detectives had been shot at.

"How many shots?" He asked me.

"I don't know. It sounded like an automatic weapon, but it could've been a semi-auto with a bump stock. I'd guess they emptied a full clip."

Davies folded his arms over his chest.

"Did you get the make or model?"

"No," I said. "It happened too—wait—it was a Ford Taurus, one of the newer ones. I could tell from the body design."

"Won't matter," Laura said. "It'll turn up stolen."

"Right," he said. "Now tell me this: why would anyone want the two of you dead?"

"No idea," I said. D'Agostino pursed her lips and didn't say anything. I knew that it chafed her to stay silent, but she'd already been pushed off the Britt Parker case.

"Bullshit," Davies said. "What are you two into?"

D'Agostino and I kept ourselves busy not saying anything. Davies stared hard at each of us, but the steely glare didn't work. I didn't melt, and neither did Laura. He turned away from us, headed back to the Explorer where his driver waited, and came back after he'd taken no more than a few steps.

"Tell me what you're working on," he said. "That's an order."

D'Agostino's eyes were wide. Davies was again using his larger frame as a weapon, trying to make her feel small. I could see what was happening, but it would do no good for her if I stepped in. She had to handle Davies herself.

"I'm on vacation," she said, her chin jutting out in defiance.

"Do you understand that I am ordering you to tell me what the hell you think you're doing here?"

"I do."

"I will have you suspended," Davies said. I could see the big cords in his neck standing out in sharp relief as he spoke. He didn't raise his voice, but the level of his anger came through loud and clear. "You can believe that. Disobeying a direct order, insubordination, any goddamned other thing I can think of."

"Yes, sir," Laura said. Her voice was small, but she didn't allow her gaze to break away from his.

I clenched my hands at the unfairness of it. Anything I might say would make it even worse for Laura, so I kept my lip buttoned tight. For the moment, anyway.

"See personnel on Monday morning. They'll relieve you of your weapon, badge, and Police ID." Then he turned to me. "You got anything to say now, Mr. Smartass?"

I flashed him a smile that didn't reach my eyes.

"I hope I run into you one night when you're not wearing that badge," I said. "I don't like bullies."

Davies snorted.

"That's rich, coming from you." Then he turned to Laura, and his tone was softer. "I'm glad you weren't hurt. Go home. Get the glass out of your hair. And then put some thought into how much you actually want to be a cop in this town. I'll call you tomorrow."

Then he got back into the Explorer and left.

I took in some air and let out a big breath, trying to manage my anger. It wasn't fair. D'Agostino was only trying to do the right thing. I'd met enough rotten cops that I could tell what a difference a good one like her could make. Out of the corner of my eye, I saw Laura wipe away a tear that had trailed down her cheek. I pretended not to see it, instead checking up and down the street carefully.

"You know he's right," I said. "You should have told him."

"I know." She sniffled. "But it does me no good either way. I tell him I've been investigating the Britt Parker murder against orders—his orders, in fact—and I'm suspended anyway. Maybe fired. Either way, if this goes in my jacket, I can kiss a promotion goodbye. Be lucky if I don't get busted back down to uniform."

I didn't know what to say. "I'm sorry" didn't seem to cut it, but it's what rose to my lips. I cut the words off before they ever reached the open air between us. D'Agostino had kept on with the investigation; she'd come to my motel room with coffee the morning after she'd gotten booted from the case. She'd been there with me, pushing just as hard as I had. She'd known what was at stake for her personally, and she kept on with it anyway.

D'Agostino was a hell of a woman when you came right down to it.

"Have you talked to Abby?" She said, breaking the silence that had grown between us.

"Yeah, before Davies got here. She's still at your place, staying put like we told her to."

"God, I bet she's going stir-crazy."

"Probably drank all of your liquor."

"Jesus, I hope not. I'm going to need something when I get home."

TWENTY THREE

ABBY WAS DRUNK when we got back to D'Agostino's place. She wasn't showing it much, just a hint of unsteadiness in her walk, a small hesitation in her words. D'Agostino didn't say anything as we came in, just headed for the kitchen and uncorked a bottle of Bushmills Irish. She grabbed a pair of lowball glasses from the cabinet above the sink and poured a generous shot into each.

She handed me the glass that held less liquor and then downed her own drink. I sipped at mine.

"You two have a nice time out there without me?" Abby asked, her tone acid "I'm here all day I might as well be under arrest."

On the kitchen table, an empty bottle of vodka lay on its side. I picked it up and tossed it into the trash can at the end of the counter. D'Agostino watched me, then poured herself some more of the Irish.

"See this, Abby? People—I'm talking about people here—use glasses. Gets you just as drunk, but you don't look like a god-damn lush."

I raised my eyebrows and dipped my lips to my own drink, being careful not to make eye contact with either of them.

"Hey," Abby said. "I gotta right, you know—"

"No, I don't fucking know. What I know is that we're trying to save your ass, and some fuckhead tried to shoot us both. And you're here trying to drink up every bit of liquor I've got, you spoiled little rich bitch."

Okay, now that was the moment for me to step in. I put my drink down and took hold of D'Agostino by the shoulders. I steered her through the bedroom and into the little bathroom beyond, where I helped her out of her clothes. Small slivers of glass tinkled to the floor as she shook out her hair.

"Don't worry about those," I said. "I'll take care of it."

D'Agostino stepped carefully over the fallen glass and got into the shower, where she ran the water very hot. By the time I returned from the pantry with a broom and dustpan, white steam had filled the bathroom and I couldn't see through the glass shower door. D'Agostino made a harsh, low sound in her throat that might have been a sob. I ignored it and swept up, then deposited the glass into the kitchen bathroom.

Abby had appropriated Laura's glass and reclined on one of the leather sofas, her lithe body appearing nearly boneless in relaxation. It was hard to think of her as a prospective mother. Hard to think of her as anything but a spoiled child herself right then. I knew without discussing it with Abby that she would have another abortion. It didn't matter to her that Alabama had one of the most restrictive anti-choice laws in the country. She was a rich white woman. She could get on a plane and go anywhere, come back like nothing had happened.

I bet Abby spent much of her life pretending that so many things hadn't happened to her.

"I guess I know where I stand," she said from the sofa. "You're out there with her. I thought you were supposed to be guarding my body and instead—"

"Instead I'm out there trying to figure out who wants to harm you and get them out of the way," I said. "You're so busy lying to everyone, that you don't give a shit, so spare me the entitled rich girl act, okay?"

Abby didn't say anything, but her cheeks flamed red, and I couldn't tell if it was from embarrassment or anger. She drank some more of her drink, and we remained there in silence until I heard the shower shut off. I went to the bedroom, closed the door behind me, and watched D'Agostino emerge from the bathroom, a towel wrapped around her torso and another around her hair. She smiled at me, tentatively, the newness of everything that was blossoming between us like a streak of rose-colored sky at daybreak. I stepped to her, gripping the plush fabric of the towel in my hands, crushing it a little, wanting nothing more than to rip it from her body and throw her on the bed.

Instead I managed to say "Hi," in a voice that was so unsteady that it didn't sound anything like me. D'Agostino put her arms around my shoulders. One shrug would pull the towel away, and there she'd be, naked and warm and fresh from the shower. Laura raised herself up on tiptoe and kissed me lightly on the lips, and electricity fired along every nerve ending and muscle in my body.

"Hi yourself," she said, tilting her head and letting the towel fall away. She shook her hair free and I ran my hands through it, burying my face in the hollow of her neck, where I could smell the fragrant mix of her soap, her shampoo, and her skin.

I began kissing along her neck line, up to her jaw, and I felt her stiffen against me in anticipation. Our mouths met, and there was no hesitation in the kiss, only the lightning that we generated with the heat and friction of our bodies, the building tension of the thunderclap of desire. My mouth explored hers with a hunger that I'd never known, and her own desire matched mine. I could feel my own reaction to her, moving with the writhing tension of her pubic bone against my thighs. The moment felt perfect in its anticipation, crystalline in its clarity. I had never wanted anything more than to take her to bed at that very instant.

And then I pulled away.

"No," she said, reaching for me. "Don't stop now." Her heaving chest did wonderful things for her body—not to mention my libido—but I had to make us stop.

"Abby's in the next room," I said.

"So what?"

Her green eyes had darkened somewhere past emerald, and if I kept staring at her, I would lose myself in them forever.

"We have a lot of ground to cover," I said. "We don't have time."

She was on me in less time than it takes to tell it, her soft fingers cupping me through the front of my jeans, her mouth tracing a line along the big vein in my neck. When she found the pulse there, her tongue flicked out to tease it. I moaned a little, probably not as loudly as I'd thought, but it was enough to encourage her.

"I don't think it would take that long," she said. She had my zipper open now, and her hand moved ceaselessly.

And she was right. It didn't. To hell with whatever Abby thought. To hell with finding out who killed Britt Parker. She bore me back onto the bed, hooking one heel behind my knees and mounting me with swift ease, and I understood that making love this time was not about me nor anything I needed. D'Agostino was on the edge, her career in the balance, her boss potentially co-opted by forces she didn't know or understand. Under the brute force of her own confusion and anger at the situation, she needed the release that our lovemaking would bring. And she was right: It didn't take long at all. She found her own pleasure, and I found mine, and we shared a brief moment of happy exhaustion afterward, kissing quietly in the dark room.

Afterward, we dressed and joined Abby in the living area. She had refreshed her drink, which D'Agostino noted with a raised eyebrow. We had no idea how much she'd had to drink throughout the day, but it had been a considerable amount. The empty vodka bottle—and now the half-empty bottle of Irish—would attest to that. In my right hand I carried the medical records we'd found at Britt's house.

"Are you two done?" Abby asked. "Like two fucking rabbits." The last word came out *rabbitsh*.

"For now," I said, and D'Agostino elbowed me in the ribs lightly.

"We went back to Britt's house," Laura said, "and we found some things that we need to talk to you about. It's gonna be hard, but we need you to be honest with us about what's going on. Please."

Abby tried to act offended, pushing herself back as far as she could go on the couch, sitting up ramrod straight, the drunk's denial posture. "I'm alwaysh honesht," she said. "I'm the only one who ish."

Laura nodded brightly. She wasn't paying any attention to Abby's act, so I decided to follow her lead.

"You told me earlier that your father is the one who got you pregnant," she said. "Is that true?"

Abby's eyes narrowed with suspicion, but she nodded. She wouldn't look at me, and I didn't blame her. We were talking about hard things, and sometimes no amount of alcohol could help you get through the hard things. Sometimes the alcohol didn't soften things; instead the liquor and the wine and the beer just made things more and more brittle. And then they broke.

"And you really are pregnant," D'Agostino said, watching Abby start to nod solemnly before she added: "Again."

"Yes, of course I—wha-wait, what do you mean *again*?"

I put the manila envelope on the coffee table in front of Abby. I didn't open it; I didn't have to. She saw what it was and tried to crawl away to the other end of the couch, and when that wasn't far enough away, she rose to her feet and began to pace the open living space back and forth between the couches and the dining table. She had one arm across her abdomen, with the fingers of her other hand pressed tightly to her lips.

"Where did you get that," she said. It wasn't so much a question as a statement of wonder.

"Britt's safe," I said. "He had it hidden pretty well, taped under a shelf where it wouldn't be easily found. It's a record of every time—"

"I fucking know what it is," she nearly screamed, and lunged for the envelope. D'Agostino was quicker than me: I reached to scoop the envelope up, but she didn't bother. Instead she caught Abby by one shoulder and kicked her feet out from under her. Abby landed harmlessly on the bigger of the two couches and flailed her way to the floor. I stuffed the envelope behind my belt in back of my waist where Abby wouldn't have to look at it.

"Son of a bitch," Abby moaned, sitting up from the floor. "Son of a bitch."

We left her there to sonofabitch for a while, listening as she wound down like an old clock. When she finally stopped, Laura helped her to sit up on the couch again.

"I'm *pregnant*," Abby shrieked. "Don't you understand?"

"I do," Laura said. "And if Carlton is really the father, we all know you're not keeping this one either."

Abby put her head in her hands and cried. Unlike the day before, when she had seemed to be unable to muster tears for her fiancé, this time the tears were real. Her blonde hair hung in strings around her face, and she blubbered wetly until I rose and went into the kitchen and hunted up some tissues. I handed her the box, and she whispered "Thank you" softly and went about trying to put her face back in order. It only took her most of the box.

When the tears were done, Laura started right back in on her.

"Are you sure the baby belongs to your father?"

Abby nodded, dabbing at her eyes with a crumpled piece of tissue paper.

"How can you know?" Laura said, and Abby barked a harsh sound that could have been a laugh under different circumstances. She still wouldn't lift her head, wouldn't look either of us in the eye.

"Trust me," she said. "I know."

D'Agostino nudged me with her knee, a signal for me to step in. I wasn't sure how to proceed. Laura wasn't being bad cop, exactly, but she was unrelenting. I wasn't equipped to play good cop, so I just decided to plunge forward.

"Why couldn't it have been Britt?"

Abby put the wet, used tissue on the coffee table and wrinkled her nose.

"Britt didn't want kids," she said, "and he made sure he wouldn't have any, so he couldn't be the father."

"Are you saying he had a vasectomy?"

Abby nodded. She was studying the tops of her knees very closely. If she didn't look at us, maybe none of this was actually happening.

"When?" I asked.

"Before we ever got together," she said. "So the first time I turned up pregnant, he thought that something had happened with his, with his, you know, procedure. Sometimes a vasectomy can reverse itself, but that's rare. He went to his doctor to make sure that hadn't happened."

I thought about it. The thing I didn't understand was what kept Britt and Abby together. If I'd been with a woman who had gotten pregnant by another man—any man, never mind her father—I would have hightailed it outta there at the first opportunity.

"It didn't have to be Carlton," Laura said, and now her voice was very soft. "What about Ralph?"

"Oh my God," Abby said, and buried her face in her hands again. "You know about that. Jesus fucking Christ would you please drop this? Can't you leave me some dignity?"

Laura knelt beside Abby and patted her gently on the shoulder.

"It's too late for that," she said. "Things have gone too far. We have to know everything if we're going to find out who killed Britt. You want that, don't you? Look at me, Abby. You want whoever killed your fiancé to pay for it, right?"

Abby nodded. Her eyes were dull with hurt and confusion.

D'Agostino fixed me with a look, and after a moment I understood. It was my turn to step in. Laura's role from here on out
would be to sympathize, to show concern without judgment or
hesitation. I took a deep breath and proceeded.

"Why couldn't it have been Ralph?"

Laura slipped from the floor up to the couch beside Abby. She
had her arm around the girl now, seeming to hold her up by sheer
force of will. Abby looked like she wanted to be anywhere but
trapped between the two of us.

"The timing wasn't right," Abby said finally. "I tried to blame
him, but Britt wouldn't believe me. He kept after me, trying to
make me tell. And one night I just had enough, you know? So I
just blurted it out."

I scrubbed a palm over the scruff of stubble on my chin.

"Where did the medical records come from?"

Abby's shoulders shook, and Laura squeezed her a little tighter.

"I don't know," she said. "One day he just had them. Told me
that my Dad wasn't going to bother me, ever again. You see how
well that worked out. I went to the clinic and, you know."

She spread her palms open as if to say "there you go."

I felt sick to my stomach. If I weren't so goddamned tough,
I might have cried. As it was, I held myself to a sniffle or two.
D'Agostino kept her arm around Abby and rocked her back and
forth gently. The alcohol and the emotional outbursts had drained
the young woman, and she eventually closed her eyes. D'Agostino
stayed where she was, like the Rock of Gibraltar that would always
be there, holding Abby as though she were a small child until her
chin tilted down into the hollow of Laura's shoulder. I got a couple
of pillows from the guest room and put them on the couch, and
D'Agostino leaned Abby sideways until her head was on them.
Then I took a throw blanket off of the back of the other couch and
covered the girl.

D'Agostino and I padded silently back to her bedroom, where

I closed and locked the door. Laura stepped toward me, slipping her arms around my waist, and I held onto her tightly.

"I need another shower," she said. "That was the worst thing I've ever heard. That poor girl."

"I don't understand why Britt stayed," I said. "I would have run for the fucking hills if my girlfriend had wound up pregnant by another man."

"Right? Anyone would have."

"So what made him stay? Do you think he really loved her?"

D'Agostino shot me the kind of look that Eve must have saved for Adam after the Fall, full of knowledge and cynicism I would never be able to understand. I felt withered and slightly ashamed under the weight of that gaze, and I took my arms from around her.

"Hey," she said. "Come back here. Maybe you're right. Maybe he really did love her."

I came back willingly enough, and when we were fitted together again like pieces of a puzzle made for one another, I kissed her forehead.

"You don't buy it, though."

D'Agostino grinned up at me and stroked the stubble of my half-grown beard.

"Wouldn't it be pretty to think so?"

I laughed. I couldn't help it, and not because she was probably right. I was able to look at the male and female relationship we were talking about and see it in softer, romantic terms. D'Agostino was a cop—and a woman—so she didn't have that luxury. In my experience, men tended to believe themselves more rational and less emotional than women, but we all lie to ourselves. When it came down to it, women were far more practical. They didn't have the luxury of looking at themselves in romantic terms like we did.

"So why else would he stay? What does he get out of it?"

D'Agostino thought for a little while, and I watched the adorable little furrow in her brow while she did it.

"Access," she said. "That's all I can think of."

"Okay," I said. "But access to what?"

D'Agostino kissed me long and hard, her hands gliding up under my tee-shirt and tracing the wide, thick muscles along either side of my spine. I responded, slipping my hands inside her shorts to cup her firm backside.

"We'll ask her when we wake up," D'Agostino said, and began busying herself again with my belt buckle.

TWENTY FOUR

IT'S AN ODD THING to wake up in a bed with one woman while knowing that there's another one waiting, lurking out in the living space with judgmental eyes and a potential grudge against you. But there I was for the second straight morning, and I've got to be honest: waking up next to Laura D'Agostino was worth whatever acid expression Abby Doyle could muster.

I opened my eyes to find D'Agostino already awake, head on the pillow next to mine. She was watching me carefully, a half-smile playing over her face. I covered my mouth and yawned.

"What?" I said.

"Nothing," she said, and waited a beat. "Only ... I never expected this. Did you?"

I shook my head and, in the process, nestled further into the soft down pillow. D'Agostino slid in against me underneath the covers, her naked thigh warm and inviting against my legs. She propped herself up on one elbow in order to see me better in the soft light of morning that streamed weakly around the blinds in her bedroom, and the sheet fell away from her breasts. We both smiled when I couldn't manage to maintain eye contact with her for more than a few seconds.

"Men," she said, and leaned forward to kiss me. I responded, and for a little while there were no words exchanged, just slow and rhythmic movements punctuated by soft moans were short by hungry mouths. When we were done, we lay on our backs, gasping for breath. Other than our hands, which were twined together between our bodies, we didn't touch at all. A thin sheen of sweat covered us. I could taste the salt of her perspiration on my tongue, smell the sweet musk of our sex, feel the ghost of her arms as they had squeezed tightly around my neck and pulled me me ever forward, as we both climaxed.

"Holy God," I said, my voice hushed in awe, as though I had just discovered prayer. And maybe in some sense I had. I had never experienced the kind of physical chemistry that I had with D'Agostino.

She rose from the bed and went into the bathroom. After a few minutes, I heard the toilet flush, and she came out with a towel. I took it from her and dried myself. Then we each hunted up our clothes and got dressed.

This time Abby wasn't waiting for us. The guest room door was closed, and the apartment was quiet. I set about finding something new to make for breakfast, mixing up some heavy cream and eggs, adding a dash of cinnamon and some sugar. Then I heated a pan to medium and dipped some thickly sliced bread in the egg mixture and let the slices cook on one side while D'Agostino made coffee.

I flipped the bread, and the smell of French toast and coffee filled the apartment. The aroma was enough to wake Abby, who wandered out of the guest room in boy shorts and a white shirt so thin it was see-through. I tried not to look—at least when D'Agostino was watching—but I don't think I had much success.

"Oink," she said, banging one hip into me when my glance

rested on Abby's chest for too long. "If I wanted a male chauvinist pig, I work with a couple thousand."

Admonished, I turned back to my French toast, using a plastic spatula to flip the slices from the pan to a plate. Soon the stack was high and my egg wash was depleted. D'Agostino watched me plate for everyone, and then she pulled a small earthenware jug of maple syrup from the pantry and broke the seal on it.

"I've been waiting for an excuse to open this," she said, and poured some syrup on her toast. "Come to mama."

We dug in. Abby hadn't said much since she'd come out of the bedroom. Her hair was still a mess, mostly covering her eyes and giving her face a darker, more shadowy cast than usual. I was worried about her mental state. She'd had to face some awful truths about herself and her father in a very short amount of time. But she ate her food and drank her coffee, and after a little while D'Agostino took out her cell phone.

"I took some photos of Britt's office," she said to Abby. "Do you think you could look at them with us?"

Abby nodded, and D'Agostino shifted over so that they could both get a good look at the photos on her phone. Laura went through the images slowly, looking from my phone back to Abby's face to see if anything registered. I was sitting across the table from them, so I couldn't see the images. Instead I looked for tells on Abby's face. But mostly she just looked puzzled.

"Can I see them again?" She said, her voice sounding remarkably like a little girl's.

Shock, I thought. *She's in shock.* I didn't blame her. I would be, too. The last few days had thrown nothing at her except one disaster after another, and I had to wonder how long she could hold up under this kind of mental and emotional strain.

Once she went through the pictures again, Abby looked at D'Agostino. "Where's his laptop?"

I stared at them. Britt had a laptop, and I knew it. I could remember seeing it sitting atop his desk the first time I made my way into that office. It was password protected, I remembered that, too. There was no way I could access the information on it, so I'd dismissed it. Apparently, someone else hadn't.

"There was a laptop in his office?" D'Agostino said.

"Yes," Abby said. "He usually kept it on the desk there, on top of the blotter, when he was charging it."

"Shit," I said. "Shit, shit, *shit*."

D'Agostino glanced at me, her eyes round.

"I saw it," I said. "When we were in the house the first time. I didn't even think about it yesterday."

D'Agostino's lips clamped together in a hard line, and I saw her start to say something, then she closed her mouth and changed tactics. She wanted to ream me out, I could tell. And I didn't blame her. But it wouldn't have done any good, so she closed that thought off and pushed on. She turned back to Abby.

"What did Britt keep on his laptop?"

Abby shrugged.

"I don't know," she said. "I guess work stuff. I was never involved in his business, so I didn't have access to his work computer, you know. And didn't want to, either. I can't think of anything more boring than accounting. God, and I was going to marry him. Can you imagine?"

I couldn't, but that answer wouldn't get us anywhere. Instead I tried to think. Who would want Britt's computer? And the answer to that depended on what kind of information he kept on there. He hadn't kept the records of Abby's pregnancies and subsequent abortions on his computer, but that may have been because the reports didn't originate with him. He probably got hold of hard copies through a crooked hospital official so there wouldn't be any kind of digital trail.

Laura touched a button on the side of her phone, and the screen went black. I refilled our coffee cups and sat back down across from her at the dining table.

"Here's what I keep thinking," she said. "You've got Doyle on one side, and you've got Martin James on the other."

"Yes," I said. "And don't forget about Becks. He's out there, too."

She nodded. "Sure, sure. But I think he may be secondary. I think the real players here are Doyle and James. You get two rich guys together in a land deal, and what do you have?"

"A lot of money," I said.

"Yeah," Laura said. "And you know the kind of guy Doyle is. Do you think all of his money is clean?"

"Of course not."

D'Agostino grinned that wolfish hungry grin that she wore sometimes, like an apex predator on the prowl for its next meal.

"So Doyle's dirty money goes into the land deal," she said.

"And Martin James's clean money comes out the other side," I finished for her. "It's so clean you could fold it and put it away in your bureau."

Abby's jaw had dropped open. She looked back and forth from D'Agostino to me.

"Are you saying that's why Britt stayed with me?"

I didn't want to look at her. Abby was already feeling shattered. I didn't know how much more she could take.

"Maybe," Laura said. "But maybe it's more than one thing. Maybe he had feelings for you. But when he found out about the Carraway deal between your father and Martin, I think he used those records to cut himself in."

"And he could be helpful to them," I said. "He was an accountant. He'd know how to hide money. It makes sense."

"But he *loved* me," Abby said. "Britt would have stood on his head for me."

D'Agostino patted Abby's thigh.

"I'm sure he cared about you," she said, trying to soothe Abby. She put her arm around the young woman and pulled her into a tight hug. "People aren't just one thing, you know. Maybe we're making it more simple than it was."

Laura shot me a warning glance while Abby wasn't looking, so I didn't say what I was thinking.

The Carraway property was potentially worth hundreds of millions. Seeing it developed would be a boon to the local economy, and it would also create hundreds—maybe thousands—of ways for Doyle to launder money. I thought our logic was sound. Unfortunately, we lacked any hard proof. Maybe if we could find Britt's laptop, the proof for the whole scheme would come out and we'd find out who had actually killed him.

Abby sat up straight then, and D'Agostino released her.

"I think I want to be by myself for a little while," she said, and without another word, she went back into the guest room and closed the door. In a little while, we heard the shower begin to run. D'Agostino and I cleared breakfast plates and pre-washed dishes, finally loading everything into the dishwasher. We didn't talk. I think we were afraid to. We went back into the bedroom and closed the door so that we could talk in private.

"So which one of them benefits from Britt being dead?" I asked.

"Carlton, for sure. The blackmail about Abby never gets out. It's the only handle I can think of that anyone's ever had on him."

I kind of agreed, but the fact was that I didn't like Martin James, and a murder of opportunity seemed his style. Maybe I was projecting. Did I fear Carlton Doyle? Absolutely. But I also respected the viciousness and violence in the man. Going near him was like getting into a cage with a King Cobra: things could go south at any moment.

"I think it's Martin," I said. "Britt and Abby have been together for more than a year, right? Carlton's used to having that handle on his back by now. But Martin, I mean, what if he saw an opportunity to take out someone who had muscled in on his deal?"

D'Agostino nodded slowly. I don't know if she bought my logic entirely, but she could see that it was certainly possible.

"We've got to talk to them both anyway," she said. "Martin first, then Carlton."

We knocked on Abby's door. She didn't open it, just called through the door to let us know that she was all right. So D'Agostino told her that we would be out for a while, and to help herself to anything she wanted, but not to venture out.

"Got it," came Abby's muffled reply. "House arrest."

"There goes my wine collection," Laura said when we were safely out in the hall. We hustled down to her Charger, and then she rocketed away from her building before I could get my seat belt fastened.

At the Tower building, everything seemed normal until we got out of the elevator. When the door opened onto the fifth floor, I could smell it: Someone had fired a gun in here, and recently. D'Agostino caught the whiff of it, too, and her weapon was in her hand before I could even draw mine. We went down the hallway cautiously and found the door of Martin James' office suite ajar. I eased the door open more fully, and D'Agostino went in high while I followed low. The smell of gunfire was thicker in here.

Jenna, Martin's secretary, would never take dictation again. Two rounds had done her in: one in the throat and one, probably fired when she was on the floor, in the center of her forehead. I looked away. D'Agostino moved through the room, looking everywhere, even in the kneehole of the desk where Jenna had late sat.

"Clear," she said, her voice low.

Martin James' inner office door hadn't been fixed since my previous visit. Going into the room, D'Agostino and I changed tactics: I went in standing, and she slipped in beside me in a scrabbling crouch to go low.

Martin James leaned back in his big leather captain's chair, a look of surprise forever frozen on his face. His white shirt had been ruined by three shots to the center of his mass, and his hands were cast wide open as if he had welcomed the embrace of death. His mouth was open, and blood had run from the corners. In death, he had soiled his gabardine slacks, and the smell was thick and clotted in the small space. Beside me, D'Agostino had holstered her weapon and drew her phone out, calling in a double homicide to the Homewood PD. We were about to be really popular.

D'Agostino was already slated to be suspended. We'd been shot at on Friday, and here on a Saturday before noon, we'd found two bodies.

And the blood wasn't even sticky yet.

"I don't understand," D'Agostino said after killing the call. "If James is supposed to launder your cash, why would you kill him? It doesn't make sense."

I shrugged.

"Doyle's going to answer for this," she said. "If it's the last thing I do."

I didn't think so. If I knew Carlton Doyle—and I did, after a fashion—he was going to be alibied six ways to Sunday. I didn't think D'Agostino would be able to connect him to the crime.

Doyle was too smart, and too connected, to do something like this. If he had murdered Britt, that was bad enough, and could get the cops to look at him a lot more carefully. Now Martin James was dead, and detectives would tease out the connection between the two and the purchase of the Carraway property.

We backed into the hallway in order to not compromise the crime scene any more than we already had.

"Did you touch anything?" D'Agostino asked. I considered, then shook my head.

"If they find you here, they'll want to fingerprint you, even if it's just to eliminate latent prints."

"I know," I said.

"I don't—I don't know everything you've done, and I don't want to." She fished the keys to the Charger out of her pocket. "Get the hell out of here, okay? I don't want to see you get arrested, Kincaid. I couldn't bear it right now."

"I can't do that," I said. "It's your department vehicle. You're probably in trouble enough."

"What will you do?"

"Same thing I always do," I said. "Make the best of it. Wish me luck."

She did even better than that, leaning forward and kissing me hard on the mouth. When she pulled away, I stared at her for a moment like I was trying to commit her features to memory. I hustled out of there, aware of sirens getting closer in the distance.

TWENTY FIVE

HERE'S THE THING about running from the cops: Don't. Running is almost always a bad idea. If first responders—and that means cops, firefighters, EMTs, whatever—are rushing toward an emergency call and see you speeding away, you won't do anything other than draw attention to yourself. So I didn't run. Around the back of the building was an empty stairwell; it would eventually take me to the rear of the Tower building and out to the soft downslope behind it. There was a narrow rim of pine trees down there, like the fringe of hair on an otherwise bald man, and past that was the half-filled parking lot of a strip mall.

The problem, of course, was that I'd be visible to anyone watching from the building, including the cops who were sure to be swarming around like hungry piranha, just waiting to take a bite out of anyone acting suspicious.

So instead of going down, I went up. I figured four more floors would be enough, and now that I was in the stairwell, I could hurry—and did—taking two or three steps at a time. By the time I'd raced up four flights, my breath was rasping in my chest and my shirt damp with perspiration. I opened the access door slowly, peering out into the hallway, where I couldn't see anything in the gloomy dark.

If we'd been in a newer building, my goose would have been cooked. There are usually video cameras in every new building, but the Tower building was old and decrepit by almost any standard. There were no cameras in the lobby nor hallways, at least as far as I could see, and I was used to looking for such things.

I hurried down the hallway, checking door knobs as I went. Most of them had a line of small silver buttons right beneath the doorknob, and the trick to unlocking them was to push the buttons in the correct sequence. The thing most people don't realize is that those kinds of keypads are notoriously easy to unlock. I found a little office near the elevator end of the hallway where I could listen in case the cops decided to search this far up and tried the three most common punch codes. Nothing. So I tried the fourth one I knew, and the lock clicked open. I opened the door and stepped through.

I snapped the lock closed. I was pretty safe up here, I thought, as long as I didn't turn any lights on. I took a moment to silence my phone, making sure that the vibrate feature was off, too. When that was done, I looked around at the office I'd burgled my way into. It was a single room—no vestibule for a secretary to sit and welcome visitors—dominated by a large oak desk with ornate carvings around the outer edge and down each leg..

Behind the desk was a large plate-glass window, covered with half-closed blinds. It let some slanted sunlight spill into the room. Enough to see by, anyway.

There were three filing cabinets lined up against one wall, five feet high, and on the walls were photos of scenes around Birmingham and Tuscaloosa. I recognized Legion Field and Sloss Furnace, as well as the Empire Building, once the tallest building in the state until the four skyscrapers that dominated Birmingham's skyline had been built. Another corner held a plastic plant made to resemble a rubber tree. *What's the point of that?* I asked myself.

Idly, I tried the filing cabinets, but they were locked. I sat behind the desk and thought about my next step. I doubted the cops would find me, and even if they did, they couldn't pin a double homicide on me. D'Agostino and Abby could easily alibi me, and I had no current warrants out for my arrest. But my first instinct, when the cops were involved, was to run.

Had D'Agostino figured out why? Did she understand that if her boss found her with me—again—that he'd begin to suspect that she was in a relationship with one of the more unsavory characters in her jurisdiction? And if that happened, she would be out. I didn't think she could be fired for being with me, but people would talk. They'd be suspicious. Promotions wouldn't come. Suspensions might become easier. And eventually she'd be driven out. Being a cop was important to her. I couldn't let that happen to her.

So I ran. And now I was holed up in this tiny office, like a turtle that's retreated into its shell. I couldn't see anything going on around me, and I just had to pray that the danger would pass before I stuck my head out again.

I was wearing a gun, which could be a problem if they found it. So I took the piece off my belt, holster and all, and took it over to the fake tree in the corner. I lifted the thing by its slender plastic trunk, and it came free as easily as a diseased tooth from a rotting mouth. It was too easy. I looked into the ceramic planter where the plant had lately stood. There was a white envelope at the bottom of the planter. I dug it up and, my curiosity getting the better of me, opened it.

Green bills in a stack. Hundreds, and they looked real. I didn't count them. Instead, I put the money back and placed my weapon on top of it. That cash looked like an emergency stash to me, something that no one was supposed to know about. So if I wanted to, I could take it with me once the coast was clear. What were they gonna do, report it stolen?

I sat back down at the desk and waited in the gloom. Eventually

I heard the elevator open and some cops—there were at least two—came down the hallway. They rattled the doorknobs of every office on the floor, but it felt like a halfhearted effort. I had a wild moment where I wondered if I had really locked it back. But the door held, and then they were past. I could hear them in the hallway, talking about what a bullshit assignment they'd drawn.

"—no way the perp's here," one said. "He's long gone."

"Yeah, gotta be. Bet you he stole a car—"

"—no way he's on foot."

Their radios squawked, and they communicated with dispatch, telling them that the fourth floor was clear. They came back toward the elevator, footsteps heavy in their thick-soled tactical boots. I heard the elevator doors open and close, and soon a faint bell dinged as the car moved on up.

Whoever was in charge was being thorough; it sounded like they had sent a team to check every floor. If the perp was still on the scene, they would have probably scooped him up. I kept my seat and watched the diffuse light in the office change. Now that the cops had passed, I could get my gun—and the little stash of emergency cash, if I wanted it—but I stayed put. There was no need to move yet.

You learn, you know? The Army gives you a lot of hurry-up-and-wait. You pass the time by checking your equipment, making sure that everything is ready to go, that there's no dust in the chamber of your weapon, that your pack is set the way it's supposed to be, that your boots are jump-laced and the pants of your fatigues are bloused just so, because you don't want water or sand or any other foreign matter getting into them.

A lot of the guys had something to keep their hands busy while they waited. I saw a lot of Rosary beads, even if the guys weren't Catholic. Some guys—and they were almost universally unpopular—played harmonicas. And a lot of us carried a deck of playing cards. Shuffling and dealing kept your fingers nimble, and I often found myself absently dealing hands of solitaire before we went out on patrol. Now, stuck in this office with nothing to do other than wait, I mentally shuffled and dealt, my hands making easy little motions as I thought about the mechanics of laying the cards out.

My breathing was slow and easy. With my hands occupied—in a way, at least—my mind could wander. Of course I thought about D'Agostino: her upturned nose, the sprinkle of freckles across her cheeks, the full lips that seemed to be slightly misaligned until she smiled. She wasn't beautiful, not objectively. I knew there were women in the world that were better looking. Hell, if you wanted to get technical about it, Abby was maybe better-looking. But she didn't have the same gravitational pull that I felt when I looked at Laura.

Abby wasn't a woman. She was an alcoholic child, a spoiled one, and one who had been badly abused and used. I tried to never think of a person as damaged goods, but it was hard to refrain from using that label when I thought about Abby.

They were both so different. I thought about the first day I'd spent with Abby, the confrontation with Britt. If D'Agostino had been in that situation, I would have never had the chance to punch him.

But D'Agostino wouldn't have let herself be put in that position, I thought. She was too tough; there was too much steel there. Or at least that was my impression. We still didn't know each other nearly as well as I wanted. I knew her body, yes, and if I allowed my thoughts to go there, it would be a pleasant rerun of some of our greatest hits. But that would only frustrate me, because I wouldn't be able to touch her, not yet, and probably not for a while.

Instead I went to the window and peered through the blinds. This office had a view, but it was the wrong one. I could see the strip club down the hill and the wide, jammed traffic artery of Valley Avenue below it. Anyone who had to look out at that view every day must feel unlovely as hell by the time they left the office.

But what I was really interested in were the cops. They were still on site down there. Three cruisers and six, count 'em, six SUVs. There was a crime scene van and an ambulance, as well. The ambulance's lights were off. Whatever help the paramedics could have offered was too little, too late, and had been for a while.I

I sat back down, blowing out a deep breath. For all my experience waiting, this was a new sensation. Things were going on out there, and I needed to know what was happening. I pulled out my phone and risked a quick text to D'Agostino.

-Status?

The message stayed unread for only a few seconds, and then I saw the little thought bubble that told me she was typing a response.

-Can't talk.

Shit.

So I texted Abby, reminding her to stay put. No one knew she was at D'Agostino's, and as long as she stayed put, no one would. She responded almost instantly, asking me to bring a bottle of Skyy vodka when we returned to the apartment, and then complaining that she was going stir-crazy, waiting there in the apartment by herself.

I looked around the dim, ugly little office. I knew how she felt. At least she could watch TV if worse came to worst. I was stuck somewhere with no way to really access what was going on. I peered through the window again and saw that a CBS 42 news van had showed up, as well as an ABC 3340 crew. Could Fox be far behind? Of course not.

I had hoped that by now—it had been a few hours at this point—I could sneak down the stairs or the elevator and get the hell out of the building. But now the news hounds had the story, and at least one blonde reporter—I think it was Leigh Garner— was doing a standup from the parking lot. The cops had kept their blue lights revolving, and Garner and her cameraman had set up so that the vehicles and the Tower building were in the camera shot.

I settled back down, closing my eyes to rest. I was in for a long wait.

TWENTY SIX

THE COLLINS BAR on Second Ave is everything the hipsters want modern Birmingham to be. The decor is funky, with indirect lighting and thin, bearded bartenders who extol the virtues of Pappy Van Winkle or Macallan 18. The bar is on the left as you come in, and you have to pass through usually-crowded outdoor seating to get into the place. It's overpriced and bougie, and as such, it's one of the more popular places in the city. D'Agostino and I were there, just past 1 a.m. on a Sunday morning, recovering after the TV crews and cops had finally packed up and gone home, and I was free of the Tower building. Forever, I hoped.

We were sitting elbow-to-elbow at the bar, drinking old fashioneds and not talking much. I could tell she had something on her mind. We'd stopped in to bring Abby some dinner and make sure that she hadn't gone anywhere. She was going a little stir crazy, which I understood. I'd guarded enough bodies to know there was a point when the body wanted to go over the wall, no matter what the danger was, just to break up the monotony.

I couldn't let her do that, though, and had extracted a promise that she'd stay hidden in D'Agostino's place for the time being.

It wasn't perfect, but it was the best thing I could think of at the moment. Like every other Birmingham cop, Laura's address was pretty well-guarded information within the department.

"I didn't like today," D'Agostino said, draining her drink and raising her empty lowball glass toward one of the bartenders. She put the glass down on the coaster in front of her and pursed her lips into a hard, thin line.

"I wasn't a fan of it myself," I said. "I was cooped up in that office for hours. But what could I do?"

D'Agostino shook her head.

"That's not what I mean."

Of course it wasn't. I knew it, and I could feel what was coming. I felt my jaw clench instinctively, as if in anticipation of a blow.

"We have to stop this," she said. "I can't be with you. You know that, right? I covered for you today, because I care about you. But I care about my job, too."

"And you care about that more than you care about me," I said softly. There was no heat in the words.

"I've only known you for a few days," she said. "I've been a cop since I was twenty-one. It matters."

I scratched at my face absently for a moment.

"No," I said, "stop. I'm not arguing. I'm not fighting about this. I'm following the conversation to its logical conclusion. Of course you care about your work, and I understand that you were in a bad position today."

"It was awful," she said. "I'm already going to be suspended Monday morning. Having to lie about you—even if it was just a lie of omission—was brutal. I hated myself the whole time I was there."

"I don't want you to hate yourself," I said. "We shouldn't, you know, shouldn't have gotten together like that. I put you in a bad position. I can understand that." I got up off the barstool and dragged my wallet out of my jeans. I tossed some of the slush money I'd found earlier on the bar, enough to cover the overpriced booze and leave a tip.

"Wait," D'Agostino said, but I didn't stop. I put my wallet away and turned for the door. She rose from the bar and followed me to the door.

"Kincaid," she said. "Come back here. Don't leave like this."

I walked out of the bar and turned right, toward the East, my cowboy boots making hard thocking sounds every time my heel hit the sidewalk. D'Agostino stayed with me, a few steps behind, as if she was cautious about the anger boiling off of me. Wise.

"Where are you going? I drove, for fuck's sake. Will you at least let me drop you at your place?"

Shit. She was right. I could call a cab or order up an Uber. But that would take time, and I'd need to duck into one of the dives around here and wait. And if I waited, I'd drink more. And if I drank more in the mood I was currently in, bad things would happen. I stopped abruptly, my hands at my sides, every muscle tense. D'Agostino touched my arm.

"I'm sorry," she said. "I really am. You know that, right?"

"Yeah," I said, and turned to face her. "It doesn't really help."

"I know."

The streetlights were glinting in her eyes, and around us the city was beginning to quiet down. The young and upwardly were leaving the bars, saying good night, walking to their secure buildings, safe in the knowledge that the BPD had cleared out most of the bad element on the streets, leaving only the hard drinkers and the lonely and the misfits at the bars. It was a time of night that felt familiar, a place where I felt I belonged.

I took in a deep breath and smelled the dank, complicated odors of the dark city. When I blew out the breath, I told D'Agostino that she should leave.

"What?"

"I need to be alone. I can call a cab to get back to my room. I'll go up to Pale Eddie's and wait."

"Are you sure?"

I told her I was, and she looked at me uncertainly in the glowering darkness. I was trying very hard to bring my defenses back up, to see D'Agostino as what she was: a cop. If I could think of her that way, I could shut out everything else. I squeezed my eyes shut and tried not to think of the way she smelled and tasted, the way she looked at me in the soft morning light, both of our heads on a single pillow, laughing and smiling at the ridiculous piece of happiness that we'd carved for ourselves in the night.

I tried not to think about it, because it had turned out to be temporary. I understood her decision, and I could even support it, in my own way. But it still hurt.

"I'll come by for Abby in the morning," I said, and turned around again. I didn't look back, instead imagining her looking after me as I got smaller and smaller in her vision until I disappeared.

Pale Eddie's hadn't closed yet, but even the barflies looked like they were ready to call it a night. I knew the bartender, a brassy blonde with a sleeve of tattoos down one arm and piercings in her eyebrows and nose, and she knew me, too. When she saw me come in, she reached for the Bushmill's and poured a long shot. I went to a small booth in the corner partially shadowed and sat down facing the door. The bartender came out with my drink and a thick china mug of coffee. I downed the whisky with barely a grimace and then sipped at the coffee.

"Again," I said, then softened my tone. "Please."

The bartender looked down at me, the jewelry in her brow and nose reflecting the muted light from the bar.

"It's gonna be like that tonight," she said.

"It is."

She nodded curtly and went away. In a few minutes she came back with the bottle of Bush and set it down on the table in front of me. Then she went away to deal with the drunks and the punks who hadn't left yet, and I got prepared to do some serious drinking.

Ahead of me, the bar door opened and a slender man of medium height entered. I didn't pay him much attention at first, because I was busy pouring Irish into my shot glass, turning the bottle slightly so that the pour spout didn't drip at all. Neat. I've always been neat as a bastard. The guy who had come in from the street looked around Pale Eddie's carefully, taking in the length of the bar and the little stage near the door. Eventually his eyes found me, and he came over. I drained my second shot of whisky and sipped more coffee while I waited for him.

He was younger than me by a handful of years, probably, and he wore a gray suit that was too boxy to be Armani. Probably Brooks Brothers, they had a shop in the Summit out on Highway 280. There was a bulge under his right arm that looked like a shoulder holster, which meant that he was left-handed. He had unremarkable brown eyes, brown hair, and if you saw him in a crowd, your eye would slide right over him without a second thought.

Unless you noticed the gun under his arm.

"You Kincaid?" He asked. I nodded and didn't say anything.

"Mind if I sit down?"

I waited for a beat.

"Yeah," I said. "I do."

It didn't bother him. He just sort of shook his head, the corners of his mouth turning up in what might have been a smile on another person. He kept his hands very still at his sides.

"Mr. Doyle sent me. I'm Joey Dykes."

I was drunk enough and angry enough at that point that I didn't care how dangerous Doyle was. And I didn't care for his lackey showing up, either. It probably showed on my face. I know it sure as hell showed in my voice.

"Yeah? So what."

The man sat down across the booth from me anyway, whether I minded or not. He looked me squarely in the eye without flinching.

"So he sent me to talk to you. I'm sorry to be the one to tell you this, but your services are no longer needed."

Dykes used his right hand to reach into his suit jacket and produced a white envelope stuffed thick. He held it in one palm, as if weighing it. Then he put it on the table between us and gave it a shove toward me. I picked it up and opened the flap, which hadn't been sealed. Inside was a stack of greenbacks, probably more than I'd found earlier in the day.

"Consider that a severance payment," Dykes said. "Mr. Doyle wants you to produce his daughter tomorrow morning at his apartment. You know where."

Yeah, I knew where, all right. I closed the envelope and pushed it back toward Dykes.

"Job's not over," I said, and Dykes cocked his head at me.

"There are things you don't know," he said, finally. "Mr. Doyle has come to an arrangement with the people who threatened his daughter."

An arrangement. I knew what that meant, in the world of a man like Carlton Doyle. He'd either had them eliminated or disappeared or bought off, and my brain flashed on Martin James and his assistant. Could be them, I decided, but probably not. However they fit into things, they weren't the ones who had threatened Abby's life.

"I don't think so," I said. "I think there's still someone out there who's a danger to Abby."

Dykes raised an eyebrow.

"What do you mean?"

I shook my head.

"You don't need to know," I said. "But you tell Doyle that I know. Tell him I know everything, and that he's not getting Abby back until I say so."

"Hold on a minute," Dykes said. "How—"

"You want a drink?" I said. "I'm gonna have another one. It's been a long night." I signaled the bartender for another glass, and she hustled over. At some point, the rest of the drunks had left, and Dykes and I were the only two people left in the bar.

"I gotta close up," she said. "You guys can stay, but when you're ready to head out, let me know. I'll unlock the door for you."

I nodded and poured myself and Dykes a shot. He looked down at the whisky like he'd never seen alcohol before. Then he took the shot glass between his fingers and tossed it off in one gulp. He didn't react to the heat of the booze at all. I drank mine and felt the little thrilling hiss of the whisky in my throat, the bloom that told me I was alive and could still feel a little something.

Dykes took a handkerchief out of his pocket and wiped the glass carefully.

"You're making a mistake," he said. "I was told to offer you the money first, as a courtesy. But make no mistake about it, sir. You *are* fired."

I smiled at him, showing my teeth, a wolf's smile, one predator recognizing another.

"What's the second offer?" I asked, knowing what the answer would be.

"You take the money, you go your way," Dykes said. "You turn it down, I kill you."

"If you can."

"Anybody can kill anybody," he said. "It's just a matter of what you're willing to do. My advice? Take the fuckin' money."

"No," I said, and then things began to happen with the easy, greasy speed of a video being fast-forwarded. Dykes' left hand flashed for the gun under his right shoulder, and I shoved the table into him hard, hearing the wind whoosh out of his chest and closing his hand inside his lapel for a moment.

And in that moment, I was on my feet. I grabbed his left wrist with both hands, keeping the gun trapped and away from me. He struggled, punching me in the side of the head with his right. Stars exploded in my vision, and he reached back for another swing. I head-butted him in the mouth, hard, and felt a couple of his teeth break. I took a chance then, pulling my left hand away from his gun hand, folding my fist in tight against my shoulder, and drove my elbow forward.

A shot like that takes the fight out of just about anybody, and Dykes was no exception. He sagged toward the floor, and I reached into his jacket and ripped the pistol free from his shoulder holster. It was a blue-steel .38 with a two-inch barrel, and if I had let him get it out when the fight first started, I'd already be dead. I stripped the ammunition out of the gun and let the shells clatter to the floor.

Dykes was barely conscious. I shook him a little as the bartender came back in, pushing a dolly loaded with cases of beer.

"Holy shit," she said. "Kincaid, what the hell happened."

I didn't know what to say, so I let go of Dykes and watched him fall all the way down. I probably shouldn't admit how satisfying that felt.

The bartender let me out, and I stuffed a few hundreds into her hand. "For the trouble," I said. "I'm sorry."

She kissed me on the cheek, as if we were old friends.

"Get out of here," she said. "Don't come back for a while. You know they'll be looking for you."

I knew. I walked down the lonely street until I found a cab idling at the curb. I got in the back, and he looked at me, a raven's glittering ravenous eyes in his face. I gave him the address for my motel, and he dropped me off no more than ten minutes later. I paid with one of my stolen hundreds and told him to keep the change. He nodded at me and drove away into the night.

I turned back to my room, taking out my key and advancing on the door. That's when they tried to kill me. Again.

TWENTY SEVEN

THERE WERE TWO of them this time, and they came at me in a kind of scrabbling rush, skulking dark figures whose shapes melded with the shadows around the motel. I could hear them better than I could see them, shuffling feet in hard-soled shoes on gritty old concrete. There was no hesitation in their approach, and the hairs on the back of my neck rose to attention. I had no time to slip the key in the lock, no time to turn the doorknob and step into the safety of my room. If I missed with the key—it's been known to happen—I was as good as dead, with a bullet or blade in my back.

I tried to draw my weapon, but the drinks earlier and the fight with Joey Dykes had left me feeling numb and slow and useless. The gun clattered on the sidewalk and then skittered into the shadows like a cockroach when the lights come on. I scanned the ground for it, but it was dark enough that I couldn't see, and I couldn't look for long or my attackers would be on me, and I would be done.

So I turned and put my back to the door and watched the two plug-uglies advance on me. Even in the dark, what little light there was seemed concentrated on the thin silvery knife blades they each carried low in one hand.

There are three things you can do against a knife-wielding attacker: the conventional wisdom is that you should press one hand over the other, forming a thick double-V with your thumbs and forefingers to try to deflect the knife blade as the attacker thrusts with the knife blade turned upward. Guys who really know what they're doing with a knife fight that way, with the sharpened blade facing up toward the sky so that they can rip your guts out easier.

The other thing you can do, if you're faced with someone intent on turning you into a pincushion, is step toward the blow, try to get inside the arc of their thrust in order to use your body as a fulcrum to either throw them off-balance or to put so much torque on their knife hand that they let go and the damned pig-sticker clatters to the ground.

I've never heard anyone say what you should do when two guys built like NFL linebackers come at you simultaneously, their knives held low like they knew what to do with them. Curling into the fetal position and screaming in fear didn't seem to be the best decision, so I told my feet to do their duty.

In other words, I chose option number three: I ran like hell.

I live in what is kindly referred to as a bad part of town. There are rows of no-tell motels like mine, a McDonald's with bars across every window except the drive-thru, and the buildings that line the street are either empty or hold small businesses whose owners are just barely hanging on.

That said, there are upsides to living in the area. Police cruisers and SUVs patrol the areas regularly. I took a hard right out of the motel parking lot at a dead sprint and tried to find an even higher gear. The two guys who were intent on skewering me followed. They were younger than me, maybe faster. But they also carried a lot more muscle. As they hit the street, I got a better look at them, two young black guys with dreadlocks that fell below their shoulders and wispy beards. Their upper bodies were thick with the kind of muscle you put on when there's nothing else much to do, and they were covered with jailhouse tattoos on their faces and necks.

They hadn't sheathed their knives, either. The blades gleamed a little brighter out here on the street, and they ran toward me in step, gaining a little ground. They didn't look like they were in a hurry, didn't look concerned that their prey had done a rabbit on them. Indeed, they looked ready to follow me as long as it took to hunt me down and kill me.

My strides were long and sure, but my chest was already heaving. I looked right and left, but there was nothing. Ahead, the buildings were even darker as the lonely businesses petered out to nothing. I skittered to a stop in front of the long, flickering fluorescent light tubes that lit up Yvonne's Wig Store. In the gutter there was a chunk of pavement that had cracked and come loose where the sidewalk met the street. I shoved my hand down through the big crack and broke a fingernail off into the quick. But the chunk of heavy black asphalt was in my hand, and I gripped it so hard that I could feel my own pulse through my fingers.

Now I had a weapon, too.

The two men skidded to a stop about twenty feet away from me and crouched, waiting to see what I was going to do next. In truth, I wasn't sure. I could use the chunk of pavement as a rudimentary hammer and try to beat their brains out, but when I went after one of them, that would leave me vulnerable to the other, and they knew it.

"Put the rock down," the guy on the right said. I didn't respond to him at all, just tracked his movements with my eyes. I was trying to keep my eyes kind of unfocused—the booze definitely helped with that—so that I could watch them both at the same time, keying on movement and trying to keep my reaction time quick.

"Come on, we just wanna talk," the guy on the left said. "We're just supposed to scare you is all."

"Oh good," I said, my breath heavy in my chest and throat. "I'm fuckin' scared. Mission accomplished. Now you guys can get the fuck outta here."

They looked at one another, bared wolfish smiles, and then turned back to me.

"Wish it was that simple," Lefty said, and moved away from his partner a little, gaining space, trying to make me split my concentration. "But we got to bring back, ah, proof."

"I'm willing to sign an affidavit," I said. "Come back tomorrow, we'll get the lawyers on it."

Righty chuckled.

"You're pretty cool for a guy can't run half a mile," he said.

"Look, you want to scare me? I'm scared. Let's call it even."

Lefty shook his head almost sadly.

"Can't do it," he said. "Our orders is, we bring back an ear."

I was silent for a beat.

"An ear?" I said, incredulity straining my voice to its upper limits. "You want to cut one of my ears off? Fuck you."

The two guys looked at each other, then over their shoulders. I could have taken off at that point, but it would have involved turning my back on the two linebackers, and I had an idea that if I did that, they were fast enough to bring me down within a few steps. I was too tired to run much further.

I felt spent, used up. The night that surrounded us was soft like a fluffy warm, wet pillow that would smother you in your sleep. The rock in my hand suddenly felt heavy. When Righty stepped forward and showed me the knife, Lefty moved away, circling, trying to get at my back. My options were becoming more and more limited, while theirs were becoming more and more lethal.

I hefted the piece of pavement, lifting it past shoulder height and drawing it back like a baseball pitcher about to throw a ninety-mile-an-hour fastball. Righty's eyes widened. And then I spun and launched the thick gritty chunk of asphalt through the window of Yvonne's Wig Shop.

An ear-splitting alarm pealed through the otherwise silent night. I followed the momentum of my throw around and took off again, while Righty and Lefty looked at one another in shock. Their surprise allowed me to get a lead, and I was planning on keeping it. I crossed First Street, feet slapping and arms pumping, and disappeared into the shadows. My pursuers ditched their knives into the gutter and took off in separate directions, and I saw two of the big white Ford Expeditions the BPD patrol officers favor roll up just a couple of minutes later.

Their blue lights flashed in the night, adding to the confusion of the alarm that still sounded from Yvonne's storefront. The officers—two from each unit—got out cautiously, guns drawn. I watched from the shadows, a block and a half away, until I had my breath back. And when I decided that Frick and Frack weren't going to be much of a danger anymore that night, I melted into the shadows and circled back toward my motel.

I took a while, because I wanted to do it right. I went down the alleys, looking for anyone who might be keeping an eye on the property. I found him in a gray Mercedes sedan, two blocks down from the motel, parked behind a big Nissan Titan crew cab pickup truck. He didn't see me, and that was the way I wanted it.

I backed away, picking my way through the alleys again until I could cross First Ave again without him seeing me. This time I'd be on the opposite side of the street, and maybe I could ID the guy. I sidled up a side street, quieter than a churchmouse, and got a good look at the guy behind the wheel.

"Huh," I grunted. Thomas, the baby rattlesnake that trailed along with Becks Towson, sat behind the wheel. I didn't know what to do with that information, at least not yet. So I filed it away with the raft of other things I didn't know. And then I moved on. I circled the motel several times in an ever-tightening pattern, making sure that the guy in the Mercedes was the only one keeping watch. When I was satisfied, I walked down the street like I didn't have a care in the world, turned into the parking lot and went to my room.

Without the pressure of a pair of attackers bearing down on me, I was able to find my weapon where I'd dropped it. I brushed it off, checked the cylinder and made sure the barrel was unobstructed. Then I held it in my right hand while I unlocked the door with my left.

There was no one inside. I checked the bathroom and the alcove-cum-closet and under the bed, but there was no one there, and there would be no one there no matter how many times I rechecked it. But the problem was that I was settled into the room now and there was nowhere for me to go. I would be safe—or mostly so—as long as I stayed in there. But I couldn't do that. I had miles to go before I slept.

The bed called to me; I needed rest, and I had to catch my breath before I could continue. My body was slick with fear-sweat, and I could smell the raw panic and anger on my skin. I patted my pockets down, but couldn't find my phone. I'd lost it sometime during the chase. Damn.

So I went into the bathroom and found the small opaque window above the bathtub. I am a man who has had to move around a lot in this life to survive, and one of the things I learned early is that you never can allow yourself to have only one way out of a building or situation. So when I moved into the motel room, the first thing I had done was remove the screws from the window frame. Now I popped the whole thing out, and the damp furry clawing hand of summer air poured through the opening. I hoisted myself up onto the windowsill and slithered out feet-first, turning as I did so and scraping the hell out of my stomach. Despite my best efforts, I landed on my ass, and my teeth clicked together hard.

Ow.

I was in a narrow little area where no one really went except the nearly nonexistent maintenance crew. There were big air-conditioning units mounted on concrete slabs, and the area was littered with candy wrappers, fast-food wrappers, and used condoms. Ick. Okay, so maybe some people besides the maintenance crew came back here. A couple of feet away was an eight-foot high privacy fence. It was unpainted and splintery and warped, but right now that didn't matter. I got up from the ground and dusted myself off, leaped and got a hand on top of the fence. I ignored the splinters and the strain, and leveraged myself over the top to the ground on the other side.

And then, for the third time that night, I ran.

TWENTY EIGHT

WHEN D'AGOSTINO OPENED the door, I nearly collapsed into her arms. She was there wearing an Alabama football jersey, gray athletic shorts, and thick white socks. She took one look at me and moved aside. I stumbled into her apartment, exhausted, with only the fumes of the spent alcohol that had fueled me to keep me upright. Laura's face was bunched tight like a clenched fist, and she held one hand behind her back. I was pretty sure she was hiding her service weapon.

"What happened?" She led me to the bedroom, locked her gun into the little safe in her closet, and pushed me down onto my back on the bed. I told her—or at least I think I did—and the last thing I remembered for a little while was D'Agostino taking my boots off and lifting my legs onto the bed. When I woke up four hours later, I was still dressed right down to my sock feet, and D'Agostino wasn't in bed at all.

I found her on the couch, a Crimson Tide throw blanket draped over her body. She was sleeping on her side and using her upper arm for a pillow. Her eyelashes were long and thick, her mouth was open slightly, and my heart ached at the sight of her.

At the same time, I hated myself for having to rely on her. I am, at my core, a lonely man. I don't have friends, exactly. I have acquaintances. I have people I do business with. I have clients. But not friends. I don't do entanglements. And now I had begun an entanglement with Laura D'Agostino, and even though it seemed destined to be short-lived, I was still relying on her.

I put my hand on her shoulder, and she came instantly awake, sitting up and sliding over on the couch. I sat next to her, careful to keep a little distance between us. D'Agostino had made her wishes clear the night before, and even if she hadn't, the fact that she had refused to share her bed with me—even while I was clothed—spoke volumes.

"You didn't have to sleep out here," I said.

"I don't want either of us to get any mixed messages."

The coffeemaker in the kitchen beeped to life. Apparently D'Agostino had set it the night before. I listened to the steady drip of coffee into the carafe, then pursed my lips.

"I understand," I said. "But someone is coming after me."

"So go to the cops."

"You *are* the cops, Laura."

She smiled at that, a sad quirk of her mouth that spoke more than her words ever could. Right then I wanted nothing more than to lean over and kiss her, but I also understood that would be a disaster. She might respond to it in the moment—after all, we'd already discovered that there was a great deal of chemistry between us—but she'd hate me for it afterward. It wouldn't be the kiss so much as disregarding the boundaries she was clearly setting. I put my hands in my lap and sat still.

"Maybe go to some other cops," she said. "Ninety-nine percent sure I'm getting suspended tomorrow anyway."

I thought about it for a little bit, then shook my head.

"I can't," I said. "If I gotta rely on the cops to get me out of trouble every time I get into a jam, what good am I? All I've got is my word and my balls, and right now that's enough."

"So what are you going to do? You can't keep Abby here. I can't—this is hard enough, Kincaid—you can't keep coming around here. I can't take it. I don't think you can, either."

She was right about that. We were both hyper-aware that we were the only ones in the room. She was still wearing her pajamas from the night before. They weren't especially skimpy, but she looked good, even after spending the night on the couch.

"It's almost wrapped up. I think it's only going to be a couple more days," I said. "You could even get her outta town if you want. And maybe you should."

"What have you heard?"

"Nothing," I said, raising my hands to try to ward away the intense curiosity that D'Agostino carried with her all the time. It was a huge part of what made her a good detective.

She looked at me intently for a time, not wanting to take my word for it. I didn't blame her. Cops want to know what other people know about them. They try not to leave a lot of trails out there for people to follow. When you're a cop, especially a good cop, in Birmingham, people tend to hold grudges.

"You want me to babysit her for another two days," D'Agostino said. She thought for a little while. "Fine. What's in it for me?"

"What do you mean?"

"Where do I end up at the end of all this?" D'Agostino asked. "You might leave me holding the bag, you know. What if Doyle or Becks—or one of their minions—gets to you? Then all I've got is some guy's little girl, and I don't even have any kind of legal right to keep her here with me."

Oh. I hadn't thought about that. I put my hands on the back of my head, straightened, and tried to pop my back to relieve some of the pressure I was feeling between my shoulder blades. I felt and heard it pop, which was a relief, but I still had to deal with the unrelenting heaviness of D'Agostino's expectations.

"I'll sign an affidavit," I said. "You hold onto it. If I don't have everything settled within two days, you open it and use the information in there however you see fit."

D'Agostino stared at me. I shrugged, not quite meeting her eyes.

"If I don't have it settled, I'll be dead," I said, "and it won't matter very much anyway, will it?"

Laura was a cop, so she knew a lot of lawyers. It didn't take her more than fifteen tries to find one willing to come to her apartment to take my statement and witness it. While we were waiting for the attorney to arrive, Abby woke up and wandered into the apartment. If she knew what was going on between D'Agostino and me, she didn't show it. She was more interested in the coffee pot. I couldn't blame her.

D'Agostino and I sat on the couch in close proximity, but not touching. I worked on my third cup of coffee while we waited. I could hear Abby rummaging through the kitchen. She came to the kitchen table carrying a family-sized box of Apple Jacks and a large mixing bowl.

She poured a lot of cereal and very little milk into the bowl and used a serving spoon to lift the cereal to her mouth.

"I swear to God, it's like having a five-year-old," D'Agostino whispered in my ear, and I smothered a laugh. We listened while Abby ate, and then the building's security guard rang the box. The lawyer had arrived.

I spent nearly two hours detailing what I had done, and all the things I had learned, since coming on board as Abby's bodyguard. Abby and Laura listened attentively to my statement, and then I wrote it all out, only X-ing out parts of the narrative in order to clarify what I had found and how I had done it. When I was done, the lawyer looked it over. He witnessed the statement and then notarized it. It went into his briefcase, a bloated and scarred brown leather messenger bag that he carried on his hip the way a woman would carry a toddler. When he was done, he looked at Abby.

"Miss Doyle," he began softly, "can you corroborate the claims Mr. Kincaid has made here today?"

Abby was very still for a moment, like a wild deer in the woods who hopes you haven't seen it yet. Then she nodded once, up and down.

"That will help, thank you."

He turned back to me.

"I'm assuming that you're worried you may not be around long enough to tell your story in open court?"

"Let's call it an insurance policy," I said. "I kind of know what's going on, which is a new experience for me, and I'm afraid some people won't care for that too much."

He nodded and went back to his bag. He dug around in it for a few seconds and came up with a business card. I took it and slipped it into my wallet.

"Call me in a couple of weeks," he said. "If you don't call, I'll release your statement to the media. We'll see what kind of traction it can pick up then."

That was fine by me. If it came to that, I wouldn't be around to care.

The lawyer picked up his bag and set it back on his hip. Then he shook my hand and Abby's, kissed Laura on the cheek, and left. The three of us sat there looking at one another, wondering what came next.

I got up from the kitchen table, where I'd written my statement. My right knee was stiff, as thought I'd been sitting for much longer than I actually had. Old age comes for us all, I suppose. I stretched out the leg, feeling the stiffness lessen a little as I did it.

"I have to go," I said. "I still don't know what the connection between Becks and Doyle is."

"You finally figured out that Becks lied to you, huh?" D'Agostino said. She followed me to the door. "Newsflash: Crooks lie. Film at eleven."

I paused.

"I never lied to you," I said quietly. I don't know what my face looked like at that moment, but it stopped D'Agostino.

"Hey," she said, "I didn't mean—"

I shook my head. "Doesn't matter. If I live through this, we'll talk about it some more."

And then I went out into the mostly quiet streets of Birmingham to see if I could finally figure out what was going on.

I parked the Mustang down the street from the address I wanted. If it had been a weekday, I might not have found parking. Finding a parking space in downtown Birmingham is like finding a four-leaf clover these days: It's rare, and when you find one, you better grab that sonofabitch quick before someone else does.

The address I was looking at was 17 N. 20th Street, and it was built in 1912. The tallest building in the city at the time. Everyone in the city knew it as simply the John Hand Building.

The first eight floors were commercial use. The next twelve floors were all residential space. Carlton Doyle lived on the 19th floor, one level above his office. I was parked facing away from the building, watching it in my rear-view mirror. That had been D'Agostino's suggestion, or otherwise I'm not sure I would have thought of it. But this way, I didn't look like I was keeping an eye on the building, and maybe no one would spot me.

I was waiting for Becks Towson. The man I'd seen the night before had been Thomas, Becks's right-hand man and apparent lover. I wasn't sure when it would happen, but the timing between Joey Dykes' visit at Pale Eddie's and the attempted hit at my hotel was too much to be coincidental. There was a connection there that I didn't know, and I needed to.

So I did what I did best: I waited. I found myself doing that more and more lately. As I got older, I saw the value of waiting for someone besides me to make the first move, to make the mistake. I wasn't scared, at least not yet. If the two guys who accosted me the night before came along, well, this time I had my weapon on me. Things might turn out a little differently, if I could get into action quickly enough.

But a couple of hours passed, and nothing happened. People came out of the John Hand Building on foot, but Carlton Doyle wasn't one of them. None of his people stirred, either. A couple of times, I took a chance and drove over to the attached parking garage, where the gate code was 4-3-2-1, and checked to make sure Doyle's vehicle was still parked there. It was.

It was nearly two p.m. by the time I saw the black Mercedes trundle up to the parking deck, and I was in dire need of two things: lunch, and a restroom. Probably not in that order. From where I was parked, I could see Thomas lower the driver's-side window of the Mercedes and lean out to punch in the security code for the parking deck. Then he went up the ramp to park.

I couldn't follow him up, but now I had my connection between Becks and Doyle. Thomas. And even though I couldn't follow him, I could still enter the parking deck. I gave Thomas a few minutes to find a parking space and cross the skywalk to the building, then I pulled the Mustang around and into the parking deck, too. I keyed the security code and drove up the ramp. It didn't take too long to find the Mercedes, which was parked on the next-to-the-top level of the deck. There were four floors of parking below us, and one more on top. I backed into a space facing the car, down the line of filled parking spaces a little ways.

And then I waited again. I had gotten so good at waiting that I could do it with my eyes closed. And did I close my eyes? Of course I did, but I didn't mean to. But it had been a long few days and I was more tired than I could ever remember being. I had been keyed up the night before, and I was simply run down. No coffee in the world could keep me awake. Soon my eyelids became heavy, like someone had weighted them down with concrete blocks. And then my head began to nod forward. And then I was gone.

They should have killed me, you know. We were in a half-filled parking deck on a Sunday afternoon. A gunshot could've been easily passed off as a car's backfire. They could have walked right up to the window and shot me in the head. Then it would have all been over, and I would've been none the wiser.

Instead I woke up when one of the ex-cons that had given chase the night before opened the driver's door of the Mustang and dragged me out by the hair.

That kind of thing is, well, unpleasant. I'm nearly fifty and have kept most of my hair, damn it. To have another man grab it by the roots and try to snatch it out was painful and insulting. But I didn't have a whole lot of time to register either of those things, because he slung me back toward the rear wall of the deck. I hit the hard, oil-stained concrete and rolled up into a kneeling position. I heard a click—the ominous sound of a knife blade opening and locking into place—and saw the guy coming for me.

My hand swept back and gripped the butt of my pistol. I brought it up with both hands, aimed for his center mass, and fired once. The slug took him in the chest, and he had a moment of awful shocked clarity where he understood that death had come for him and not me. There would be no more tomorrows, no more long days and pleasant nights, no more chasing the neon until the night was gone and the sun rose high in the east. No more great meals. No more women. No family. His engine was stopped somewhere along the track of time and would never reach its destination.

The man bent his head forward, looking for the hole where the .38 slug had entered. I don't think he ever found it. His legs collapsed first, and then his body went limp, slipping to the ground with the splattering sound of boneless ease.

The gunshot had been very loud, so what followed felt like a perfect vacuum of silence. That lasted for maybe ten seconds, and then I heard the slap of feet running away.

I listened carefully and heard the pounding echo of footsteps finally stopped abruptly. For whatever reason, the second man hadn't gone down the ramp toward the street. Panic had driven him upward, to the roof.

I kept my weapon in my hand as I staggered up the concrete ramp to find him.

TWENTY NINE

THERE WERE STAIRS that could lead all the way to the street, positioned at diagonally opposite corners of the parking deck. If the man I chased had used either of those, he could be on the street by now or—here's a happy thought—sneaking up on me from behind right at that very moment. Okay. I knew those were possibilities. But I went with the probability: He was on the rooftop with me, hiding behind one of the cars parked along the building's edge.

The sun was high in the deep blue sky, and somewhere along the horizon, white cumulonimbus clouds promised late afternoon thundershowers. To the South I could see the WRBC call letters on top of Red Mountain near the Vulcan statue. Vulcan himself looked on, impassive and steely eyed. At night, the TV station's call letters glowed crimson and the Vulcan would be silhouetted by moonlight coming over the peak of the mountain.

Sweat ran down my face, big rivers of perspiration that pooled where my throat and collarbone met. My armpits were damp, and the bright sun made my skin feel like it had just been taken straight from the furnace at Sloss.

I blinked sweat away from my eyes and squinted around the roof of the parking deck. On the way up the ramp, I had moved in a shuffling gait—left foot mostly forward, right foot perpendicular—holding the pistol in a two-handed grip. It was the classic Weaver stance, and I was committed to it. Until I got tired, at least.

Now on the roof, with the sun beating down on me, I let my gun arm dangle at my side. I felt a little like Gary Cooper in High Noon, a man alone against more enemies than he knew how to handle. I remember the framing shot of Cooper—tall and slim, long legs encased in black broadcloth, black boots—walking down the main drag of that dusty western town while Grace Kelly waited and fretted. There was no Grace Kelly for me. D'Agostino wasn't waiting, and she wasn't fretting. She was done with me. I understood that, and it reinforced the loneliness I felt up here eight stories off the ground with the world falling away on all four sides.

There was movement to my left, and I turned in time to see the other man from last night—was he Righty or Lefty?—slip toward the stairwell on the far side of the parking garage. I walked that way, and the slow clop of my cowboy boots echoed against the waist-high concrete wall surrounding us.

He was thirty or forty yards ahead of me, but I couldn't bring myself to hurry. Something about the showdown on this rooftop felt inevitable. He reached the stairwell, hit the safety bar on the door, and staggered back. It was locked. He scrabbled at it, trying to find a way through, but it kept on being locked. His fingers scrambled for purchase as he panicked, and my lips split into a wide grin and I came on, drawing nearer with every step. The stairwell seemed to be his last hope. He turned toward me, put his back against the door, and sagged a little. I stopped about twenty feet away from him, the gun still dangling from my hand. I didn't lift it. Not yet.

"Leave me alone, man," he gasped. His chest was heaving, and I couldn't tell if it was from fear or exertion, or some combination of the two. I didn't respond, either. I just stood there with the gun in my hand, thinking, trying to figure out what to do.

"Somebody will see," he said and waved a hand at the John Hand Building behind me. "You can't do this."

If somebody was watching us, they were probably already on the phone to the police. I was very aware that eleven floors above us, Becks Towson's right hand was probably meeting with Carlton Doyle. But would they look down? If they did, could they do anything about me?

Answers: 1) Unlikely; and 2) No.

Momentum combined with a rage I didn't know I'd held—rage at being put into this position, rage at Doyle, rage at Thomas, rage at even D'Agostino—made me feel invincible and carried me forward.

I raised the gun, aimed it center mass. He raised his hands in supplication, a prayer to ward off bullets. My knuckle was white on the trigger from the strain of trying not to shoot him. He and his buddy would have ended me the night before, and they would have done it today if I hadn't been armed. Every reasonable fiber of my being wanted to get him now before he could get me.

Instead I kept the gun steady on him.

"You want to live?" I asked, and he nodded his head up and down fast, uncontrollable, like a bobble head doll. "Tell me what the hell is going on with Thomas and Doyle."

"I don't know, man."

"That's too bad." I cocked the hammer on the revolver. I didn't need to, because the .38 was double-action and would fire when I squeezed the trigger, but as a dramatic device it worked really well.. The sound was loud in the still Sunday air.

"Wait," he moaned. "Please, man, come on. He'll kill me."

"Him later or me now."

"Fuck, please."

"I've been walking around the last week not knowing what the hell is going on," I said. "You know something, you tell me.

You don't know anything, you might as well lie down and die right here."

"Okay, okay. They're cutting the old man out," he said. "Becks has got old and slow, man. The money's drying up. World's changing, and Thomas is taking over. He's doing a deal with Doyle so everybody can make some money."

I grunted.

It made a kind of sense.

"So Becks didn't greenlight me," I said, and before I could even finish the sentence, the guy was shaking his head.

"Naw, he said let you honkies kill each other, we pick up the pieces."

I rolled my shoulders a little. I was tired of holding the gun extended at shoulder height. I lowered it a little, still gripping it tightly.

"Does Becks know any of this?"

"What you think, man? Becks been around a long time. He run numbers and whores in this city before I was born. He got eyes and ears everywhere. That's why Thomas keeps things on the downlow, don't want the man to get any ideas, you know?"

Becks Towson had been a kingpin in Birmingham for a long time, that was for sure. And he didn't get to the top by being a nice guy, either. I was pretty sure that Thomas wasn't the first usurper to try to occupy the throne. The difference was that Thomas was still alive. But if Becks knew, that could change some things. And it could throw a wrench into whatever plans Carlton Doyle was making.

Dreadlock boy shoved himself off the door, standing up to full height. I hadn't put a bullet in him yet. Maybe he was thinking that I wouldn't. But there wasn't enough room between us now for him to be making sudden movements like that. I pointed the gun at him again.

"You got another blade on you?"

He hesitated, then gave a little tilt of his head in acquiescence. Of course he did.

"Take it out," I said. "Toss it over the side."

"Sure, dude, whatever you say." He put his hand in his front pocket and came out with a gravity knife. Before I could react, it clicked open and he used the door to the stairwell for leverage, pushing off and accelerating toward me in a long dive. One hand held the knife, the other reached for my shirtfront. If I had let him get his hands on me, it would have been all over but the shoutin', as my Granny used to say.

But that's not what happened. Instead, I struck him across the temple with the butt of the gun, keeping pressure off of the trigger, and he went down. My cupped hand had partially cushioned the blow, so it didn't knock him out. He staggered down onto all fours with the knife still in his hands. I stomped the knife with my hard-soled cowboy boots and got some fingers in the process. I heard them snap, and I'm not gonna lie: it felt good.

I put the gun back into the holster at the small of my back. I didn't want any more gunfire if I could help it.

He was game, give him that. He doddered up to his feet, lunging for me again, and I kicked him in the kneecap. His leg buckled, made him lurch to one side. I used his momentum to slip behind him and grab him by the thick mane of dreadlocks and the waistband of his pants. I took four running, lunging steps and heaved him over the waist-high wall of the parking deck down to the pavement eight stories below.

I heard him when he hit the pavement. I made a face, but by that time I had already turned away. I hustled back down the ramp toward the Mustang. There were a couple of thick, ropy dreads clinging to my fingers, and I tore them away, shoving them into the first trash can I saw. A floor below, I stepped over his partner's corpse and into the driver's seat of the car. I didn't look at him. Thankfully I could avoid the body as I pulled out of the parking space. Then it was down, down, down to street level and out the parking deck.

I drove south on I-65 driving through Homewood and Hoover, taking the exit for Pelham and Helena. The whole way, I drove the speed limit and kept a weather eye out for any cops. Hoover is infested with them, and they're the kind of boys in blue who will cite you for damn near anything. I took a state road into Helena and then drove onto Morgan Road, following it up toward I-459, which would eventually lead me back into east Birmingham or over to Tuscaloosa in the West, in case I ever wanted to go back there again.

There's a little creek that runs through Helena. It's deep enough that even in a drought, it never completely dries. The bottom is sandy and dark, maybe twelve or fifteen feet down. A long time ago, I used to kayak the river. I found the turnout still located where it always was, and spun the steering wheel hard. The Mustang was the only car there. The parking area was shaded by a small copse of hardwoods. In a few months the weather would turn the leaves gold and red and brown. But right now the leaves were lush and the grass was thick. I walked out to the creek, kicking my booted feet through the tall grass and stayed alert for snakes. The water in the creek bed was deep brown and moving slowly. Eventually it would tie in somewhere with the Black Warrior, but I couldn't quite remember where. Nearby, a woodpecker hammered his head into a tree, and I thought I must know how he felt. There were other birds chirping, while flies and mosquitos and noseeums flitted around my head, hoping to take a bite out of me.

I took the gun out from behind my belt, shucked the spent brass out of the cylinder, and tossed the gun into the middle of the creek, where the water was deepest. I'd stick the brass into a garbage can at a convenience store. No muss, no fuss.

Then I breathed the soft, warm air for a few minutes, letting the proximity of the water and the wildlife calm my chattering brain.

In a little while, I went back to the Mustang, knocked the mud from my boots, got in, and drove toward I-459. When faced with the choice, I always drove back toward Birmingham.

When I stopped to gas up and get rid of the brass from the .38, I dragged my wallet from my back pocket and pulled out the business card Becks Towson had given me. There was no name, just a number. And it was a number I didn't want to call from my own phone. So I wasted a little time finding a working pay phone—there's one near the 16th Street Baptist Church, for the record—and pumped a couple of quarters into the coin slot. Then I dialed the number Becks had given me. When he answered, I told him that I had news he needed to hear.

"What makes you think I want to listen to you?"

"I don't know," I said into the sticky, hot receiver. "I know you're getting old, Becks, but I thought you wanted to stay alive for a little while longer."

"You threatening me?"

"You know I'm not," I said. "But there's someone gunning for your seat. You know the only way that happens is if you fall down first.

He was silent for a moment, and I watched the cars on 16th Street pass by while he thought.

"Where you at," he said. I told him.

"You know where Eagles Restaurant is?" I did, and said so. He grunted into the phone, in satisfaction or pain I couldn't tell. "Come alone."

"I be there in half an hour."

And he was.

THIRTY

EAGLES RESTAURANT is a low-slung, narrow building, gray-painted cinderblock with a somewhat darker shingled roof. Inside, there's a long steam table filled with soul food and a special that changes daily. On the opposite wall is a row of comfortably sprung vinyl booths. It's dark, but clean, and the food is the best-kept secret in Birmingham.

Unfortunately, I didn't feel like eating. When I opened the door, the aroma of slow-cooked oxtail and fried okra hit me, and my stomach turned. I kept thinking about the men I'd killed, kept seeing the first one fall bonelessly to the concrete floor. The .38 had made a small hole going in. The exit wound? I couldn't have covered that with my hand. I didn't want to think about the blood on the ground, and I definitely didn't want to think about the other guy, probably concussed—certainly wobbly on his feet—rushing headlong toward the sidewalk some eighty feet below us.

I shook my head, trying to clear it, and cast a glance along the steam table. There was Salisbury steak in gravy, oxtails, catfish, mashed potatoes, cornbread, okra ... any other day, I would have grabbed one of the lunchroom-style platters and lined up for a heaping plate.

Not today.

Today I was lucky to keep the bile down. My saliva glands were working overtime, and I swallowed a couple of times, nearly gagging. I didn't want to eat, didn't even want to think about eating. I waved off the counterman who had stepped forward to fill my nonexistent plate. Instead I looked around and found Becks Towson at the back booth, tucked into a plate piled high with oxtails and okra. There was no one with him. No bodyguards, no hangers-on. His hair was white and sparse, his mustache neat, his cheeks clean-shaven. There was a small scar from the corner of his jaw to halfway across his throat where someone or something had cut him a long time ago. Whoever—or whatever—had tried to slit Becks's throat hadn't finished the job. The old man was still here and still dangerous.

I sat down across from him. He sucked the marrow from one of the oxtails and I nearly gagged at the sound. But I didn't. I tried to make my mind go somewhere else, somewhere away from the two men dead at the parking deck, away from the bodies of Martin James and his secretary, away from the corpse of Britt Parker. So many people dead. And for what? All so Carlton Doyle could get a little richer, a little more powerful.

Becks wiped long, slim fingers onto a white paper napkin, then patted the corners of his mouth. He seemed in no hurry.

"Get you some food," he said. "I can wait."

I shook my head.

"Not hungry. I know some things you probably should."

Becks grunted. He didn't say anything, though, just went back to eating.

"You've lost control," I said. "You don't know it yet, but there's a coup in the works. You're not the most dangerous man on the block anymore, Becks."

He lifted his dark brown eyes from his plate and stared at me intently.

"Is that right?"

I looked around us.

There was no one else in the restaurant, just the lone worker behind the counter: a tall, rangy black man with a gleaming shaved head and a sharply defined goatee. His hands hung below the counter, out of sight.

"You know about it," I said.

Becks smiled a small, self-satisfied smile and nodded his head.

"I know somebody's been nibbling at the edges," he said. "But they always are. You don't get to be a man like me and know when something's coming. I can feel it. I just can't see it yet."

"You know where Thomas is right now?"

Becks thought for a moment, relaxing back into the vinyl booth as if he owned the place. Hell, he probably did.

"At church with his mama," he said finally. "Sunday's his day off, and he go with her every week since he got outta Bibb Correctional."

I shook my head.

"I saw him an hour and a half ago going into Carlton Doyle's building."

Becks was too world-weary to act shocked, but I could feel the news hit home. From what I had seen, Thomas was more than just payroll help. Becks ate some okra, chewing thoughtfully.

"What's he want with Doyle?" He asked, but I could tell he was talking to himself. "Kid got two skills: giving head and killing people. Doyle don't want him for blowjobs."

I didn't say anything. I didn't really know much about Becks other than the fact that he was considered just about the most dangerous man in the state. Becks came up in the sixties, when being black and gay were two strikes against him already, even in the hateful businesses that he ran. But Becks never let it stop him from carving out a kingdom of crime in Birmingham. If you wanted horse or weed or a woman in a dozen neighborhoods in Birmingham, Becks Towson was the one behind the action. He'd taken two falls, including one for manslaughter. But it had been years since Becks had even been arrested. He had learned since those early days, and he put layers between himself and the street crime his lieutenants ran.

Layers like Thomas.

"He tried for me last night," I said.

Becks carefully looked me up and down.

"It looks like he missed."

"He sent two hitters to my room," I said, and described what had happened the night before. "I managed to get away."

"That sound like Bloomfield and Weddle," Becks said. "You won't have to worry about them anymore."

"I know," I said, and told him the rest. While I told it, Becks resumed lunch. He had cleaned his plate by the time I was done and signaled to the counterman for some dessert.

"No wonder you don't wanna eat," Becks said. He paused as his dessert was delivered: pecan pie with a white perfect scoop of vanilla ice cream on top. Becks picked up a fork and dug in. "First time you killed somebody?"

I shook my head.

The first time had been in the war, looking over the barrel of my M4 carbine and watching the Taliban sons-of-bitches trying to sneak forward in the sand. I had flicked the selector from single-shot to three-round bursts. And then I'd fired. I could still see that man, the first one I'd ever killed, jerk as the bullets hit him. He didn't scream. Just laid down and died.

Afterward, once the fighting was over, I had thrown up. I hadn't wanted to eat anything then, either, but an old infantry sergeant handed me an MRE and told me to open it. I did, and was suddenly ravenous. I ate everything and wanted more. It took me a long time to realize that in the act of eating I had simply been affirming that I was still alive.

Becks pushed aside his finished plate and steepled his fingers underneath his chin.

"So now tell me: what do you want?"

I thought about it for a moment, rubbing my hands over the stubble on my face. I was going to have to shave soon or grow a full beard.

"You threatened Abby," I said. "That's why Doyle hired me in the first place, right?"

Becks didn't say anything. It was as good as an admission.

"You were putting pressure on him to give you a piece of Carraway, right?"

Again, Becks stayed silent. I didn't blame him. What if I were wearing a wire? But his silence still spoke volumes. If I had been wrong, he would have denied it.

"Thomas going to Carlton changes the game, doesn't it?"

Becks's eyes crinkled a little. That was the closest he came to a smile.

"We're getting to it now," he said.

"I've got an idea that Thomas isn't going to be a factor much longer."

"Could be," Becks said. "He's young to be retired. But it happens."

I nodded.

"What if I told you that Carlton Doyle isn't going to be a factor much longer either?"

Becks smoothed his mustache with a thumb and forefinger.

"That ... would make for some interesting developments."

"Abby wouldn't be a danger to you," I said.

Becks nodded. He didn't say anything. I waited and let the silence sprawl out between us, but Becks never rose to the bait. Finally, I got tired of waiting.

"I need to know if you would be a danger to her," I said. "Or me."

Becks thought for a minute before answering. He still wasn't sure whether I might be wearing a wire.

"If her father weren't a factor in my business going forward," Becks said, "I can't see what interest I'd have in the girl."

He waited a beat, and then smiled at me, a real smile. It was disarming in its charm.

"Or you," Becks added.

Just what I needed to hear. I nodded and rose from the booth. I thanked Becks and walked out of the restaurant with the pleasant smell of fried food following me as I opened the door. I breathed it in deeply. I no longer felt sick to my stomach. Maybe I'd come back another day. But not today.

Today there were other things that had to be handled. I had to get another gun. And I had to finish things with Carlton Doyle. He was the only real danger to Abby now.

THIRTY ONE

SLOSS FURNACE LOOMS over the North Lakeview Industrial district to the south and the Avondale neighborhood to the north. At night, the place is eerie and the oxidized ironworks glow a sullen red. At one point it was the central financial hub of the city, shipping pig iron, steel, coke and other iron-related products throughout the south. If Pittsburgh is truly the steel city, Birmingham was—at least at one time—its ambitious little brother.

But there are no fires to power the furnace anymore. Steel is mostly a memory in Birmingham, but the ironworks are still there, and someone put the damned place on a historical registry. That means that schoolchildren and bored tourists sometimes visit during the day. At night, Sloss is a different animal. The big water tank with S L O S S printed in huge block letters looms over the place like one of the aliens out of H.G. Wells' *War of the Worlds*. Because of the steel and the asphalt, heat never seems to leave the furnace. Despite the fact that the fires no longer burn, Sloss is almost always hot.

This night, it seemed especially warm. I had climbed the chain-link fence earlier in the evening, tossing a blanket over the barbed wire atop the fence and levering myself unharmed to the ground on the other side. I took the blanket with me and found a hidden spot among the pipes and vents and waited. While I was waiting, I realized that my position might be too perfect, so I moved a little farther back into the shadows where I didn't have a clear view of the gate into the property.

Carlton Doyle hadn't been happy to hear from me when I called him that afternoon. I told him that I'd taken care of every-thing—and that his daughter was no longer in danger from any-one but him.

"What did you say, you son of a bitch?"

I spoke carefully and clearly into the phone.

"You're a kiddie-diddler, Carlton," I said. "I know all about you. Abby told me everything."

And once I had him off-balance like that, it had been simplic-ity itself to set him up. He told me that I was a dead man the next time he saw me, and I told him I'd be waiting that night at Sloss.

"Ten o'clock. Come alone," I said. "We can finish this man-to-man."

I figured he wouldn't come alone, though. That's why I'd gotten there early to search the place. I settled down on the blanket in the shadows. In a little while, I heard the gate rattle and roll back. Whoever Doyle had sent, he'd made sure they had a key. I watched a long, lean shadow stalk past me, the weird light around Sloss bending and mutating the shadow into something unearthly.

And then I moved. I'd changed out my boots for a pair of Adidas running shoes, and they made no sound on the poured concrete as I stalked my prey as he moved around and looked for the perfect place to ambush me.

He found it, too: the place I had originally chosen. I smiled in the dark, even though no one could see. I was behind him on his left, and I carefully snaked my way to a point where I was thirty feet back. And then I crept forward slowly.

At the last second, he heard or felt something wrong. He turned as I chopped down for the side of his neck and took the blow on the thick hard muscle of his bunched trapezius. After that, the fight was on. It was a mad scramble as we struggled, each understanding that this was life or death. He reached into a pocket—for a gun or a knife, I was sure—and when he did, I hit him in the throat with the edge of my hand.

He gagged and sagged forward onto his knees, his face momentarily illuminated in the soft weird light. Joey Dykes. I was able to get behind him with one hand on his forehead and the other on his jaw. The tendons in my forearms stood out like cables as I made sure of my grip. And then I tore my hands in opposite directions as hard as I could, and broke his neck.

Joey fell with no sound at all other than the wet noise of his body slapping against the cement. A quick search of his pockets revealed a .38 revolver under his arm and a .380 semiautomatic pistol on his ankle. I took both guns and stowed them away on my person. At some point I realized that his body had voided, and I moved away from the smell and took up my position in the darkness.

Doyle never showed, the son of a bitch. The plan, then, had been for him to send Dykes ahead of time, to have him lie in wait for me and then kill me. Probably from ambush. Good plan, and one that would have worked if I hadn't gotten there first. I stayed until eleven, waiting. Then I went to Dykes's body and took his wallet. There was three hundred dollars in cash, and I added that to my own wallet. He had ID cards in different names: John B. Allen, Charles Willis, John Rumsey. Each had his photo and a different address in suburban Birmingham. His watch, a very nice Patek Philippe with no inscription, transferred easily from his wrist to mine, and I also grabbed his cell phone. He had one of those new phones that needs a fingerprint to unlock, so I got his cooling hand in mine and used his index finger on the button. The screen popped up with text messages from a number I recognized.

Doyle.

There were three messages, but the last one was the one that mattered most.

-Is it done?

The text had come fifteen minutes before. I opened the contacts list on the phone, found Doyle's cell phone number, and called it. It rang three times, and I expected the call to go to voicemail. I have no idea what I would have said. Instead, Doyle's waspish voice answered.

"Well?"

"He's dead," I said, keeping my voice neutral. On the other end of the line, Doyle was silent for a beat.

"This isn't Joey."

"That's right," I said. "You tried to set me up, Doyle. But it didn't work out. You need to keep that in mind for the future. I'm going to walk through as many of your boys as you can send until we see each other face-to-face."

There was silence on the other end of the line for a few long seconds, and then Doyle laughed.

"Go to hell," he said, and I could hear the cold satisfaction in his voice. "I can squash you whenever I want, and there's nothing you can do. I've got everything I want. You can go to hell, and take your cop friend with you."

The line went dead, and I stayed very still. I had gone out of my way to keep D'Agostino out of things. The fact that Doyle had even mentioned her sent a chill down my spine. I looked down at Joey Dykes and wondered where he'd been earlier in the evening. I went out the gate that Joey had left open. Probably he would have come back and closed it to keep from alerting me that someone was there. But he never got a chance.

By the time I got to my Mustang, I was running. I leaped the hood, half-sliding across it and landing catlike on my feet on the driver's side. Eat you heart out, Bo Duke. I tore the driver's door open and jumped in. D'Agostino's place was only minutes away, but it felt like hours.

When I got to her building, I rang the bell for the security guard to let me into the lobby. He wasn't there. I looked around carefully, but there was no sight of him. I took out one of the guns I'd found on Joey Dykes's body and used the butt to break one of the glass panels near the doorknob. I reached through, careful of the jagged pieces of glass that stuck in the frame, and unlocked the door. I maintained my concentration as I withdrew my hand. An old burglar I'd once known had told me that most people cut themselves after they'd broken a window that way. Even though I was in a hurry, I tried to keep my patience. When I finally stepped into the lobby, I found the security guard down on the floor, a small trickle of blood trailing from his temple. I knelt beside him, slapping his face gently to wake him. When that didn't work, I pinched him on the leg as hard as I could, hard enough to leave a bruise.

He moaned and started to come around. Groaning with effort, I helped him into his chair.

"Buzz 306," I said. He looked blankly at me with no indication of the words I'd said. I repeated myself, and when he still didn't respond, I hit the big button on the console of his desk that unlocked the interior door of the building. Then I was through and bounded for the stairs.

Three flights of stairs is not easy at a dead run. By the time I got to D'Agostino's apartment, I was gasping for air and sweating hard despite the air-conditioning in the building. Her door was slightly ajar, and I slowed down enough to keep from hitting it full speed with my shoulder. A good thing, too, since Laura was down on the floor, just inside her apartment.

She was conscious, and that was good. But she was bleeding from a cut on the scalp and another on her lip. One of her eyes was bruised and swollen shut. The other rolled in its socket, and she moaned in pain. Her left arm lay motionless at her side, and it looked like she had grown a second elbow somewhere above the first. I winced. That was a bad break, but it didn't look like the bones had come through the skin. Thank God. My first instinct was to go to her, to help her, but I knew it was the wrong thing to do.

Instead, I stepped past her with my weapon level, sweeping the room beyond her for anyone who might still be there. I checked the small kitchen, both bedrooms and bathrooms, and when I was satisfied that we were alone, I came back and knelt beside her, taking her good hand in mine.

I made an emergency call on Dykes's phone, requesting an ambulance for D'Agostino and for the doorman. Then I called 911 to report an officer down. I stressed that she was injured but not shot. Nothing seemed to be life-threatening. As I talked to the operator, D'Agostino seemed to come around a little. Once I ended the call, she squeezed my hand.

"I'm sorry," she said. "I did everything I could."

"I know," I said. "It's all right."

She tried to shake her head, then squeezed her eye shut when she couldn't. A tear ran from her good eye, and she choked back a sob.

"It's not," she said, her voice catching in her throat. "Doyle showed up with some muscle. I couldn't—I couldn't—"

She collapsed into tears, leaning hard against me, and I kissed her forehead. I understood. There had been two of them, and D'Agostino—who could generally leap tall buildings in a single bound—couldn't overcome two larger, stronger attackers on her own. In her own mind, it was a failure. And even if no one would blame her for it, D'Agostino held herself to an impossibly high standard.

Wonder Woman.

But she wasn't a cartoon hero. She was a woman like any other. She was strong and skillful and smart, but she was human. She was as prone to mistakes as anyone else, even if she didn't let herself think so. I held onto her and felt my rage grow quiet and white-hot. Doyle's attack had done more than just break Laura's body. It had also broken her spirit. And even if that—like her body—could repair itself over time, it would always leave an ugly scar on her soul.

Sirens blared in the night, and my first reaction was to run. The ambulance would be first, and then the cops. I'd be busy answering their questions all night, and they'd have reason to look into me and into what I'd been up to the rest of the night. I wanted to be out the door and on the hunt. I wanted Doyle's throat in my hands. I wanted to watch the life seep out of him.

Instead I sat down next to D'Agostino and put her head in my lap. I held her still and stroked her hair and said words that I'd never said to another woman as we waited for help to arrive.

THIRTY TWO

THIRTY MILES EAST of Birmingham on I-20, there's a 17,000-acre reservoir on the Coosa River. It's called Logan Martin Lake, and it sits between Logan Martin Dam to the south and Neely Henry Dam to the north. It's a man-made lake, built by Alabama Power in 1965. Even though the lake itself is a little more than forty-eight miles long, it has nearly three hundred miles of shoreline. The lake is so sinuous and crenelated that the locals sometimes refer to it as the Lake of a Thousand Coves.

In one of those little coves, Carlton Doyle had a lake house, a place to get away from the city. Even though Birmingham is only around thirty miles away, it can seem like a lifetime. The closest civilization is Pell City, the kind of place you'd expect the extras from Deliverance to move their mobile homes when the movie royalties came rolling in.

There are several small islands on the lake, and if Carlton Doyle had his lake house on one of those, my efforts to reach him would have been in vain. Instead, he owned a three-story Alpine cottage on one of the many pieces of shoreline on the eastern side of the lake. It's amazing what you can find out when you have a friend who works in the public records office.

I had no such friend, of course, but D'Agostino did. That's why we had rented a place on the other side of the cove from Doyle. There was only three hundred feet of water between us: brackish, black, filled with freshwater eels, catfish, copperheads, and snapping turtles. Laura had insisted on accompanying me, so we were holed up in much more modest accommodations. Our house had only two floors, but the roof didn't leak and the indoor plumbing worked.

We were taking turns watching Doyle's house. He and Abby were in there, hidden from the world. We saw them on the dock every morning, taking coffee and looking out at the natural beauty of the lake. And we saw them when Doyle would untie the 18-foot ChrisCraft from the dock and start the nearly silent motor. The boat left twin trails of white water in its wake, but it made so little sound that the lapping of its wake against the shoreline made more noise.

Logan Martin is a reservoir, but it's also an outdoorsman's paradise. You can boat, or fish, or swim, or waterski. You can watch the variety of waterfowl that call the lake home. And if you're lucky, you can watch the deer and raccoons and foxes that populate the area near Talladega National Forest come down to the lake for their morning drink. Once I saw a bear, thin and not yet ready for the coming winter. He spotted me out on the little deck on the second story of the rental house, tilted his head, and moved on about his business.

Our dock faced the other direction from Doyle's house, so we found ourselves sitting outside at dawn and dusk, fragrant with the smell of bug repellent. D'Agostino had taken apart a wire clothes hanger and fashioned a kind of scratching device that she poked underneath the cast on her left arm. The first time she had used it, her face was nearly orgasmic in its relief. Now she kept the mostly straightened hanger with her most of the time. And every day I was aware of the danger Carlton Doyle posed. Always I wore a gun.

There didn't seem to be much going on at Doyle's place. The first couple of days, I watched. The house would obviously have a security system. I could occasionally see Doyle arming it before he and Abby went to bed. And they did go to bed together. The last thing I saw from the house every night was the bedroom light on the top floor. When it winked off, my stomach sank.

Poor Abby.

At night, I prowled around Doyle's property. The driveway was crushed oyster shells, and although it wasn't gated, the pale white path led between two large, dark-painted wooden posts. Down low, maybe a foot off the ground, was an electronic eye. Anything that broke the beam would alert the house. I stepped carefully over it and listened.

There was no sound but the lake. I crept along the property, peering into the dark house. There were security lights inside, and in their dim glow I could see a well-appointed space, lush with furnishings and art. The first floor was dominated by an open space used as a living area. The ceiling was high and almost peaked, and the second floor was built around a landing that circled the big open space. In the center of the main floor was a fieldstone fireplace. The chimney ran straight up to the third floor so that a fire built on the first floor would warm the whole house.

A Land Rover registered to Doyle sat in the driveway, and the house itself was surrounded by greenery and immaculate landscaping. Must be nice.

I'd made the trip around the property for three nights in a row, and I was getting a little stir crazy. So was D'Agostino. If she scratched her arm any harder, she'd probably start bleeding.

That night I made us dinner, pan-searing some steaks in butter and tarragon, listening to them sizzle and testing them occasionally by pressing the first two fingers of my right hand against the browned crust I'd managed to create on the beef. When I thought they were medium rare, I pulled the steaks from the pan to rest and put some sliced mushrooms in. They sautéed in the butter and spice, and while they did, I used butter and shredded cheddar cheese and boiling water to create something mostly edible from a box of instant mashed potatoes.

I sliced the steaks and they were pink with a warm center, just the way I'd intended, so I put a large dollop of mashed potatoes on a plate and put some steak on top of them. Then I poured mushrooms and the melted and browned butter over the whole thing. We each had a can of Good People brown ale, and there were fresh blackberries and clotted cream for dessert.

"I don't know how to get him," I said, forking some steak into my mouth and chewing thoughtfully. "He's not hiding, exactly, but he'll see me coming no matter what I do."

I'd cut D'Agostino's steak for her because of the bad arm, and she wasn't pleased about it. But she ate some anyway and thought.

"I don't know how you manage to make instant potatoes taste halfway decent," she said. "You'll make a lovely hausfrau one day."

"It's a talent."

We ate a little more, comfortable in the silence between us. Neither of us commented on the moments that passed between us as she lay injured on the floor of her apartment.

Hell, as far as I knew, she might not even remember what I'd said. Or maybe she didn't want to remember it. We slept in separate beds in the rented house, and in the dark hours of the night I thought I could hear her breathe in the next room.

D'Agostino finished her dinner and asked for more, which I took as a good sign. After I refilled her plate, I passed by the window in the kitchen.

I want to say that there was something that warned me. I want to tell you that it was training and toughness and pure street smarts that saved my life. But it wasn't. I felt the bullet strike home at the same time I heard the glass in the window break, a millisecond after I heard the sound of the gun.

It was like I'd been punched hard in the top of the shoulder. I fell, dropping D'Agostino's plate, and I can remember thinking *oh no I'm going to have to clean that up.* And then time caught up with me and I hit the floor, rolling over onto my hurt shoulder and coming level with my own gun, firing wildly, fear and anger overtaking me as I put six shots into the blackness where the kitchen window had been.

The silence following the gunfire was eerie. I could smell the spent rounds in the air, that peculiar burnt gunpowder smell that everyone assumes is cordite, but it's not. Cordite went out of use after the 1960s. I was pretty sure I was in shock, but that wasn't going to last. I could feel the pain from my shoulder seeping in, and there was blood on the floor around me where I'd been shot.

"Kincaid?"

D'Agostino's voice came from the kitchen, and I hated the fear I heard in her voice.

"Still here," I moaned, and scrambled on my knees to the little dining room we'd shared. D'Agostino was under the table, trying to keep to the shadows. Her face was pale, with bright spots of color under each eye. It might have been pain from her bad arm or shock or both. Blood from my own wound leaked from my shoulder onto the hardwood floors.

Thank god there was no carpet. I'd lose my deposit. I giggled madly in the dark, the sound just on the wrong edge of sanity.

"Doyle?"

"Has to be," I said. "Do you still have your coat hanger?" She did. I took it from her and pressed my revolver into her hands.

"Get upstairs. Reload."

"What are you going to do? Jesus, you're bleeding. You didn't tell me you were hit."

I stared intently at the front door as I wrapped the unwound clothes hanger around my right forearm.

"When I say, run for the stairs," I said. "Don't stop for anything. I don't care what you hear."

"Jesus fucking Christ, are you crazy?"

"I'm in love with a cop," I said. "Of course I'm crazy."

D'Agostino narrowed her eyes and shifted her weight so that she favored her injured arm. She held my weapon in her right hand.

"Ready?" I asked. She nodded. There was a moment more of silence that seemed to stretch out forever, and I heard a hesitant, tentative step outside the house.

"Now," I screamed, "go, go."

D'Agostino bolted for the stairs, and I ran straight for the front door. I clawed at the knob and yanked it open to see Carlton Doyle standing there, a raised gun in his hand. He pulled the trigger, and I threw myself aside. He was so close that the muzzle flash from his weapon caught the front of my shirt on fire, and I felt the bullet sear my side as it went past.

He had been no more ready for me than I was for him. I could see that he was off-balance, so I helped him along by driving a shoulder into his armpit. He twirled an ungainly turn on the porch, flapping his arms and trying to get his balance, and then I kicked him hard, straight up the ass with one of my pointed-toe cowboy boots—god, that was satisfying—and he launched off the little porch and into the bushes that surrounded the house. In an instant he was up and running, and so was I. We splashed into the water that separated our houses, and I caught up with the son of a bitch at last.

His gun was gone. My shirt was wet and still smoking. I grabbed him by the throat, and he tried to gouge my eyes with his thumb. His nails tore grooves into my cheek, and they welled with fresh blood. He tried to knee me in the groin, but I turned my thigh to block it and took the knee on the big quadriceps muscle there. The blow was so hard that it made my leg spasm in a charley horse, and I nearly lost my grip on Doyle's throat.

But I didn't. I head-butted him in the face instead, what the old-time brawlers used to call the Liverpool kiss. He tried to claw at my arm, and I head-butted him again. This time there was the satisfying crunch of a bone breaking. It got him on the cheekbone, so maybe I'd exploded his orbital socket. I tried for his nose next, and pulped it. I knew I'd feel those head-butts in the morning, but at that moment I didn't let myself care. I couldn't.

My wound hurt like fire, and I could tell that it was still bleeding. I had to end things quickly, or else I'd pass out from blood loss and exhaustion, and then Doyle would be alone with Laura.

I wasn't going to let that happen. Not that night. Not any night.

He bit me hard when I got a little too close, and that's when I let him go. He scrambled toward the shore and I followed, unwinding the coat hanger that I'd managed to carry with me through the fight. I couldn't see well in the dark, but Doyle was splashing and thrashing so much that it didn't matter.

In the end, I wrapped the wire coat hanger around my hands and looped what was left over his head. A hard twist and the makeshift garotte was tight. I dragged him to shore, then turned and got my uninjured shoulder underneath his back and lifted him bodily out of the water so that he hung himself with the weight of his struggling body against the wire.

It didn't take long. It never does. The wire bit into his throat and into my palms. It hurt, and I could feel my hands bleeding from where the nasty narrow wire hanger cut into my palms. It couldn't have taken Doyle five minutes to stop struggling as the life force left his body, but by the time he was done, so was I. My hands let go, but I couldn't get the wire unwrapped. My fingers wouldn't work. In the pale moonlight they looked like thick purple sausages.

I collapsed next to Doyle on the shore. His eyes were blank and empty. Whatever evil had lurked in the man, it had left along with his soul. Good fucking riddance.

And then I closed my eyes and there was nothing left.

THIRTY THREE

THE AFTERLIFE, or what I thought it was, turned out to be pretty uneventful. I woke up in a room I didn't recognize. The bed was huge, the size of a football field, with clean white sheets and thick, heavy blankets. Above me there were cedar roof beams and a ceiling fan that turned as slowly as the hands of time. My shoulder itched, but when I tried to scratch it, I discovered it was covered with a pressure bandage. My hands were bandaged, too, with particular care taken with each of my palms.

I tried to get up, but there wasn't enough strength in my body. So I settled back onto the fluffy pillows and did what I did best: I waited for what came next.

When D'Agostino opened the door a little while later, I wasn't surprised. Her arm was still covered in a cast above the elbow. In her other hand, she carried a rectangular-shaped white bag with a red cross-shaped logo on the side. A first-aid kit. Of course. But for D'Agostino to administer first aid, she would have had to have some help. At first she didn't realize I was awake, so I could look at her without her knowing.

I liked what I saw. She didn't look haunted the way she had as we waited to make our move against Doyle, and she moved better. I was willing to bet that she was on her road to recovering, not just physically, but mentally, too.

"Hey," I said. The words came out in a croak, but she jumped anyway.

"Oh my god," D'Agostino gasped. She dropped the first-aid kit to the floor and held her right hand to her mouth. "It's about time."

Abby came in a moment later with a bowl of steaming broth on a sterling silver platter.

"Oh," she said, watching Laura and I stare at one another in silence. "I can come back."

I looked over. I could smell the broth. My stomach growled at the thought of food, and my mouth watered.

"Don't you dare leave," I said.

Abby helped me sit up, plumping pillows behind me until I was mostly comfortable, and then putting the bowl—platter and all—onto my lap. I wasn't sure I could manage a spoon, but the bandages on my hands worked fine as oven mitts. I lifted the bowl to my lips and drank some broth.

"How long have I been out?"

"You went into the lake with Doyle on a Thursday," D'Agostino said. "It's Tuesday now. Do you remember anything?"

I thought about it, then shook my head. The entire time between then and now was one dark, blank space on the map of my brain. I wasn't sure I wanted that place filled in, either.

"I came out of the cabin and there you were. Doyle was dead, and I thought you were, too. Then you coughed, and I nearly jumped into the lake myself."

I grinned weakly.

"Shut up," she said. "I couldn't handle you on my own, so I did the only thing I could think of." She turned to Abby, who had resumed her place near the door of the room.

"I ... I didn't know what to do," Abby said. "But Laura said you needed help. That my—that my father was dead—and that I didn't have to be scared anymore."

"She came back with me," D'Agostino said. "Helped me fish the bullet out of your shoulder, helped me patch it up, whole nine yards."

"Jesus Christ," I said.

"Yeah, you jumped a lot when we poured alcohol on the wound," Abby said. "I mean, I thought you'd come out of it then, but you were way, way under."

"It was just a little bullet," D'Agostino said. "A twenty-two. I found Doyle's gun in the bushes afterward. I thought you were tougher than that."

I snorted, a hollow half-laughing sound that made D'Agostino giggle. When she did that, her whole face brightened, and she looked younger again, lighter, as if the weight of some of the events over the last few days had been lifted from her shoulders.

I hoped they had.

I drank some more soup, right down to the bottom of the bowl. My stomach, which had felt shriveled and empty, now felt full. The room was warm and clean and I was safe. I shifted a little in the big bed, snuggling down onto my back again and looked up at the ceiling fan. It wasn't on very high, just enough to keep the air circulating in the room.

"You're all right," I said to Abby, and she nodded.

"Yes," she said in a very small voice. "I am."

Something hit me, and I struggled to sit up.

"Shit," I said. "The body."

D'Agostino had a hand on my chest in an instant, pushing me back down.

"Taken care of," she said, and looked purposefully at Abby. The younger woman studied the nap of the plush carpet on the floor. She wouldn't meet our eyes. I had no idea how hard the last few days must have been on her.

"Can you give us a minute alone?" Laura asked. Abby nodded,

took the silver tray with the bowl on it, and stepped out of the room. She closed the door firmly when she left.

"Middle of the lake is a hundred and ten feet," D'Agostino said. "We dragged his body onto their boat and then drove out to the middle of the lake around midnight the next night. Abby tied him to an anvil and we pushed him over the side."

"Jesus," I said. "I can't even imagine the kind of therapy that kid's gonna need."

"Me either," Laura said quietly. "But she's got enough money for it, for the rest of her life."

"And her father isn't around to molest her anymore," I said. "I guess that's something."

"Yeah, something. You know, she cried the whole time she was tying him down. We had to both do the lifting to get him overboard, but the cinderblocks? That was all Abby. She's stronger than either one of us gave her credit for being, I think."

I didn't know what to say. While I'd been lying on the ground unconscious, D'Agostino had rousted Abby and gotten her to help dispose of her father's body. And she did everything with only one arm to work with. Maybe she really was Wonder Woman.

And then there was Abby, who was some kind of superhuman herself. Even though her father had been her molester, he was still her father. It couldn't have been easy to do what they did, under cover of darkness, under the demanding pressure of a time crunch to get the body tied down enough to actually sink ... and then to help muscle him overboard.

We didn't talk about the fetus Abby carried in her belly. We knew that, no matter what the law said, she would have enough money to go away and have her little problem solved. Hemingway had written that it was a really a very simple procedure, and maybe it was. Abby was able—because of her race, because of her wealth, because of her status—to deal with her problem in a way that many women couldn't. But the psychological damage from her father would be harder to undo.

Maybe she had grieved in the days since. But in the few minutes she had been in the room with us, I had seen no evidence of it. I closed my eyes and tried to relax against the pillows. It was more difficult than I had imagined it would be.

"I'm sorry," I said.

"What, for getting shot?"

She punched me playfully in the uninjured shoulder, and I grinned up at her. Then we were quiet for a little while, the two of us just sitting there and getting used to one another's presence. D'Agostino held one of my hands in her good hand. Even through the bandages, her hand felt warm and full of life, and I knew that no matter what happened from here on out, I was better off for having known her.

"You talked a lot in your sleep, you know."

"Oh. Uh. I did?"

D'Agostino smiled.

"You did." She waited for a beat. "So you meant what you said before you got shot? That you're in love with a cop? Is it anyone I know?"

We both laughed. Now it was my turn to go quiet. D'Agostino looked away until I squeezed her hand.

"I meant it," I told her. "I love you. I don't know where this will lead, but I want us to figure it out together."

"Together?"

I nodded.

"Together."

ACKNOWLEDGMENT

WHILE I WAS WRITING THIS BOOK, I had *The Drive-By Truckers* playing on a nearly continual loop. Their Southern gothic brand of rock-and-roll really powered me through the writing process, especially the song 'Birmingham' from the album Southern Rock Opera. Many thanks to my friends and fellow writers, Emily Guy Birken, J.B. Stevens, James D.F. Hannah, and Mark Westmoreland for their ideas, insightful readings, and encouragement. Having writer friends means that someone cheers you on during the hard times. I have been inspired by a long line of writers like Donald Westlake, Robert B. Parker, Elmore Leonard, and Lawrence Block. If some of this work feels like an old friend, it's because I wrote the book in homage to them. Thank you to Ron Phillips, who believed in my work and offered me the chance to show it to the wider world.

In 2022, I lost my mom, Mavis Mathews. This book is dedicated to her, and I wish she was around to see it come to fruition. She was the first person to believe that I had some small talent for writing, and she always encouraged me to write and tried to nurture my interest in it. I owe so many other people, like Janice

Morgan at Enterprise High School, who encouraged me and believed in me even when I was a terrible and recalcitrant student. Gil Kelly is another one of those teachers, and Jim Strength, too. It's probably cliche' for a writer to say how much their high school English teachers affected them, but there's a reason it's cliche': It's true.

And, of course, thank you to Misty, who does so much stuff behind the scenes that allows me to "be a writer."

BOBBY MATHEWS knew exactly what he wanted to be when he grew up: a writer. That led him into a career path as a journalist in Alabama, New York, Wyoming, Georgia, and finally back to Alabama before he called it quits. He's won General Excellence, column-writing, newswriting, and sportswriting awards from press associations in all four states. In addition to his journalism career, Bobby has been a PR flack, a bartender, an investigator, and roustabout.

Bobby lives in suburban Birmingham, Alabama—which truly is the Magic City in more ways than one—with his wife and two sons.

SHOTGUN HONEY

2012 · 2022

CELEBRATING 10 YEARS OF
FICTION WITH A KICK

THE ROAD IS JUST BEGINNING
shotgunhoneybooks.com

9 781956 957105